Double or Muffin

Books by Victoria Hamilton

Vintage Kitchen Mysteries

A Deadly Grind
Bowled Over
Freezer I'll Shoot
No Mallets Intended
White Colander Crime
Leave It to Cleaver
No Grater Danger
Breaking the Mould
Cast Iron Alibi

Merry Muffin Mysteries

Bran New Death
Muffin But Murder
Death of an English Muffin
Much Ado About Muffin
Muffin to Fear
Muffin But Trouble
Double or Muffin

Lady Anne Addison Mysteries

Lady Anne and the Howl in the Dark
Revenge of the Barbary Ghost
Curse of the Gypsy
Lady Anne and the Menacing Mystic

A Gentlewoman's Guide to Murder

Double or Muffin

Victoria Hamilton

Double of Muffin
Victoria Hamilton
Beyond the Page Books
are published by
Beyond the Page Publishing
www.beyondthepagepub.com

Cover design and illustration by Dar Albert, Wicked Smart Designs.

ISBN: 978-1-950461-97-4

Double
or
Muffin

Cast of Characters

Merry Muffin Mystery Series

Merry Grace Wynter: newish owner of a real American castle, and muffin baker extraordinaire!
Virgil Grace: her husband, former sheriff of Autumn Vale, and now private investigator.
Gogi Grace: Virgil's mom and owner of Golden Acres Retirement Residence.
Lizzie Proctor: Merry's teen friend.
Pish Lincoln: Merry's best male friend, and partner in a new venture.
Doc English: Irascible senior who is Merry's living link to her past.
Gordy Shute: Autumn Vale resident and local conspiracy theorist.
Hannah Moore: Autumn Vale librarian.
Zeke: Gordy Shute's best friend and Hannah's boyfriend.
Dewayne Lester: Virgil's PI partner and old friend.
Patricia Lester: Dewayne's newish wife and cake baker extraordinaire.
Sheriff Urquhart: Autumn Vale sheriff.
Janice Grover: Merry's eccentric opera-loving Autumn Vale friend.
Leatrice Pugeot/Lynn Pugmire: Model and Merry's former boss in New York City.

Cast of Characters

Double or Muffin

Opera DivaNation Producers, Judges and Mentors:

Anne Parkinson: Helping Hand Network—HHN—producer
Sparrow Summers: HHN associate producer
Anokhi Auretius: Composer and judge on *DivaNation.*
Sir Daffyd Rhys: LOC—Lexington Opera Company—lyric tenor and judge on *DivaNation;* Welshman.
Giuseppe Plano: LOC baritone singer and judge on *DivaNation.*
Liliana Bartholomew: LOC soprano/mezzo-soprano and *DivaNation* mentor.
Carlyle O'Connor: LOC baritone and *DivaNation* mentor.
Roma Toscano: LOC lyric soprano and *DivaNation* mentor.

Opera DivaNation Finalists, and Others:

Kamile Markunis: Lithuanian-born soprano; exceptionally talented but very quiet.
Darcie Austin: struggling actress/singer, mezzo-soprano.
Brontay Bellini: teen opera prodigy, lyric soprano.
Zeb Wolfe: African-American graduate of Juilliard, lyric tenor.
Alain Primeau: French-Canadian tenor.
Lachlan McDermott: Scotsman; dramatic tenor; former member of the Scottish Tenors, an operatic performance group.
Pam Bellini: Brontay Bellini's mother.
Gilda Greenwald: Journalist.
Moze Markunis: Kamile's Svengali-like uncle/protector.

One

It started out as such a *beautiful* autumnal morning; a little chilly, as November is wont to be, but bright and clear.

Don't you love stories that begin like that? *It started out . . . It had been . . . It was a lovely day* . . . all with the implication that something bad is coming around the bend. In truth, had I but known what was coming in the next week—most of it exhausting and some of it life-threatening—I probably would have gotten out of bed anyway and forged on. It's what I do. There have been tragedies and frightening moments in these last three years, but for every bad thing that has happened, I have been overwhelmed by *good* things that also happen. I arrived at Wynter Castle over three years ago feeling alone and desperate; I now have a husband who adores me, and I'm surrounded by wonderful people who I love.

Anyway . . . it was a November Tuesday, and a beautiful autumn morning. Virgil and I indulged in a longer than normal breakfast after a fun sunrise surprise under the covers in our wonderful sunny bedroom in our gorgeous Craftsman home. I was feeling pretty blissful. If you like food descriptions I can tell you that he had extra-crispy bacon, eggs, hash browns and toast, a big breakfast to suit his big appetite. I ate my favorite morning meal, a toasted everything bagel with olive schmear and lox, brought back two days before from a too-brief trip to the city with Pish, my friend and now business partner.

Virgil had a teleconference call coming in at ten—he was still working with Sheriff Baxter of the Ridley Ridge Sheriff's Department, his former father-in-law (don't ask)—and Sheriff Urquhart of the Autumn Vale Sheriff's Department. Virgil and his PI partner, Dewayne, were helping in the formation of a task force to investigate a too-long list of missing local young females. So with a full cup of coffee he retreated to the office and I ascended to our master suite and dressed in boyfriend jeans, boots and a gorgeous cinnamon cable-knit long sweater.

"C'mon, Becket!" I said as I threw a cape over my sweater, grabbed my favorite Birken bag and headed out toward the castle. Pish and I were working toward the finalization of our business plan for the Wynter Woods Performance Center . . . if that's the name we settled on. Despite being still in the planning stage we had secured much of the funding necessary, some of it so far promised, not guaranteed. It made me nervous. Promises needed to turn into checks.

Becket, my marmalade cat, pranced at my side as I did my usual long slog from our house at the far edge of my property to tour the houses we had moved from Autumn Vale—homes that would soon be occupied. We are creating our own mini village that will be filled with creative types and their financial backers from the Lexington Symphony Orchestra and the Lexington Opera Company (the LSO and the LOC, respectively), all in support of the performing arts center we are building back in the woods. We'll open next summer, if all goes well.

I walked past the foundations where two more houses would soon nestle and stopped in front of the two already built, ready to be occupied. They are lovely, two distinct styles surrounded by nicely landscaped property. Behind them is a wall of forest, a few brilliant leaves still clinging, while more fluttered on the breeze; on the edge of the forest a white-tailed doe stood completely still and stared at me with a steady gaze. I held my breath, but then Becket leaped at a mouse and at the sound and flash of movement the deer whirled and fled into the woods. I let out my breath and smiled, but my smile died.

I had one of those inexplicable chills run down my back. Life was too good; my day had already been too perfect. *Something* was set to mar it. Looking back, the foreboding feeling was justified.

I turned away from the forest view and followed the path toward the castle. Leaves crunched under my booted feet along the worn path, and the nutty aroma rose to my nose like a perfume I'd never tire of. The view of the castle front is now partially screened when approaching from that direction by a hedge of arborvitae, a fast-growing evergreen, which hid the new parking lot from the castle. I walked along the edge of the parking lot, where Pish's car was the only vehicle.

In two weeks a documentary company was filming establishing shots of my castle for a docudrama on the robber barons of the nineteenth century. The producer was bringing a full crew, with cranes and drones and cameras, but they would only need a few days to film because establishing shots in this case meant exteriors only.

Brad and Dani, the owners/operators of Batavia Sparkle Clean, were scheduled to begin a thorough cleaning of the windows. We have a lot of windows: gothic arched windows line the dining room, French doors line the ballroom terrace, there is a magnificent stained glass rose window that takes up a large portion of the back wall of the great hall staircase, and a gothic diamond-paned window panel dominates the entry wall over the big oak double doors. It was going to take them the better part of a week.

I took a deep breath and rounded the hedge. The Batavia Sparkle Clean van was not yet parked in front of the castle. However, what *was* parked there made me yelp in dismay. *Three* Helping Hands Network cube vans crowded the crushed gravel circular drive, along with two more vans and a couple of Lexuses, and the castle doors were propped open with equipment boxes. "No, no, *no*!" I muttered and hastened on, hugging my Birken bag to my chest, my long cape like wings flapping in the breeze as ominous clouds began to muddy the clear blue sky of moments before. A storm was brewing, both in the weather overhead and in my heart. I'm sure I looked the very image of a vengeful Valkyrie on the warpath, but there was only one thought in my mind . . .

HHN vans should *not* be in front of my castle.

Inside, I wove through streams of people bustling back and forth, carrying totes and roles of wire, and found Pish. He stood by a gothic arched window in the dining room. He was holding one end of a measuring tape; a plump gray-haired middle-aged woman was holding up the other end, and jotted a note as she let it go. I recognized her; she was Anne Parkinson, the senior producer for the network, Rudy Alblom's partner. They had collaborated in creating the failed ghost-hunting show we had hosted a while ago, though she had not been present for the debacle. We had met in the past briefly, and I did like her, however . . .

"What is going on, Pish?" He explained. I bristled. "What do you *mean* you've volunteered the castle to host the finals of a reality TV competition show about opera wannabes?" I waited for *"Ha-ha, I'm just kidding"* to fall from his mouth. Instead, my dear friend, mentor, father figure and sometime trouble maker in chief shrugged and smiled. "Pish, tell me you're joking," I pleaded, clasping my hands together in a child's prayer attitude.

"I imagine the presence of the HHN crew is evidence that I am not joking."

My whole body vibrated with an odd mixture of trepidation and fury. "Explain, please."

"Rudy called from New York late last night," he said. "He was quite *quite* desperate. He told me—"

I held up one hand to halt him. Rudy is a nice man who is not above a little manipulation between friends. We've been through this before—the television crews, the mix of weirdoes and attentions seekers—with the ghost-hunting show and, as I've said, it did not end well. However, we have had *other* filming crews at the castle in the three years or so I've owned it; it has stood in for an English castle, an abandoned haunted manor, and the interior has been used in several television shows, docudramas and historical films. Nothing bad happened with *those* crews so, there's that. Not *all* TV people are nuts.

"Pish, can we take this conversation into the kitchen?" I muttered, giving Anne Parkinson the side-eye. She kept glancing over our way and waved to me. I waved back. She looked worried and tired and frazzled. I knew how she felt. "I have muffins to bake."

"Happily," he said, clearly *not* happy. He sent a look to Anne—one I couldn't evaluate—and followed me to the kitchen.

I needed tea. Wine would have been better, but wine and baking don't mix; I have the burn scar to prove it. Also, it was not even eleven a.m. and we do have standards. Wine in the morning is for dedicated wine-a-holics and I'm not there yet, though this project might drive me to it. Maybe a mimosa. *That's* a morning drink, right? Or a mojito . . . that had fruit, so I could call it a fruit salad in a glass. Distracted by thoughts of alcohol at eleven in the morning . . . not good.

So as I had already had my morning quota of coffee . . . *tea*. Becket preceded me into the kitchen huffily looking back over his shoulder every couple of steps. He does not like his routine disturbed. He had no doubt expected a peaceful ramble through the castle. I was in complete agreement with him; I had expected a morning meeting with Pish while I baked the muffins I supply to my mother-in-law's retirement and nursing home and the local coffee shop. However . . . Pish is my beloved friend, and I can't stay mad at him.

So by the time we reached the kitchen I was ready to be

convinced. There was no point making myself any crazier than I already am, I thought, taking off my cape and sweater and slinging them over a chair. I *knew* I'd cave, so I said, as I put the kettle on for tea and began to assemble my muffin ingredients, "Ten days, Pish. That's all we can give them; ten days, absolute *max*. We have a crew coming for the externals for the docudrama on the robber barons of the eighteen hundreds and after that a film crew coming for the news piece on our deal with the Lexington Opera, and the fundraiser the week of Thanksgiving. We need the place cleared out at least a day or two before the docudrama crew." It would take a couple of days and a cleaning crew to get rid of the residue from electrical lines taped on the floors and to return the rooms to order. I knew that from experience.

He took a seat at the trestle table with a complacent smile. "It should be five days, tops. Or seven at the most. Absolute max, ten, I agree. These are the final steps. They *were* working from a hotel in Rochester but—"He broke off suddenly and looked shifty.

I set down the enormous teapot with a clunk. "Why didn't they stay there, Pish?"

He sighed, fidgeted, then bent over to pet Becket, breaking eye contact. "They were evicted."

"Evicted from a *hotel*? What did they do, pee in a plastic aspidistra in the lobby? Play a rousing game of Nicky Nicky Nine Door?"

"No, though there was an unconfirmed report of one crew member lighting up a marijuana cigarette in the elevator."

I poured boiling water over tea bags and then sat down opposite him. "Pish, I'm serious; the window washing crew is scheduled to start today, and we have Gordy coming to clean up the property before the docudrama crew gets here. The landscaper is coming next week to tidy the gardens. What are we going to do?"

Pish gave me a look filled with asperity. "Darling girl, I'm *well* aware of what we need to do."

Chastened, I smiled at him. He was right, of course. No one knew what needed to be done better than Pish. And there was not a more business-minded individual; he had come from a family of some wealth, but Pish had quintupled his family's fortune with astute speculation and his work as an investment counselor to New York City stars. He was the trustworthy kind, with more connections than any Hollywood mogul. I took a deep breath and let it out, like a hiss of steam from a kettle, then got up to start my baking. "I'm sorry. It surprised and freaked me out. It's not a great time to have this happen."

"But remember, Rudy and HHN are the ones who will be doing the *Making the Music* documentary on our Wynter Woods Performance Center project. When he called last night he was desperate, so I told him yes, and in return he's offering a three-part series rather than one hour."

I turned back to him from the commercial fridge, where I was taking out a bowl of Honeycrisp apples, preparatory to making Honeycrisp streusel muffins, a new favorite for the folks at the Autumn Vale Variety and Coffee. I carried it back to the counter and poured myself a cup of tea, sitting down opposite him at the table. "Three hours? That's a lot of time to fill, Pish. Can we do this?"

"Of course!" he said.

I drank my tea then made the muffins while he talked, also baking a batch of pumpkin streusel muffins. In autumn you can't get enough pumpkin anything, I find, and I did have a lot of streusel topping made. By the end of Pish's explanation I was convinced. I had to trust him more completely. He had thought this through and wrung the absolute best deal from Rudy, signing himself up as a producer and creative consultant. He is the perfect business partner because he never takes offense when I underestimate him, and he is patient explaining his plans to me.

He then explained the opera contest while I made another batch of muffins, this time savory sweet combo maple bacon muffins. Of course, I had to bake bacon first, which filled the kitchen with the aroma of bacon and the coffee I was brewing in the huge urn. I know TV folk; we were going to need coffee . . . a *lot* of coffee.

The competition was in its final stage after a month of whittling down the contestants to six, three male and three female, he told me. The three judges were all known to me: Anokhi Auretius, the great African-American composer; Sir Daffyd Rhys, a Welsh tenor; and Giuseppe Plano, an Italian basso profundo. Of the mentors, I knew one and not the other: Liliana Bartholomew was not only one of America's greatest soprano divas, she is also our tenant in one of the two houses on our property, along with her even more famous son,

Blaq Mojo, rapper and producer extraordinaire. The second mentor was someone I've never met, though I've heard his name, Carlyle O'Connor, an Irish tenor of solid reputation.

The six competitors would be receiving their final mentoring, then singing one song, recording a video of it, and being judged. The actual awarding of the prize would happen at the HHN studios in New York City. I turned it over in my mind, considering all I had learned. I popped the tins of muffins into the oven then set the timer and turned to my friend; Pish was watching me. There was more. "What is it, Pish? You may as well tell me now."

He set his phone down on the table and cradled his drip-brewed cup of Kenya blend coffee—off limits to anyone but him—staring down into it. He then looked up and gave me a squinty-eyed gaze. "Would you be up to maximizing our profits from this little venture?"

I sat down across from him again. "How?"

"Would you consider catering the craft services table? It would be much simpler if we could do that in-house."

I bit my lip and thought about it, calculating the electricity bill for the month and weighing it against how much I could soak HHN for. A new thought popped into my head. "Pish, are *all* of these people staying here, at the castle?"

"Of *course* not. Remember the motel that the crew from the ghost-hunting show used, the one out on the highway?"

I remembered that dingy cave—I've seen it once or twice—but I'd camp in the wilderness and sleep in a bear's den before I'd lie down on one of their bed coverings. I nodded.

"The HHN crew will be holing up there. Anokhi has her own house, as does Liliana, who has graciously invited Sir Daffyd, Giu and Carlyle to stay with her. But we *will* be hosting the six contestants."

"And who else?"

Pish set his mug back down and ticked off on his fingers as he said, "Anne Parkinson, of course. There's also Sparrow Summers: she's the associate producer. Pam Bellini is one of the contestant's moms—"

"Mom?"

"Brontay Bellini is fifteen, so legally she needs a chaperon, her mom," he said, waggling the third finger. "There will also be Moze Markunis; he's the uncle of one of the contestants."

"How old is *that* contestant?"

"Kamile Markunis is twenty-three or so, I believe? But she's Lithuanian, and her uncle is protective. It's nonnegotiable; Anne asked if we'd let him stay as a special favor. Anne says they don't want to lose Kamile. She's a front-runner, a star in the making. We do have an extra room, so I said okay."

"Favoritism?" I smiled. "And I thought all competition-based reality shows were run so fairly!"

He rolled his eyes at my sarcasm and smiled. "Anokhi's home *is* ready to use, correct?"

I nodded.

"She's trying to finish *African Meditation Suite*, her next work, while they tape *Opera DivaNation*. Moving the competition here, where she has a home ready for her, is fortuitous. I was surprised to hear she'd agreed to be a judge, and even more surprised she never mentioned it when she was here last." He paused, then said, "I'm pleased that Liliana is acting as a mentor to the singers."

I brightened and smiled in agreement. "She's *perfect* for that, so kind and warm and knowledgeable." Liliana Bartholomew had been with us one week ago for a meet and greet for the townsfolk. She performed on a stage in the woods near the performing arts center site, first a lovely version of "Amazing Grace," and then a stirring, haunting, *rousing* rendition of "Go Tell It on the Mountain" with the choir from the local Methodist church. After, she had greeted the choristers and had a lovely chat with them all. The video my young friend Lizzie had posted of the event had in a week garnered hundreds of thousands of views.

"She's graciously agreed to host the other mentor and the other two judges."

"This is kind of exciting," I said, a trickle of anticipation racing down my backbone. "We've seen both Sir Daffyd Rhys and Giuseppe Plano perform."

"Giuseppe is the world's sweetest man," Pish said, with a fond smile. "We saw him play Escamillo in *Carmen*."

"So we'll do a craft services table–type lunch, and dinner for the contestants?"

"And for the two producers, Anne and Sparrow. We can hire outside help."

"On HHN's dime?"

He nodded.

"You're going to love this, aren't you? Being around so many singers and opera greats?"

He grinned and nodded, looking about twenty, with his divine skin and longish light brown hair.

"You know who else would love this? Janice," I said about our opera aficionado friend Janice Grover, who is an amateur singer and the owner of Crazy Lady Antiques.

"Well, of course she can observe, but—"

"I was thinking more along the line of she could be my hired culinary helper for the week. She has catered Brotherhood of the Falcon lunches for twenty years or more. And maybe we can hire Patricia, too," I said about the woman now married to Virgil's business partner, Dewayne. Patricia is a wizard with baked goods, especially cakes. With me rounding out the threesome, we should be able to handle it.

"As long as Janice doesn't pester the judges and mentors too much, I'll agree to that."

"Because opera singers never enjoy fawning fans," I said.

He smiled. "You have a point. Oh, there's one more person we have to host . . . I forgot about her. Gilda Greenwald is a reporter for *Modern Entertainment Monthly*. She's doing a spread on the competition. The contestants will be here within the hour and are starting work right away, but Gilda isn't coming until tomorrow morning. She stayed behind in Rochester for some reason."

I got out my clipboard and took the order sheets off the top to expose clean lined paper underneath. "The mother and daughter need a room together. The two female contestants have another, then one room for the male contestants. The female producers can share a room. That's . . . five rooms for the show people."

Lynn Pugmire, formerly Leatrice Pugeot, came in stretching her long slim frame, yawning and sniffing the air delicately. Lynn is a retired supermodel, was once my boss, and at one time my archnemesis. Despite all the dirty water under our mutual bridge, I was beginning to like her rather than pity her. She snatched a piece of bacon and I handed her a muffin and poured her a cup of tea. I stood and sighed, grabbing my sweater. "I'll be back in to introduce myself to the crew, but right now, I have window washers to talk to."

Two

"I'll walk with you," Lynn said, dusting crumbs off her hands, then drinking down the last of her tea and putting her mug into the dishwasher. "I've been talking to Anne for the last twenty minutes. One of the *Opera DivaNation* stylists had a plumbing emergency and left—"

"Plumbing emergency? Surely she could have had someone else take care of it," I said as we headed out of the kitchen.

"*Her* plumbing, not her home's . . . you know, she needed a doctor and all that. So I'm filling in. I need to talk to Anne and Sparrow to see how they want me to work."

"A stylist? Why wouldn't they ask me?" I asked. I was once a stylist on fashion shoots, after all.

"They all know you're too busy to take on styling, too," she said.

That was true.

We parted as she returned to the dining room and I exited the castle. The clouds that had scudded in and concealed the sun had thickened, and a breeze had come up. I huddled into my sweater and sought the window cleaners, who had wedged their van into the minuscule space left by the HHN crew. Brad and Dani, dressed in jeans, steel-toed shoes and Batavia Sparkle Clean windbreakers over hooded sweatshirts, unloaded equipment from the back of their van; squeegees, buckets, chemicals, orange cones and a couple of signs for the work area. Together they lifted down a gigantic extension ladder from a roof rack. I waited until they had, together, carried it around to the far side of the castle, and returned, and then waved. Dani approached while Brad kept unloading.

"How are you, Dani?" We shook hands. Hers was warm. I gestured to the HHN vans. "There have been changes since we arranged the schedule."

"I see that," Dani said.

I told her about the HHN *Opera DivaNation* shoot. "There will be shoots outside," I said. "We may need to adjust the schedule. I hope that's not a problem."

She sent a hostile look at the cube vans and cars crowded around them. "It's only a problem if it causes a delay," Dani said, as Brad looked up from his toolbelt with a frown. "We have a job set up in

Batavia on the fifteenth, and we pride ourselves on getting the job done *on time.*"

"I understand. I'll do everything I can to keep them from delaying you. But if it comes down to it, the absolute most vital windows to be cleaned are the stained glass and the rose window. Those will be in most shots of the documentary and need to gleam. Just do the best you can."

"Got it," the fellow said. "Can you ask the TV crew to move their vehicles so we can get the rest of our gear out?"

Dani looked at him with a frown, but he just stared at me. I glanced between them; it appeared to me that they had all of their equipment out, but I *did* want HHN to move their vans, so I wasn't going to quibble. "I'll get them to move the cars, at least, to the parking lot right away, and they can move the vans once they've unloaded." An HHN crew member came out and got in the cab of one of the cube vans. It looked like they were going to move the vehicles on their own. "I'll leave you now to get started," I said.

As I started to walk away, I heard the chugging of a heavy motor, and a burgundy dark-windowed motor coach pulled around the bend, up the lane and stopped on the graveled parking area. There was a hiss of air brakes being released, and the motor stilled. This must be the contenders arriving. I was confirmed in this guess when Anne burst from the castle and hustled out to greet the contestants as the door swung open.

I moved to stand next to her and said, "Why don't you introduce me as they come out?"

Bounding down the steps first, with a bag slung over his shoulder, was a slim young man, more wiry than skinny, with big glasses on a beaky nose that was centered on a long narrow face. "Bonjour, Madame Anne!" he bellowed. "Allo, allo, this is our new home? C'est le fun, yes?"

"Alain Primeau, this is your hostess, the owner of the castle, Merry Wynter," Anne said.

"Ah, t'es ben chix. La la . . ." He smiled and bent over my hand, which I had extended to shake, but he placed a kiss on my palm.

I jerked my hand back. It was unexpected, and I was taken aback. He smiled and cocked his head to one side.

"Don't mind him, he's French," said the next person down the steps, a girl younger than Lizzie and chunky, with dark eyes and dark curly hair pulled up in a high ponytail.

"Actually, he's French Canadian," Anne leaned in and muttered as Primeau strolled off, "and he doesn't mean any harm. He said you're beautiful."

"Actually, he said you're hot." A tired-looking woman followed the young girl down the steps. "I'm Pam, and this is my daughter, Brontay, the winner of *Opera DivaNation*!" she said, resting her hand on her daughter's shoulder.

"Mo-om, do you have to do that every single time I meet someone?" Brontay, who was quite a bit taller than the other woman, shrugged away from her mother, slung her duffle over her shoulder and stomped after Primeau. Pam shrugged, tossed her long brown hair back, rolled her hazel eyes, then followed her daughter.

A young man with smooth dark skin stepped down and looked around with interest.

"Merry, this is Zeb Wolfe," Anne said with a smile. "Zeb, this is Merry Wynter, your hostess and owner of the castle."

He met my gaze and smiled. "You've saved the show, I guess," he said, taking my outstretched hand and shaking. "We're all thankful."

"I'm delighted." He was nice-looking; middle height, dark curly close-cropped hair, full lips and kind brown eyes. He had a delightful smile, warmth emanating from him.

After him came a pretty blue-eyed blonde: thirtyish, slim, dressed too lightly for the weather. She shivered and glanced around. "What is this place anyway?"

"My ancestral castle," I said tightly.

"This is Darcie Austin," Anne said. "Darcie, say hello to the owner of Wynter Castle, Merry Wynter."

Neither of us put out our hand and she sailed past me without a word.

"Isn't she a treat," said the next to disembark the bus. He was a tall, sturdily built fellow, with a friendly freckled face topped by reddish curls. "Lachlan McDermott, milady, at your service," he said, a lively Scottish lilt to his delicious voice, as he jumped down from the last step. He bowed over my hand and I smiled.

"Lachlan, where is Kamile?" Anne asked, mounting the few steps into the bus and looking down the aisle. The driver ignored her. "Where *is* she?" she asked, stepping back down. She sounded a little panicked, her eyes wide.

"Ah, now there's a tale. Don't worry, milady . . . she's on her way. But the lovely Kamile would not be conveyed by such plebian means, ah, no, she is being carried hither by . . ." He stopped and smiled. "There they are now."

A black Escalade pulled around the bend and up to park by the bus. A long pair of slim legs draped in flame-colored silk, the skirt emblazoned with a peacock feather image, emerged from the passenger side; it was a young woman, lean, very tall, big sunglasses concealing her eyes. She shouldered a Birken bag that made me want to snatch it from her, and sailed past all of us without a word, toward the castle door. The driver of the car got out and stood, thoughtfully watching her go. He was a stocky man, with wild, bushy salt-and-pepper eyebrows over deep-set eyes and a shock of iron gray hair that stood straight up from his pink scalp. He had bulky shoulders and no discernible neck.

From the backseat emerged another man—this one I recognized. It was Sir Daffyd Rhys, the Welsh tenor who had played every tenor role in opera, and had a dozen or more albums as well as Grammy Awards. Handsome, with an elegantly styled mop of white hair, a white beard and piercing blue eyes, like the Welsh sky, he was breathtaking in that way that stars often are, polished to perfection.

"That, madam, was the front-runner, so I've been told," Lachlan said, eyeing Anne with acerbity.

"I beg your pardon?" I said, my attention pulled back from staring at Sir Daffyd.

"That's Kamile Markunis and her uncle or lover or *something*, Moze Markunis."

"Lachlan, enough," Anne said angrily. "Don't be a jerk and stop making insinuations. It's an open competition, all fair and aboveboard." She looked worried, and frowned at the two men who, despite arriving in the same car, seemed to only tolerate each other.

"And yet you let Kamile have a companion with her, whereas the rest of us can't? I'd say *that* is favoring her, Anne. Brontay I understand; she's a baby and has to have her mama. But if Kamile can have a companion or guardian, then we should all be able to."

"Why did they come together?" Anne muttered under her breath.

"The others had a full car. Sir Daffyd wished to come earlier and managed to cadge a ride with the Markunises," Lachlan answered. "Not the Lithuanian gentleman's preference, but I believe the ride was offered in the spirit of buttering up the judges."

Anne sighed and shook her head.

I stepped forward as Rhys got his suitcase out of the back of the Escalade. "Sir Daffyd," I said. "How lovely to have you here. I'm Merry Grace Wynter; this is my home," I said, sweeping my hand over the whole of Wynter Castle. I was peacocking, I'll admit, excited to welcome a star of his importance to my abode.

"Ms. Wynter, how *charming* to meet you." His voice was gorgeous, plummy and full-throated, yet soft and caressing. He set his suitcase down on the flagstone step and took both of my hands, cradling them in his, chafing them to warmth. "I know Percival, of course, and I look forward to reanimating our old acquaintance, as well as to making yours."

Percival; I smiled. I hadn't heard anyone call Pish by his given name in quite a while. He had been on the LSO/LOC board in past years, so of course he knew all of these luminaries and counted them among his friends. "I hope you enjoy your stay at Ms. Bartholomew's Wynter Woods home."

Anne had been speaking with Moze Markunis as Lachlan brushed past them toward the castle. For a moment they appeared to quarrel, but the gentleman shrugged and said something under his breath. The producer nodded, then beckoned to me.

"Moze, this is Ms. Merry Wynter, the owner of Wynter Castle. She has graciously invited us here to finish our program."

"How fortunate," he said, in a heavy accent. "I promise not to trespass on your hospitality for long, madam. I will be here tonight and tomorrow, but I have business elsewhere, and will be departing once I see my niece settled."

"You and your niece are welcome, of course."

Sir Daffyd had already proceeded into the castle. Moze and Anne followed while I watched. I had that tingling in my neck, that presagement of trouble; the worry in Anne's eyes concerned me. I hoped the tingling was just muscle strain. Brad and Dani were carefully extending the huge ladder that reached the second-floor windows. I waved to them, then followed the others inside, past the closed door to the turret library to the dining room.

The dining room, along the east side of the castle between the parlor and turret room library, is across the great hall from the ballroom. It overlooks the lane on an angle. Where the ballroom is lined with large French doors, the dining room—only half as long or less—has three sets of gothic arched windows that almost reach the floor. They are diamond-paned with beveled glass and flood the room with light, a good thing because the dining room is paneled in dark wood. The room is anchored with a huge fireplace on one end, actually in the corner of the room. We have added a lovely piano that Pish plays when we have company. There is an enormous eight-foot-long Eastlake buffet along one wall, and the rest of the room is taken up with round tables that seat five or six people each. We use those when we have a tea party or event of twenty or more people.

The HHN crew had clustered most of those in the dark northwest corner, leaving only a couple near the center, while along the whole east side of the room, by the gothic windows, they had set up a performance area for the singers and a spot for judging and mentoring. Behind the performance space there was a broad opening taken up with lights on stands, microphones angled to catch sound, sound equipment like mixing boards and computers on rectangular folding tables, and wires snaking everywhere. Technicians wearing headphones bustled back and forth, unwinding coils of wire and hooking up the equipment.

Lynn was chatting with two women, and beckoned me over. She grasped my arm with her iron grip. "Merry Wynter, this is Anne Parkinson and Sparrow Summers."

"I know Anne," I said, smiling at the plump middle-aged woman.

She now held a clipboard, with a bullet list printed on it of initial shots needed. "Merry, we have a drone operator here for today and would like to do establishing shots. If we clear out our trucks, can you have those window cleaners move their van? Maybe to the parking lot?"

I sighed, thinking of Brad and Dani, who were even now expecting to start the job. They'd have to take the ladder down; that would not go over well. "I'll see what I can do."

"Also, if you don't mind, our people may move the outdoor furniture around, for clean shots."

"Okay," I said.

"And we'll be painting your double doors—"

"*No*. Do not touch the doors, do not paint *anything*," I said, starting to feel the tension creep up my back. "I mean that. Not a *thing*."

The producer chewed the end of a pencil, glanced down at her list, then met my gaze. Whatever she saw there, she caved. "All right. No painting."

"And the window washers have already started to set up. I wish you'd said something about the drone footage earlier. If you want them to move stuff, I suggest you get your crew to help them."

Anne opened her mouth, but I held up one hand to stay her protestations. She shut it and nodded, bustling off and beckoning a couple of her crew members to join her.

I turned to the other woman.

"So pleased to meet you," Sparrow said. She was a younger woman than Anne, probably in her thirties, slim, ponytailed, with wide eyes and an air of enthusiasm. She looked over my shoulder and waved; when I turned I saw some of the singers entering. "Now, Merry," she said, glancing down at her clipboard, then refocusing on me. "If you don't mind, we'd like to interview you for background on the castle and your ownership. We'll use the information in our voice-over, and for questions we'll pose to our contestants as they get ready to compete."

"Sure," I said.

Lynn touched my arm. "Merry, they were also wondering where you think the best place to set up wardrobe and makeup will be?"

I considered it carefully. Upstairs would be the only option. There were, officially, seventeen bedrooms upstairs, but we had not remodeled all of them yet. Still, for makeup, hair and wardrobe, it wouldn't matter if the room was painted and carpeted, just that it had functioning bathroom facilities and space. "You'll actually need two rooms, at least."

Anne, who had returned to stand with us, nodded with an appreciative look. "Lynn, can you coordinate with Merry and work it out? Then give the okay to our guys, and they can move all the trunks to the rooms." She checked something off her list, then looked back up. "If you have one more room as a staging area for the trunks, it would help."

I led the way, out to the great hall and up the grand two-direction staircase that splits, winding up to the gallery, off of which are all the bedrooms and suites. For the next half hour Lynn and I toured upstairs and jotted down room assignments. I gave her access to my office and the printer, and she made signs for each door so she could direct HHN staff to the appropriate place, while I made sure that the contestant and staff rooms were supplied with everything they needed. Pish was in his suite and poked his head out a few times, looking more and more perturbed. The last time he had his phone to his ear.

Finally he emerged and caught me by the arm as I was rushing past along the gallery. "Merry, dearest, I did not realize how much work this was going to be and that it would require so much from you," he said.

"It's okay, Pish, it won't be so much once we're organized."

"It *will* be a lot of work, especially since I convinced you to supply craft services as well as meals for the contestants. I called Rudy and made him give us a better deal. He's forwarding a big deposit. Your name will be listed in the credits as a consultant." He quirked a sly smile. "Also in the credits under craft services it will list Wynter Castle Catering."

"You're a prince, Pish," I said, giving him a quick hug. "Your friends are downstairs, you know. *Sir Daffyd Rhys!*" I said, eyes wide. "He's every bit as impressive in person as on stage or TV."

"Has someone got a bit of a crush?" he said with a wink. I rolled my eyes. "By the way, I spoke with Anokhi. Once she, Giu, Carlyle and Liliana are here Daffyd can have his luggage taken over to Liliana's house."

"I hope they find their homes comfortable." I had welcome baskets prepared with local products, from honey to jam and wine, as well as Pish's contribution, a pound of his favorite coffee beans and a pour-over coffee maker.

I had a million and one things to do, as well as delivering muffins to town and Ridley Ridge. And I had to stop and ask Janice and Patricia if they wanted to sign on as my co-chefs. I descended to get started in the kitchen, taking a deep breath in and letting it out slowly, quelling a wave of panic. There *was* a lot to think of . . . much more than I had even considered when I agreed, Pish was right about that.

He had been wise to push for a better deal. We were doing them a huge favor, after all, in giving them space.

As long as I stayed organized we would get through this. It was just a few days . . . a week or so at most. Lizzie, alerted to what was going on by Lynn, I supposed—the teenager and the model had struck up an unlikely friendship—bounded into the kitchen chattering nonstop about the singing competition and her first sight of the contestants, an unusual burst of buoyancy from one who was often so dour. I half listened as I took inventory of my cupboards and pantry, seeing what we had and what we'd need.

"So, can I stick around?" she finally said. "Lynn said I needed to clear it with you—"

"Really? Lynn said that?"

"Of *course* she did," Lizzie said crossly. "So, can I stay?"

"You can stay on one condition," I said, eyeing her squintily.

She eyed me back, equally squint-eyed. "*What* condition?"

"You can stick around and observe, but you have to help me get the rooms ready, and do chores around here."

"Not—gulp—not cooking?" she said, wide-eyed, with a curled lip.

"Good *grief,* no. I wouldn't subject anyone to that. I've eaten your burned eggs. I'll get other help for that."

"Good," she said, snatching a muffin. "Mmmm . . . maple bacon. Yum." She bit and chewed, watching me.

"Bed making, bathroom cleaning and laundry." She shrugged in answer, which I took to mean she'd do it. "I'll pay you hourly, of course, and I expect you to keep track of your own hours and bill me. Now, you've finished your muffin; let's get moving."

"Can't I go and watch them set up the cameras?"

"No. Let's start with the contestants' bedrooms first."

Three

I sent Lizzie upstairs with fresh linens and told her which bedrooms to start with, then grabbed my sweater and ran out to apologize to the window washers for the interruption they were going to experience. The crew had helped them move their stuff and loaded most of it back into their van.

"I'm so sorry about this," I said, hugging my sweater around me against the wind.

Brad glowered over at me, his lip curled, as he slammed the van back door then rattled it, to make sure the latch had caught. Dani accepted my apology with a nod. "Look, it's not something you could avoid," she said with a sigh. "We talked to the drone guy and he said that his footage would take three hours. So we'll be back in four hours. Hopefully we can rescue an hour or so of daylight, but I doubt it."

I returned inside and found Anne, telling her that her crew had exactly three hours to do the drone footage and not a second more. I spotted Lizzie lurking. Without me to ride herd she had snuck back downstairs and was hiding in the shadows of the dining room watching the camera operators set up and go over shooting lists with Anne and Sparrow. The girl is hungry for knowledge in her chosen field, anything to do with photography, taping or filming. How could I be angry?

I watched, too. The production crew members were now busily staging a couple of performance areas by the big fireplace and near the piano, dressing the space with silken cloth over the piano, and urns of (fake) flowers by the fireplace. To conceal wires they had several gorgeous patterned Turkish rugs on the floor, layered in angles by the tall gothic windows that lined the far wall. That was going to be tricky to light, I thought, but they were professionals and knew what they were doing. Key light, fill lights, back lights and various deflectors were all being set in place on tripods. I crossed my fingers behind my back, hoping the electrical panel could handle it. The film crew had a couple of steady cams on mounts, and other camera and equipment cases lined the far wall. The judges' three director chairs had been set up in a row, with a big *Opera DivaNation* banner as their backdrop.

Despite myself, I was intrigued; this was a much more professional production than the ghost-hunting show had been. I knew I had to shoehorn Lizzie into it as a learning opportunity, so I cornered Anne, pointed to my teenage friend, and told the producer how she had worked with a camera crew before and was passionate and hardworking when it came to anything to do with film or photography. Could she shadow the camera operators? "She could be an intern. She'll do anything you say," I urged.

"You're lucky I have a soft spot for young people," Anne said with a smile. "If she'll fetch and carry and do their grunt work, I'm sure our video guys will be happy to show her the ropes."

"Thank you," I said.

Lizzie had been lurking and watching me with that odd concentrated light in her eyes. She's intense, possessed of a single-minded passion I respect but that can be unnerving at times. She no doubt knew what I was doing—she knows I'll always go to bat for her—and was awaiting the outcome.

She practically jumped with joy when I told her the deal we had made. "But *my* work first," I said. We returned upstairs and moved swiftly through the bedrooms, making beds and supplying towels, and I then directed the moving of the luggage from the luxury bus to the appropriate rooms. I ordered Lizzie to take the gift baskets to the two houses—Becket followed her out, unnerved by all the activity and noise—then returned to the dining room.

Moze Markunis idled by the craft services table I had set up along the wall closest to the door. He drank coffee and smoked. I stiffened and held my temper. I didn't have *No Smoking* signs posted, I reminded myself, and he didn't know the house rules; no smoking in the castle for about three million reasons, one of which was that it was a two-hundred-year-old castle and irreplaceable.

"Mr. Markunis, how are you doing?" I said, using my pleasant but cool tone. "Your room has been prepared. Pish Lincoln is upstairs and can show you where it is."

"Thank you," he said. He had what I thought of as a Slavic face, the kind with Spock eyebrows that spiked over deep-set wintry blue eyes, a lip that seemed to curl naturally, and a wrinkled forehead topped by spiky hair that was receding in deep Vs just above the temples. He had an interesting face, commanding and secretive, and was impeccably dressed in a Hugo Boss suit and tie.

"May I ask one thing?" I said. He eyed me, one brow raised. "May I ask that you not smoke inside the castle? I have a smoking area on the side terrace off the ballroom that I will ensure is fitted with ashtrays but . . . absolutely *no smoking inside,* please and thank you."

He nodded. "Certainly, madam."

"You can extinguish that in the toilet of the half bath that is off the butler's hallway just beyond the kitchen."

He nodded and departed the dining room. Kamile had been watching us with an unhappy look on her lovely face. She was striking, one of those born models with a still and yet expressive face: high cheekbones, full mouth, smooth skin marred only by the over-application of makeup and a thick coating of maroon lipstick. Her eyes were light brown and topped by a thick fringe of fake eyelashes. She caught my steady gaze and appeared torn. Finally, she slipped off the stool, where she was awaiting instruction from the producers, and approached me.

"Mrs. Wynter?" she said, in a husky melodic voice that I looked forward to hearing in song. "I hope my uncle was not bothering you?"

"Not at all, Ms. Markunis," I said, copying her formality. "I was simply informing him of the house rules . . . no smoking inside these walls. I'll be making a general announcement to that effect." *I'll be damned,* I thought; those eyelashes weren't fake, they were real and luxurious, though heavily caked with mascara!

She nodded. "Good. One or two of the crew smoke, as does Sparrow, I think. Pamela Bellini, though she doesn't let her kid see her. Darcie as well, although she will let no one see her."

"Please call me Merry."

"Kamile," she said, putting out one long-fingered hand; we shook. "You have a beautiful home. I feel almost like I'm back in Lithuania."

"We're old for a European American build, but not old by Euro standards. I've never been to Lithuania, though I have traveled close by, a short cruise on the Baltic."

She nodded, her expression grave. "Do you like opera?"

"Very much. I look forward to hearing you all sing. What made you enter this competition?"

"My uncle," she said, with a half smile that died quickly. She watched Lynn, who was consulting with Anne Parkinson. "The others are saying that Lynn Pugmire was once a famous model; is that true?"

I smiled. The gossip was probably started by Lynn herself, and why shouldn't she put it out that she was famous? Sometimes it is the only thing that will get you respect in entertainment. "She is Leatrice Pugeot, a world-famous supermodel since she was a teenager. She's transitioning to a new career. If you ever need any advice on navigating the world of entertainment, she knows it all."

"Hmm. I did not suspect it."

"What is going to be your performance song for the competition?"

"I am singing 'Voi che sapete' . . . it is Mozart."

"Yes, from the *Marriage of Figaro*! A so-called trouser role . . . Cherubino, correct?"

She looked at me with respect. "You *do* know your opera!"

"Pish Lincoln has been my mentor. He took me to many operas over the years. I didn't appreciate them at first, and still don't know as much as most opera lovers, but I have enjoyed many great performances, some with your judges, Giu Plano and Sir Daffyd Rhys, as well as one of the contest mentors, Liliana Bartholomew."

With increasing animation, she sat up straight, a light in her lovely eyes as she said, her words only faintly accented with a Middle-European inflection, "I'm hoping to perform the piece with Agnes Baltsa's warmth, her specificity and lovely vocal quality for the song."

I smiled at Kamile. "I'm going to disappoint you now. I'll confess I am not familiar with that singer. I have exposed the totality of my knowledge of the Cherubino role at this point."

She threw her head back and her throaty laughter was warm and soft and yet with an earthy guttural quality I found most attractive. Others did too, looking in our direction and staring. Kamile noticed their stares and shrank in on herself, making a hasty farewell and hustling back over to the producers, behind whom she hid.

"What was my niece laughing about?" Moze Markunis asked, approaching from the doorway.

"Nothing in particular," I said, staring at the man, whose brow was knit and mouth turned down in a frown. "Surely she's allowed to laugh?" I said, nettled, as he frowned and stared over toward his niece.

His lip curled in contempt and he walked away from me without further comment. I was perturbed. His question could have been innocent, mere curiosity, but I didn't think so. He exuded an aura of absolute authority—the Euro strongman vibe—and it made me antsy.

I have seen too many women controlled by the men in their life, made to explain every laugh, every comment, every glance. I didn't like it one bit, but maybe I was overreacting. I hoped so.

"He's a piece o' work, isn't he?" said a voice at my side.

I turned and found Lachlan McDermott beside me.

"I feel sorry for the lass, I truly do. She's got a lovely voice, perhaps the best here, and he makes sure everyone knows it. It makes her uneasy, the way Moze pushes her," Lachlan said.

"You confirmed what I was worrying about."

"Aye, he's no' someone to tangle with."

I smiled up at him. He was good-looking in a redheaded, freckled Scottish way; he had laughing blue eyes and was broad-shouldered. I could picture him wearing a kilt and tossing the caber, he appeared so strong, with bulky shoulders and a strong jaw. "You look so familiar. Have I seen you on stage or TV?"

He grinned and leaned down close to me, so close I could smell his aftershave. "Perhaps. I was with a group called the Scottish Tenors for seven years," he said, as a swell of music echoed, then was quickly turned down, as the sound techs fiddled with the volume. "We made records and toured the U.S. What a braw time we had. American girls are *lovely*!"

"Ah, yes, the Scottish Tenors! I remember you now," I said, not confessing how much I loathe the Three Tenors copycat groups. "Did you disband, then?"

"The boys are still goin' but without me. They added another singer two years ago after I left."

I was startled into staring up into his blue eyes, fringed by reddish eyelashes. "Why would you leave?"

He shrugged and straightened, looking off toward the other contestants. "I get that a lot, the questions. No one realizes how difficult it is to tour with a bunch of lads who only want to get wi' the groupies and don't take the art seriously. I want to perform on stage. I want to do *Don Giovanni*."

"You wouldn't play Don Giovanni—"

"I'd play Don Ottavio, the tenor role, of course."

"Lachlan, can you come now?" Anne said, summoning him with a flap of a handful of papers.

"Aye, I'm on my way." He turned and bowed to me. "Thank you, milady, for your hospitality toward this weary suffering group of players. After wearing out our welcome in Rochester, I feel we have ascended from purgatory to heaven."

"What exactly happened in Rochester?"

"What didn't?" he said lightly, and departed.

Lizzie, who had been lurking about in the snaky background of camera and lighting cords, was now off talking to the youngest competitor, Brontay, while her mother, Pam, argued with Sparrow, hands waving, face contorted and red. I made my way over to them, where they all stood by one of the windows.

"Lizzie, introduce me?"

To give her justice, she did the job nicely. Brontay eyed me with trepidation—adults are sorted into allies and enemies at that age, or that's how it was with me when I was a teen—so I thought I'd try and put her at her ease. "It's unusual for a teenager to be interested in opera. How did that come about?"

She pushed back her wild mop of gorgeous natural hair and haltingly told me about her mother's ambition and push. They saw a ten-year-old girl on a TV talent show sing opera; when Brontay began to sing along with the music, Pam decided her daughter would become a star.

"Do you like it?" I hate to see kids pushed into things they hate to fulfill the parents' ambitions.

"I think so," she said, hesitating, frowning down at her booted feet. She chewed her full bottom lip but then met my eyes. She had an almost adult determination in her eyes, a presence and calm resolve rare in one so young. "I didn't at first, but I love the feeling of the voice coming up," she said, using both hands to signal a rising within her. "It's like a spring, you know, that bubbles out of the earth. And I like that other people like to hear me sing."

"Tell me about the other contestants?" I asked, curious about her take on them all.

She grinned, her dark eyes sparkling. "Boys first. Lachlan is too, too Scottish, you know, all *aye* and *dinna* and *lass* and *laddie*. And Alain is so *annoyingly* French."

"He's actually Canadian," I said.

"I know, but he acts French, snooty to me, you know, because he considers me just a kid and not competition."

I raised my brows. Alain could live to regret underestimating this determined teen. "And the last guy?"

"Zeb . . . he's cool," she said, looking toward Zeb Wolfe. Her cheeks pinkened. "He *gets* me. My dad was Black. He was a famous football player in the NFL. He died two years ago—"

"Oh, I'm so sorry! My dad died when I was five. I know what it's like."

"—and I can talk to Zeb about . . . about being torn, like, not fitting in. His friends, when he was young, didn't get him either because he was into performing. He got called a lot of names. So did I, because of that and because I'm too tall. I was always too big for my age." Her lip quivered. "It wasn't easy. I ended up going to a private school, and now I'm homeschooled."

I touched her shoulder. "It will get easier," I said. I, too, had been big and tall for my age, taller than any of the guys I liked until I went to college. "What about the other two women?"

"Darcie is a total bitch," Brontay said.

I choked back a laugh.

"She *is*!" Brontay said, her brows knit. "She acts like I'm not even alive, and she's just . . . she's just . . ."

I had been eyeing Darcie, and I said, "Self-absorbed?"

Brontay nodded. "Except sometimes. Sometimes she's *awful*, but then once in a while . . ." She frowned and sighed, her brows drawn down. "Once in a while she, like, *sees* me, and she's nice to me. I don't get her."

"I imagine she's focused on this competition. What about Kamile?"

The teenager twisted her mouth and tilted her head. "I can't think of the word. It's like she's not even of this world, you know? Like she landed here from a place where everyone is cold and careful and quiet, and walks on tippy-toes." She demonstrated, rising up on her toes and carefully navigating a few feet before collapsing back to her full foot.

I wasn't sure I understood. The Kamile I had met was warm and sweet. "Have you ever talked to her without her uncle around?"

Brontay shook her head. "At the hotel we all had our own rooms, so I never saw her except on stage. And her uncle is *always* around."

"He's apparently going away tomorrow for a time. Try talking to her without Moze nearby. I think there's a nice person hiding in a shy shell."

The girl's attention was claimed and she hustled away without another word.

"What did *you* two talk about?" I said to my young friend, who had her camera slung over her shoulder, of course; she never went anywhere without it.

Lizzie looked shady and shrugged. "Stuff."

I regarded her for a long minute as music began to fill the dining room. The engineers were doing sound checks with each competitor. "I'm happy Brontay has you to talk to."

"You are?"

"I am. She could not have a better role model than you, Lizzie." I meant it. My young friend had gone from public nuisance vandal to ambitious and mature woman in the three years I had known her.

"She wants to get a tattoo of a bird of paradise on the back of her neck," Lizzie blurted out.

"And you told her . . . ?" I waited for Lizzie's words of wisdom, that a tattoo was permanent, a big step, and that Brontay would have to wait until she was eighteen.

"I told her I'd hook her up with my tattoo artist in Ridley Ridge."

"Lizzie!" I squawked.

Lizzie grinned, laughed, and strode off to bug the film crew.

Four

I was tired already, and it was just after noon. Anne and Pish were close by and talking; my friend was earnestly trying to impress upon the producer how important it was that they wrap this up in five days. Seven at the most. Ten, tops. She nodded and smiled, but her attention was divided, and she ended up abandoning Pish in mid-sentence.

We were going to have trouble with them, I knew it. I retreated to the kitchen to box my muffins and found Lachlan there, snagging one from the cooling trays. "Hey, those are my bread and butter, so to speak," I said.

"How much do you charge?" he said, smirking around a mouthful.

"Five bucks apiece," I said, giving them a New York City price.

"Then I owe you fifteen dollars." He waved the half-eaten muffin. "Third one. Pure dead brilliant, these are," he mumbled around a mouthful of maple bacon muffin. "You, lass, are a bonny genius of the baking pans." He dropped a wink, and I smiled, his good humor impossible to resist. "Best be off, or the bosses'll beat me arse," he said, energetically bounding out of the kitchen.

I retreated upstairs to finish readying the bedrooms, placing baskets with toiletries—locally made artisanal soaps, shampoos, moisturizer—on the antique dresser in each room with the laminated sheet of instructions for the castle. I hoped they would read it. It was informative, with a guide to the rooms and the rules, including the one about no smoking—tobacco or other substances—*anywhere* inside.

Lynn found me and together we worked on the two rooms that would be utilized by wardrobe and makeup, with a third for storage. Both dressing rooms were bright and well lit. The wardrobe and makeup people—who were arriving any moment—would have extra lighting. I shoved the last piece of extra furniture up against a wall and glanced around. We needed more dressing tables. Lynn, stronger than she looked, helped me carry two folding tables and two dressing tables down from the attic.

She was quiet, and more thoughtful than she had been earlier. "What are you thinking?" I asked as I shoved a dressing table against a wall, scraped clean of paint and blotchy with fresh plaster. The scraping sound echoed in the nearly empty room.

She shook her head. Her somberness made me wary. She struggled with addiction, and I realized for the last couple of weeks, despite her determination, I had been waiting for what I felt was her inevitable backslide. This job, with the TV people, and this atmosphere was potentially the very thing that would be her undoing. But how to approach her without undermining her progress?

I touched her shoulder and caught her eye. "Lynn, I'm on your side always. If there's anything you want to talk about, tell me."

She sighed and stared at me for a long moment before finally nodding. She hoisted herself up on one of the dressing tables. "I'm not sure I can do this," she said, swinging her feet. She put one hand over her concave stomach. "A few pills or a slug of Jack would calm me down, but if I do that—if I cave—I'll end up where I was again."

I watched her, but stayed silent. Her expression was lost, her face, devoid of makeup, pale and drawn by anxiety.

"I've tried so many times, and every time I thought I could handle one drink. I don't want to screw this up. I worry that with all this going on I might."

"Lynn, if it's too early for you to take this on there is no shame in that. If you need to step back, or walk away altogether, it's okay. I'll cover for you until they can find someone else. And they *can* find someone else. You make the decision this time that's right for you."

Her face cleared and tears welled. She slipped down off the dressing table and we hugged. She sat down on a stool we had dragged in front of one of the dressing tables and clasped her bony hands between her knees, staring at the floor. I went about more organizational work and let her think. Giving her space and time was the best approach. I had to stop trying to fix things for people, letting them fix things for themselves. After I had tidied the room to my satisfaction I came and sat beside her. I took her hand and we sat for a moment.

"I'd like to try working," Lynn said wistfully, petting my hand in hers like it was a kitten. "I'm not sure I can. These people . . . they're all so intense, like nothing matters outside of what they're doing. I remember being so driven to perform, to be what everyone saw, what everyone needed me to be." She shook her head. "I think I'm going to go phone my therapist."

"Good idea. But remember, we *will* keep talking, and if it ever feels like too much, you can quit. You can stay at my house instead of the castle and take whatever time you need."

She nodded and stood up, giving me another hug. She's a tallish woman, but rail thin. I hugged her back and was surprised to feel the energy emanating from her. She was stronger than she had been. "You're going to be okay," I said, and for the first time I believed it.

We descended together. Laughter erupted from the dining room and I smiled. It was good to hear people enjoying what they were doing. Then I stiffened; *that laughter* . . . I recognized it. "No. She *wouldn't*!"

"What is it, Merry?" Lynn asked.

"Roma Toscano is back."

• • •

I learned in a hushed conference with Pish that Roma had managed to get herself invited to join the cast as a "floating mentor" who could advise anyone about anything. I would bet she had pressured the LOC board. She had arrived with Anokhi's group, but had pointedly not been invited to stay at Anokhi's home on the grounds. So that was another room I'd need to prepare.

"Are they sure they want her?" I asked Pish, my tone acid.

"My darling, despite your personal feelings about her, Roma is a talented and capable singer with a sterling résumé. She's well qualified for this role," he said mildly.

Grudgingly I acquiesced. But I was *not* happy about it. Roma had stayed with us before when Pish invited her to the castle to recover from vocal paralysis. He had made it his mission to help her, and he had succeeded; she owed him a great deal, but she and I do not get along. I find her sneaky and manipulative. *And* I didn't appreciate that she had tried her damnedest to steal Virgil from me. Fortunately for them both he viewed her desperate flirtation with amused irritation.

I peeked in the dining room. They were about to have a meeting and had pushed several of the tables into a semicircle. The technical crew stood in a cluster to one side; the judges and mentors sat together at one table, the contestants at another, with Moze Markunis and Pam Bellini joining them. Anne Parkinson strode to the front, with a nervous Sparrow clutching a clipboard to her chest pacing behind her.

I stood in the shadows and listened to how the week was going to go. The rest of this first day would be devoted to technical run-throughs, Anne said. The contestants would rehearse, if they wanted, which would give the technical crew a chance to get levels and work on lighting and sound in the new environment. The next morning would be final details, and the rest of the day would be rehearsals—this time filmed for footage to edit in later—and contestant interviews, which would be done in the Rose Parlor. If there was enough time they would start filming performance videos, snippets of which would be released online during the televised competition. They would also be taping the mentors giving advice and support to the performers. This stage would last for three days.

The last two days of the shoot would be final performance videos alone and in front of the judges, video of the judges conferring, then wrap-ups, exit interviews, that kind of thing. I counted on my fingers, and if they kept to their schedule then it would take seven days all told. I was impressed by Anne Parkinson's management, and how she answered questions from the mentors. I stood and cleared my throat. There were things they all needed to know, and since they were gathered . . .

"Merry, welcome," she said, eyeing me with concern. "Would you like to say a few words to the cast and crew?"

"I would." I strolled to the front and introduced myself to everyone. I welcomed them to the castle and said, "I'd also like to introduce you to other folks who will be here and helping to make your stay better. We have Lynn, who will be working with the style crew. She is better known as Leatrice, a world-renowned model. She lives here, so if you have any style questions, she is the one to speak with." I pointed her out where she stood near the back of the room, and she gave a nervous little curtsey.

"Pish Lincoln lives here as well and is my partner in the Wynter Woods Center for the Performing Arts—or whatever name we finally choose—project. He is your go-to guy for almost anything, and one of us will always be here. We'll have additional staff working during the day to keep the craft table stocked for all of you; they will also produce breakfast, dinner and snacks for those staying here. If you have any specific dietary needs or food allergies, please let me know. My house is on the property, and I can be here swiftly if need be."

I paused and glanced around, meeting Roma's neutral gaze and lingering for two seconds before moving on. I surveyed the producers, the judges and mentors, and finally the contestants. It was going to be an effort not to fangirl over Sir Daffyd Rhys—such magnetism!—but I'd keep it cool and professional. For the moment. I smiled, meeting each one's gaze. "Please note . . . there is absolutely no smoking on these premises, no exceptions. If you wish to smoke, you must go outside to the designated area, which any one of us can point out for you. When that area is off-limits because of the window washing crew, I will find another temporary spot." People nodded. "I wish you all the *best* of luck. I look forward to hearing you."

There was a smattering of applause and I retreated. Time to get on with my day, and with recruitment of Janice and Patricia, and shopping for all of these people!

Wearily, I retreated to the kitchen and texted Virgil about the surprise that had awaited me at the castle, made sure there was fresh coffee and that Pish was available in case anyone needed anything. He had brought his laptop to the kitchen and was ordering supplies online from a commercial restaurant supplier who could also rent us fridges and a commercial coffee system. They would deliver it later in the day.

I made lists, one for Autumn Vale and one for a much larger Costco run, and then I packaged the muffins and exited. The drone operator was working diligently, and I looked over his shoulder at the monitor. I was awed; the above angle presented my beautiful castle in a way I had never seen. He promised to ask the production company if I could have the drone footage for reference in planning the Wynter Woods estate.

Five

I drove to Ridley Ridge, dropping off muffins at the coffee shop, then headed to Autumn Vale. I dropped muffins off at Golden Acres, the retirement home my mother-in-law owns and operates, pausing only to say hello to Doc English, my late great-uncle's best friend. I vowed we'd have a proper visit in the near future. I then headed downtown to the coffee shop, where I had to drop off muffins anyway.

In quick succession I went to the butcher and Binny's bakery, where I was fortunate enough to run into Patricia; I quickly secured her and Janice's help in the kitchen at the castle. She said she would take care of speaking with our mutual friend. I headed back to the castle in a better mood and with the car laden. It was becoming evident how much work the next week would be, but I would have plenty of help, as I learned when Patricia texted me that Janice was on board, thrilled to death to be asked to help opera folk. As I drove up the lane to the castle I was relieved to see that the drone operator had finished. Brad and Dani were already back on the job, cleaning windows. I retrieved my purchases from the car and headed inside.

Everything was falling into place.

My good mood lasted until, weighed down by bags and a box and my Birken, I entered the castle and was set upon from two different directions by Pam Bellini and Roma. Pam, phone to her ear, actually caught me by my sweater sleeve, almost causing me to drop the bags of baked goods, while Roma smirked, hand over her mouth, eyes glee-filled.

"Wait a minute . . . no, stay on the line, I have to talk to this lady first," Pam Bellini said into the phone. "Ms. Wynter, I've had a look at the room Brontay and I share and it's not adequate. I looked at the one Kamile and Darcie have and it's bigger."

I pointedly yanked my sleeve from her scrabbling hand. "The rooms vary in size. There's nothing I can do about that."

"There's no bathtub in our bathroom!"

"The guest room ensuites have showers. The only tub for guests is in the common bathroom at the end of the hall. You can use that."

"No can do. It's not me that needs the bathtub, it's Brontay;

steamy air helps clear her nasal passages. How can you not *know* that? No, I'm still here, hold on."

I stared at her; the last part had been said into the phone to whomever she was speaking. "I can't help the lack of a bathtub," I said loudly. "I'm sorry, Ms. Bellini. Now, if you'll excuse me—"

"Not good enough!"

"Well that's too bad," I snapped.

"Not *you*," she said, flapping her hand dismissively at me. She gestured to her phone and turned away. "No, it's not good enough. You tell that Gilda Greenwald that I expect Brontay to be *featured*. She's a star in the making, not an elderly hack like Darcie, or a weird Euro-trash like Kamile Markunis." A tiny hurricane of activity, she headed back toward the dining room still yelling into the phone.

"Fun times," Roma said lightly. "Let me carry the box," she said, taking it from me. "Kitchen?"

"Yes. Thank you, Roma. I'm sorry I don't have your room done up yet."

"It's okay. I don't need any special treatment."

I squinted at her in the shadowy light of the great hall as we made our way to the kitchen, suspicious at how pleasant she was being. "Your room is smaller than the one you had last time."

"That's okay."

We entered the kitchen and I plunked the bags down on the counter. Roma followed me and put the box down carefully, then smoothed the front of her elegant one-piece jumpsuit. It was a lovely merlot color that looked good with her brown hair and hazel eyes. She had dyed her hair darker from its previous auburn since I last saw her, wasn't wearing her usual green contacts and had lost weight; she looked svelte and elegant, while I felt disheveled.

"Hello, my darlings," Pish said, looking up from his laptop.

Aha, Pish had read Roma the riot act, which was why she was being so nice to me. Okay, I'd take it. "We have Janice and Patricia on board," I said to him as I unpacked a bag.

"Good, good," he said, tapping away on the laptop. "I'm making up a request to HHN for an up-front payment in advance for the money we're putting out for food and wages."

"I have my bills here," I said, grabbing my Birken and fishing out the receipts from town. "And I'll make up an estimate for hours and wages for others." Pish and I chatted a moment, and when I turned, I noticed that Roma had unpacked the box and stowed the meat in the big refrigerator.

"Wouldn't want this spoiling," she said, hefting a butcher-paper-wrapped pot roast.

"No, wouldn't want it spoiling." My voice sounded ghostly, and I turned my gaze back to Pish and raised my eyebrows. He shrugged. I was still waiting for whatever it was that Roma wanted from me, but she never did ask. She finished putting the meat away and drifted off. "I guess I'll see if all is well with the production," I said.

"Okay, you do that," Pish said.

They were finished setting up in the dining room. Lizzie, I discovered, had not only endeared herself to the contestants and cast, she had befriended the gentle giant bespectacled hulk who manned the cameras and managed the camera crew. He had her running errands and making herself useful. The judges, mentors and contestants had retreated to their respective houses and rooms upstairs to settle in.

I headed upstairs and checked to make sure all was well. Everyone seemed content with their rooms, so far. The cube van carrying the trunks of clothes had arrived, along with the makeup, hairstyling equipment and the wardrobe mistress and hairstylist. Lynn was helping them unpack and orient themselves. They did not need my help, they all chorused distractedly. It was good to see Lynn engaged, busy and happy. I slipped back out and into the quiet gallery and leaned on the railing overlooking my magnificent chandelier, taking a deep breath and letting it out. No fires to put out, no tempers to soothe, no problems to sort. I was free . . . for the moment at least.

• • •

Pish's order came two hours later, with packaged goodies, bottled water, cases of assorted cold drinks, three rental mini fridges to keep the water and soft drinks cold, and two men to carry it all in for me. I had them set up much of it along the wall in the great hall, with a smaller table in the dining room close to the doors, to keep it out of the filming and technical area. On the table in the dining room I filled baskets with packaged muffins and granola bars and other goodies, carried in the giant coffee urn I use for big events, filled it and turned it on, setting out sugar, artificial sweetener, milk, cream, paper cups and stir sticks. As I finished up, the scent of fresh coffee filled the air. Technicians sniffed and looked up with hope and a greedy gleam in their eyes. All productions run on the powerful fuel of caffeine.

Patricia and Janice had offered to do a Costco run, so I texted them both a lengthy list, telling them we'd make do for the evening if they could do the run in the morning with Janice's big Crazy Lady Antiques van and come directly to the castle. I returned to the kitchen—Pish had retreated to his office upstairs—and checked the big side-by-side fridge freezer. I had recalled correctly; I had three large lasagnas in the freezer—one vegan—as well as salad ingredients and a delicious assortment of pastries from Binny's, so we'd be good for dinner.

Everything was going so *well*! I was amazed, relieved, and pleased.

I should have known better.

Six

Virgil strolled into the kitchen and wrapped his arms around me from behind as I chopped romaine, cucumber and other veggies for the dinner salad. "That is quite the production out there," he murmured in my ear, rocking me in his arms. "Pish gave me a tour. He's like a teenager he's so excited."

I leaned back against him. "It's old home week for him, surrounded by friends new and old." I sighed. "Mmmm . . . this morning seems a lifetime ago."

He turned me around in his arms. "You sure you're not taking too much on?"

"I don't know," I said, staring up into his warm brown eyes, filled with concern. "We'll get through it. I like Anne Parkinson, the producer; she runs a tight set. I've got my gals pitching in starting tomorrow morning. But," I said, kissing him, "I'm going to be home late tonight. I have to have everything set up so the morning will start smoothly for the contestants and producers, who will be having breakfast here." He kissed me again and my toes curled.

"Then don't come home," he said against my lips.

"What?" I drew back and glared up at him. "Since when do you not want me to come home? Is this what our marriage has come to, a shambles of its former glory?"

He chuckled, and I could feel the rumble of laughter in his chest. "I have a hockey game this evening, and then Dewayne and I meet with Urquhart. The taskforce is ramping up with new leads. Tomorrow I'm heading to Buffalo and Rochester; Dewayne and I are both going and it will be at least one overnight stay. We have a lead on an old investigation he's been trying to finish for a year."

"That's all good, right?"

"All good. I was thinking I'd grab a duffel and stay with Dewayne overnight to head out early." He caught my worried glance. "Unless you need me here?"

"No, no, not at all. In fact, that will work out perfect. I'll stay here overnight to make sure at least the first couple of days go smoothly, until we have it all under control." I reserved one of the turret bedrooms for us, and we both have clothes and toiletries in it for quick changes. "I'll miss you."

He kissed me again. "You're going to be so busy you won't even notice I'm gone," he murmured against my lips.

"Wanna bet?"

"I'll get out of your hair. Don't forget, Gordy is coming to do a last cut of the long grass and weeds and a cleanup of our yard. He's putting away the barbecue for me and tuning up the snowblower, too. I talked to him today and asked him to bring his uncle's chain saw to clear brush by the arboretum."

"I did remember. We need the property to look good for the film crew next week. Are you sure he's up to all of that?" I asked. "And working on his own?" Gordy had had a rough time lately and I worried about him.

"Honey, he's not a child," he said, putting his hands on my shoulders and fixing me with his gaze. "He's been working on this property for years; once he's on task he's steady. And he's good with small engines . . . better than I am. You can't *coddle* everyone. What he needs more than anything is to be needed."

"You're right, of course." I trust Virgil's assessment of people. He was a cop for many years, and his judgment is impeccable. *And* he's known Gordy all his life. "Okay." I put my hand on his cheek and stared up into his brown eyes. "You're a nice man, you know that?"

He kissed me again, lingering, then sighing and releasing me. "See you day after tomorrow, late. Okay?"

"Okay."

I turned away and he smacked my bottom. I laughed as he slipped down the butler's pantry hall to the back door, the better, I suspected, to avoid Roma. Becket, who had been hiding back there, came slinking into the kitchen and slipped over to Lynn, who had just come in, rubbing up against her jean-clad legs. She bent over to pet him and murmured words of kitty chat.

"How is it going?" I asked her.

"Good, so far," she said. "I wanted to ask your opinion. Pam is trying to force Brontay into wearing a slinky gown that isn't . . . it's going to make her stiff and uncomfortable. Lizzie says Brontay told her she didn't want to wear anything that sheer and clingy. Oh, by the way, Lizzie said she had to go, but that she'd be back tomorrow morning. Anyway, I don't know how to handle Pam. She's such a . . . a *diva*."

"Anne seems to have a handle on the whole thing. She might have suggestions on how to control Pam."

Lynn nodded. "I'll go talk to her now. We need to head this off early and not let it slide."

"You're doing well, Lynn; I'm proud of you."

"I am too . . . proud of me."

When she left I had the kitchen to myself and sat in one of the wing chairs by the fireplace with my laptop, clipboard, phone and a cup of tea. I did a planning chart. I made lists. I arranged by text to have orders arrive in a timely manner since I didn't have storage space for everything I'd need. After a few years of living in the castle I was better organized.

I heard a noise over by the sink and turned to see Sparrow Summers, the assistant producer. She leaned against the counter, eyes closed, taking deep gulping breaths. I didn't want to startle her, but needed to announce my presence. "Do you need anything, Ms. Summers?"

She jumped and turned. "I'm good, thanks. And it's Sparrow, please, and you're Merry. I'm catching my breath. It's been a hectic day so far, with the early move from the hotel in Rochester and the travel and setting up here."

"I'm sure it's quite the change." I eyed her; she was close to the edge, I thought. "Come, sit down for a moment. Ten minutes of hiding out will give you back your equilibrium."

She brought her bottle of water and sat in the other wing chair. "Good advice," she said. She put her head back and closed her eyes for about thirty seconds, but she was not a restful sort. She asked me questions about the castle, then said, "Why are those window washers here? How long are they going to take?"

"They'll be here all week. We have a crew coming to film footage of the castle and we're planning upcoming events. Everything needs to be in tip-top shape."

"I can't imagine doing what they're doing! That girl is up on a ladder that's so tall . . ." She shuddered.

"Dani is a strong young woman. Sparrow, I'm curious. No one has told me yet what went on to get the production evicted from the hotel in Rochester?" The offense must have been egregious for the hotel to renege on a contract and pass up such a moneymaker.

She squinted toward the door, then leaned forward to confide. "Don't say I told you, but Sir Daffyd is a dirty old *lech*."

I didn't know how to respond.

"I shouldn't have said anything," she said, with a feverish glance toward the door. "Oh, gosh," she said, practically vibrating with dread. "You'll probably tell Anne and then I'll be fired!"

"No, no, I won't, I promise. I'd never heard that of him before, though. I mean, he's *famous*." And famous people never do any dirty business, right? I frowned, surprised that even came out of my mouth when I had seen enough bad behavior in the past to know better. "But what does that have to do with you all being thrown out of a hotel?"

She shook her head, anxiety oozing from her in waves. Taking a deep gulp of her water, she sighed and sat back, taking another deep breath and letting it out slowly. "I don't know how Anne does it, catering to all these weirdoes and artistes. Who knew opera people had such big and fragile egos? They're worse than boy bands."

"You've had experience with boy bands?"

She smiled. "*Have* I? Hah! Have you ever heard of One 4 All?"

I shook my head.

"Neither has anyone else, but I worked with them. Have you ever heard of Gurlz N Guyz?"

I shook my head.

"Neither has anyone else, but I worked with them. I could name a half dozen more, not a one of them memorable. I thought opera—and opera *people*—would be easier." She sighed. "Boy, was I wrong!"

"So what did Sir Daffyd do that got you all kicked out of the hotel?" I asked, refusing to let my question be sidelined.

Sparrow stared at me for a long moment. "I have an NDA, a nondisclosure agreement. It's worth my *career* to say anymore, and I've been through enough crap in my life to not want to risk this. Gotta go," she said, leaping to her feet and heading to the door.

"Wait, you forgot your—"

She was gone, leaving behind her clipboard. I examined it with interest. It was a list of shots and a timetable. I flipped through the pages. Her signature at the bottom of a note to Anne was "Sparrow," with a stylized diagonal line of small V-shaped birds taking flight and oodles of white space. Cute. She was a character.

But what had she meant when she said that Sir Daffyd Rhys was a lech?

I opened my laptop and did a quick search; I didn't find anything nefarious, but there were a few articles that hinted that the knight liked the ladies, wink wink. *Many* ladies. More than one at a time, if one were to believe the most scandalous of scandal sheets. Well, to each his own, but unless the women were unwilling it didn't seem a crime, nor something that a hotel would cancel a profitable enterprise over. So yes, maybe he was an operatic Romeo, but as far as hotels went, they were there to provide a room, not judgment on one's lifestyle. There *had* to be more to the eviction.

I went back to my organizational task and was joined by Lynn, who was taking a break, as were the crew, she said. She made tea—something she had never done for herself until recently; it was as though she was starting life anew of late—and we sat in silence as she sipped.

"How are they doing?" I finally said. "So far it's just technical, right?"

"So far. The contestants are still upstairs settling in."

"Wardrobe and makeup arrived; how is the setup going? If you need anything, let me know."

"So far, so good. The wardrobe mistress is wife to the big guy, the head cameraman. They've taken a room at a bed-and-breakfast in town rather than stay with the crew at the motel."

"Good call," I said with a smile. "The motel is kind of a rat trap. You'll have to work with her closely. What is she like?"

"She's nice. She's also doing hair and makeup. Nothing elaborate, she said. She's happy to have my help, and I think I can learn a lot from her."

"I'm so happy. Is it all okay for now?"

"I think I'll be okay," she said, meeting my gaze and smiling. She understood the subtext of my words.

"I had an interesting conversation with Sparrow Summers," I said, and told her what the assistant producer had said about Sir Daffyd Rhys. Lynn got silent and thoughtful, and I felt a twinge of unease. Watching her carefully, I asked, "Do you know anything about him?"

"He was friends with my manager. Do you remember my manager?"

"I do." I never liked the guy who acted as her manager, agent and even financial adviser until Pish stepped in to make sure she was protected.

"He's ignoring me lately; I'm not making him any money, I guess. Anyway, he was good friends with Daffyd and took me to his parties. It was after you left."

I got a prickle of unease down my backbone. "Parties? What kind of parties?"

She was silent.

"You can tell me anything, Lynn; I hope you know that."

She nodded, but there was a troubled look on her face.

"Did you see anything there? Anything we should know about?"

"My memory of that time is not good," she said with an apologetic glance. She shook herself, like a dog shedding water, and brightened. "Anyway, this has been fun so far! I'm glad I'm working with the wardrobe mistress. She's been with the production since the beginning, so she can tell me a lot."

I cocked my head and watched her face. "I assume it is interesting gossip?"

"*Apparently* the rules are that the judges are supposed to stay away from the contestants except when the judging is taking place."

"That makes sense. It has to be fair, and also be *seen* to be fair."

"But she says *someone* was seen with a judge away from the production site."

"Which singer? And which judge?"

"She wouldn't say."

"Did she have anything to say about why the production was kicked out of the hotel in Rochester?"

"I haven't asked her, but I did hear that—"

I jumped at a noise and looked toward the kitchen sink. Lachlan McDermott glanced over, smiled, and said, "Rinsing out my water bottle. I pay close attention to it since I don't want to take a chance on bacteria. Got to look after the throat, you know!"

Lynn waited until he was gone and then jumped up. "I'd better get back to work. I want her help in sorting out how the makeup will coordinate with their clothing for the video shoots." She hustled out of the room.

I spent the rest of the afternoon adding to the shopping lists, coordinating details with Pish, and answering questions about the castle and rooms as people flitted in an out. Finally the crew departed to get settled in to their motel—I wished them luck, but one crew member assured me they had likely seen worse accommodation—and the contestants and producers retreated again to their rooms. Roma had offered to play den mother, as she was familiar with the castle and my expectations. I was pleasantly surprised.

Pish and Lynn joined me in the kitchen so we could talk about dinner service. We sat at the trestle table, with the two of them opposite me. I told them the menu, then said, "I think we can use the breakfast room if we put two leaves in the table." After coordinating our dinner service, I asked Pish if he had heard any of the contestants sing yet.

"I sat in on a sound test in advance of tomorrow, and though the singers were only doing snatches of songs, it was interesting, to say the least."

"Who would you say is the most talented?"

As I made us a pot of tea and fed Becket, he gave his thoughts on the contestants, ending with the one male and one female he considered most likely to win. "From what I've heard, while Lachlan McDermott is the most practiced, Alain Primeau is the superior operatic talent. He has a beautiful voice, and the best emotional inflection of any of them. He *feels* the words; I wonder if it's because he appears to understand the languages?" He paused and pondered that, then continued. "However, if they are only going to choose one winner, I must say Kamile Markunis is my bet to win it all, hands down. Her voice is *lovely*. She can go from an exquisite contralto to an effortless soprano. And her glissando . . . it is haunting." He sighed, then looked down at the table with a frown.

"Why the look?"

"I wish . . ." He twitched his lips and tossed his hair back. "She seems *unhappy*."

"I thought that too."

"I can't put my finger on it, but there is something . . ." He frowned and shook his head.

"I noticed a difference in her personality when Moze Markunis was not present. I think he makes her nervous. Anxious, even. He's going away tomorrow morning, so maybe Kamile can relax and give it her best." I looked up at the big kitchen clock. It was already six, and I had told everyone that dinner would be at seven thirty. I put my hands on the tabletop and pushed to stand. "Okay, crew, time to get busy. We're it for prep, cooking *and* table service tonight, so let's get started."

As Pish gathered everyone in the breakfast room for pre-dinner drinks and hors d'oeuvres, Lynn and I stood at the counter doing the last prep work. "After spending the day with them, I'd be interested in *your* take on the contestants . . . not their singing, their personalities," I said, sliding a glance over to her. "Lachlan seems pleasant, but he was definitely peeved that Kamile was able to have Moze with her when the rest of them have to be without a companion. I see his point—fair is fair—but he was perturbed."

"He's used to having someone doing stuff for him, I think. You know, from when he was in the Scottish Tenors. They had an entourage."

"He said as much."

"He's self-centered," she said. "And *that's* coming from another self-centered person," she said, rolling her eyes. "When you talk to him it feels like he's waiting to hear what it is that relates to him, you know? Like . . . *where's my part in this.*"

I smiled. Her level of self-knowledge was improving. "Maybe it's the perceived unfairness?"

"Probably. But only as it relates to him."

"Brontay seems like a nice kid, even if her mother is a pain."

Lynn frowned and screwed up her mouth. "I suppose."

I waited for her to go on, but she didn't. "What is it?" I prompted.

"I like Brontay, but she's way smarter than she lets on. And I wonder why, you know?" She paused and put her head to one side, slotted spoon hovering over a jar of olives. "She acts like a normal kid, but Brontay watches *everyone* closely. That's the last thing I wanted to do at her age, hang out and watch adults."

"She must feel out of place in an adult competition," I said. "Maybe she's trying to fit in. I remember what I was like as a kid. Don't all teenagers watch adults to emulate them?"

Lynn shrugged and plopped olives in a dish. "Not me. Anyone over twenty was dead to me when I was fifteen."

"What about Zeb Wolfe?"

"He's nice. When you talk to him he listens."

I rolled thin slices of prosciutto. "Darcie Austin?"

Lynn smiled, a sly look, but shook her head. "She appears professional."

Appears . . . hmmm. When I asked her to elaborate, she shook her head again.

"Alain Primeau?"

She rolled her eyes again, then giggled. "What a flirt! He thinks he's God's gift to women, you know?"

I laughed. That had been my impression too.

"And he's flaky. But there's no *harm* in him. I mean, he's flirty and over-the-top, but not in an icky way, if you know what I mean, once you get past the palm kissing." She shuddered.

I laughed. "Nice to know I wasn't singled out for the wet palm kiss."

"He was so sweet when I told him I wasn't up on makeup for men. He said to consult Zeb, who has a background in theater, and Lachlan, who has been on stage a lot. They're all experienced and will be able to help, he said."

"Well, *that's* nice."

"I'm probably lucky that the wardrobe mistress seems happy to pick up the slack. She told me to worry mostly about dressing them."

"Pish seems to think Primeau is the best male singer of the three. I'm curious about Kamile and Moze. Is he really her uncle, do you think? Lachlan hinted at something fishy."

"He would, wouldn't he? He's the worst gossip in the group."

"I hate when people cast doubt like that with no foundation . . . or even *with* foundation, I guess."

"It's a cheap shot," Lynn said. She frowned and looked down at the cheese tray she had arranged neatly with wedges of Brie, Stilton, and a sharp local cheddar, plump figs and the kalamata olives. She moved a pretty jar of fig compote to the middle, then fiddled with an array of crackers on another tray. She met my eyes. "You know, I *do* think Mr. Markunis is her uncle, despite what Lachlan implied. They have the same features, you know?"

"You're right . . . there is the nose and cheekbones."

"I'm glad the guy is leaving, though. He gives me the creeps, the way he tries to control Kamile. I hope he stays away."

I was silenced by her somber manner. Lynn is intuitive and I had learned, working for her, that no matter how unpopular her impressions were about people, she was often right. And yet other times she mistrusted her gut and displayed a blind spot, letting herself be used.

Pish came in at that moment and said, "We're ready for antipasto. I'll take it to the table."

Seven

Lynn preferred to eat alone most of the time, and so took a plate upstairs. Pish and I sat opposite each other and did our best to encourage general conversation. However, such a varied bunch of people who had spent a lot of time together could not dine without there being friction, inside jokes, and gossip. I tried to delicately raise the topic of the Rochester hotel, but beyond a few glances traded among them, no one offered any information and I was not about to dig too hard or too deep.

So I chatted across the table with Pish, and watched. I got to see the group's relationship dynamics. Sparrow and Anne sat beside each other and talked shop. Alain and Zeb had a lively discussion about their respective performance pieces. Moze ate with single-minded intensity, drinking many *many* glasses of wine. Kamile was quiet and didn't eat a lot, while Brontay watched with avid interest. Lachlan issued pointed barbs, particularly aimed at Darcie and Pam; Brontay's mom ignored him, spending most of her time with her phone.

Darcie sniped back at Lachlan, but then fell silent and played with her food on her plate. She picked up her cellphone, sighed heavily, and dropped it back on the table.

"What's wrong, Darcie? Someone not getting back to you?" Brontay said.

"Mind your own business, little girl," Darcie said.

"Stop picking on her," Roma—who had so far been diplomatic and neutral—snapped.

"Who asked *you*?" Darcie retorted.

"Ladies, *ladies*!" Pish took a sip of wine, then said to the table at large, "So . . . what do you all think of the flood of little girl opera singers that pop up on competition shows?"

"D'you mean why not little boy opera singers?" Lachlan said, and there was general laughter.

Pam said, "Are you aiming that at Brontay, Mr. Lincoln?"

"Mo-om!" Brontay said with an agonized moan. "He didn't mean me!"

I struggled not to laugh, and caught Brontay's eye, winking at her. Pish, horrified that he had been misconstrued, babbled to explain that he meant to ask about all the little girls as young as five warbling "opera" in televised competitions when their voices weren't ready. It was a rare moment when I saw him flustered as he tried to explain and only made it worse by talking about parrots, and how they didn't understand the words they were saying, instead mimicking.

"So you *are* talking about Brontay?" Pam said, her face tight with anger.

"Of *course* not." Pish took a deep breath. "From what I have heard, your daughter appears to have, for her age and experience level, an exceptional grasp on the material."

I bit my lip to keep from laughing at my discomfited friend; Alain Primeau, across the table, winked at me. By the time dinner was done it was late enough that everyone was content to retreat to their rooms. It had been a long exhausting day, and it wasn't over yet. Lynn brought down her plate and helped Pish and me carry the dirty dishes to the kitchen, then we tidied the breakfast room, ready for the morning, and returned to the kitchen. I stared at the stack of dishes on the counter and yawned. Lynn said she would help me clean up, but Pish and I exchanged a look. She was gray and wan and I was worried, after the conversations we had, that she was doing too much too early.

I put one arm around her shoulder and squeezed, pushing her toward the door. "Honey, you go to bed. You're already working for the show and you don't need this on top of it. One job is enough. This is just tonight," I said, motioning at the dirty dishes piled high. "Tomorrow I'll have Janice and Patricia's help. Pish and I will do the dishes." She looked mulish, determined, perhaps, to follow through on her therapist-prescribed regimen of taking responsibility. Firmly I said, "I prescribe a hot bath and bed for you. You've done enough for one day and tomorrow will be a long one."

"Go on, Lynn," Pish added, his tone gentle. "We've got this covered."

She nodded, too weary to argue further.

I turned off most of the lights, leaving the pendants directly over the sink. Becket had been an angel all day, only getting underfoot a couple of times, and he deserved a treat, so I opened a can of tuna. "Have at it, buddy," I said softly, setting his bowl on the floor near the wing chairs.

As the dishwasher churned with a load, Pish and I took care of the china and crystal that could not go into the dishwasher. Talking in soft murmurs, washing dishes and handing them to Pish, who dried and put away, it reminded me of the first year or so at Wynter Castle when he and I—and Shilo, with her pet bunny Magic, for a time—lived together here in the castle, strangers in a strange land with just each other for company. How much had changed!

As much as I love my life, there was something intimate and cozy about that time that I miss. It was simpler. Or was I remembering it wrong? It had only been a few years and I was already waxing nostalgic. Maybe that was because of how much had happened in those few years.

Becket raced ahead of us as we climbed the stairs; he headed off to sniff at each closed door. So many strangers, so little time. After a kiss and hug goodnight, Pish and I retreated to our separate bedrooms. I slipped on a cotton T-shirt nightgown and climbed into bed. It felt empty without Virgil. He had been away plenty—his new private investigation business with Dewayne took him away overnight more than I would like—but here, in the castle, I felt especially lonely.

There was a creak and I sat up in bed. My door was opening all by itself! I was about to yell *Who is it?*, but Becket jumped up on the bed. "Good grief, you scared me, fella. You don't like all these strangers on your turf, do you, buddy? I'd think you'd be used to it by now." He kneaded the plush cover then curled up near me—unusual in itself—and purred, falling into kitty snores, not nearly as loud as Virgil snores.

I don't know if it was missing Virgil, worry over our business, being restless because of all the strangers sleeping in the castle, or a mixture of it all, but I could *not* sleep. I kept hearing noises: doors, footsteps, coughing, sneezing . . . whispers, even. I got out of bed more than once and crept to the door to find a restless guest tiptoeing downstairs. It made me antsy to have strangers wandering the halls, but I had to give them the latitude to get a drink of water or tea, or to go to the library for a book. It was all on the sheet I had left them; their freedoms, my expectations, house rules. Some would inevitably need to go outside for a cigarette, so I had left three castle keys on a hook inside the double doors, a fact that was also on the sheet for their reference. In big red letters I also said that I expected all three keys to be on that hook unless someone was outside.

I tossed and turned, checking my phone a few times. Virgil had already sent me a good-night text so I don't know who else I expected would be up. I finally decided I needed a cup of herbal tea. Shrugging on a housecoat and pushing my feet into slippers, I crept from my room and descended to the kitchen, made my tea and sat in the wing chair by the fireplace. It was after midnight. I scrolled through texts and thought about the next day. It was going to be hectic, but with Janice and Patricia we'd be fine. However, they wouldn't arrive until midmorning, so breakfast would be my task. I went through the options: we had dozens of eggs, and there were frozen muffins galore, so I would do a breakfast bar of scrambled eggs kept warm in a buffet tray, toast, muffins, rolls, sausages, ham and a couple of vegan options, yogurt, fruit, cold cereal, plus coffee. *Lots* of coffee. I got out the warming trays for a breakfast buffet and left them on the counter.

What HHN was paying would be enough, with the other shoots I already had lined up, to see the castle through the winter as far as utilities, taxes and maintenance costs. We were having a ceremony to officially break ground on the performance dome, and we were doing a big benefit over Thanksgiving to fund the renovation of the carriage house, but we already had that planned. There was another production company that had asked that I contact them the moment there was considerable snowfall in the forecast, as they wanted shots of the castle in winter for their production. Then in the spring construction of the domed performance theater was scheduled to begin. Finally! It felt like we had been planning it forever, though it was just a year or so.

Sometimes it felt like too much, like I had thrown two dozen balls in the air and didn't have a shot of catching them all. I took a deep breath, fighting back the anxiety that constantly gnawed at me. Pish was the most levelheaded and cautious person I knew, financially, and he had this well in hand; I had to keep reminding myself of that. And I needed sleep. It was one thirty; my alarm was set for six a.m. so I could get a jump on what would be a long and arduous day.

I padded out of the kitchen and through the great hall to the stairs and was about to mount them when I heard the *beep* of a car alarm being turned on, and a few seconds later the thudding bang of the big door knocker. My heart leaped and pounded. Who could that be? I tiptoed to the door but jumped back when the knocker was again employed. Thieves and murderers don't bang the door knocker, I reasoned. I unlatched and jerked the door open.

It was windy and raining; a woman stood on the doorstep struggling with a giant purse, a laptop case and a suitcase. Her frizzy hair was dripping in her eyes, her glasses were misted, and she was in a sodden long sweater, her wet feet in serviceable black pumps.

"Finally!" she said, and pushed in past me. "Look, I know it's late and I wasn't supposed to be here until morning. I tried to text you but you didn't bloody answer. I started out at eight or so from Rochester but then my stupid rental stalled on the highway, and I had to get a tow into Batavia—whatever the hell that is, a backwater town—and luckily the rental company there gave me another car, but then I got lost on the way here, which, again, is in the freaking middle of the freaking middle of *nowhere*—"

"Who *are* you?" I asked as she dripped and sniffed and swiped at her wet hair, making a puddle on my great hall floor.

"Oh! I'm Gilda Greenwald," she said, finally swiping the last locks of lank coiled hair out of her eyes. She took her glasses off and shook the raindrops off the lenses as she squinted and peered at me. "I thought you were Anne. Same . . . figure," she said, waving her hand up and down my body. "Who are *you*?"

"I'm Merry Wynter, owner of Wynter Castle. You're the journalist from *Modern Entertainment Monthly*. Leave your bags there and come on in to the kitchen and get dried off." I led the way, retrieved towels from the half bath off the back hall, and bid her sit down in one of the wing chairs by the fireplace. "Tea? Or coffee?"

"Coffee would be *heavenly*!" she exclaimed, aggressively towel drying her hair. It was matted and frizzy, and the toweling was making it worse.

"Are you hungry?"

"I could eat," she said, taking off her saturated sweater coat and draping it over a chair.

I took it and put it on the kitchen counter, trying to mitigate the damage from her soggy arrival. I then got her a cup of coffee, and put a hunk of lasagna from dinner onto a plate, heated it in the microwave, and gave her a tray. She ate voraciously as I had another cup of tea.

I turned sideways in my chair and examined Gilda Greenwald.

She was in her thirties, I'd estimate, slim, tall, with a long oval lightly freckled face and that great mop of curly hair. Oversized glasses perched on her nose. She was dressed in jeans, the soaked pumps—which she had kicked off—a sweater, and with no rings on her fingers, but tiny Star of David earrings in her ears and a gold cross around her neck.

She caught my gaze and shrugged as she swallowed. "I'm a Catholic Jew. Confusing, right? My dad is Jewish but my mom is a Polish Catholic, so I was raised in the church." She fingered the small cross at the hollow of her throat. "I don't believe in any of this nonsense, so it's a superstition now, to wear it, I guess. I feel naked without it." She fished in her huge purse and pulled out a glittery black velvet bow. Pulling her hair back in a ponytail, she fastened the bow to it, and then sat back and sighed. "That lasagna was *so* good. The best I've ever had."

I smiled. "It was baked from frozen and then reheated for you in the microwave. I guarantee it was better fresh. I'm happy you liked it though."

"After that rotten hotel in Rochester—their food literally stunk, and as a writer I take the use of the word *literally* seriously—this was like five-star dining."

"I didn't know the hotel was that bad," I said. "The others didn't mention the food being off."

She rolled her eyes. "It was terrible . . . chemical-smelling, you know? Like something was poured over it. I couldn't eat it."

"That's awful!"

"It got worse! The service was terrible and the amenities nonexistent. The place is a death trap!"

"What do you mean by that?"

"Get this," she said, leaning forward, her dark eyes sparkling behind the glinting lenses. "I'm having a shower one morning and I reach up to grab hold of the curtain rod and *zap*! Electricity surged through me, I *swear*! Maybe that's why my hair is particularly frizzy today," she said with a grin, touching her restrained mop. "Just one of a long string of mishaps, let me tell you."

"No one is out to kill you, are they?" I asked, half serious, half joking.

She rolled her eyes again. "Of *course* not." She then frowned.

"Though there *is* a guy cyber-stalking me, posting mean tweets and sending vaguely threatening letters."

"What? Why?"

"He's an up-and-coming classical pianist. In my 'Classical Beat' column I reported on an incident between him and his husband when he was arrested for domestic battery." She shrugged. "I was doing my job, reporting on the entertainment industry."

"Did you tell anyone about the threats?"

"Sure, I told the cops. He was detained. My magazine backed me up and I provided proof."

"Is he in jail?"

"No, he was released on his own recognizance, but I have a restraining order against him, as much good as that will do me."

"Is he a threat?" I asked, alarmed both for her and us.

"I don't *think* so. I'm pretty sure it was the heat of the moment that he made the threats, and they were kind of half-hearted. If he behaves I'll drop the charges. I don't want to ruin anyone's career. Unless they deserve to have it ruined, you know?" She quirked a grin.

I was taken aback; what did that mean, exactly, *unless they deserve to have it ruined*? I opened my mouth to ask, but she spoke again.

"He's trying to get his career back on track, so I don't imagine harassing me is high on his to-do list." She smiled. "Besides, he's back with his husband. Better things to do, and all that."

"Well, that's good." I had a feeling Gilda was one of those women who trouble follows. "Why did you stay behind in Rochester and not come with the rest of them?"

"I wasn't done there." Her eyes widened with significance.

She was also one of those who loads her words with significance and expects you to plead to be let in on the secret. I was exhausted and longing for bed, but I played along. "You weren't done doing *what*?"

"Investigating, of course." She winked. "I *am* a journalist, even if I cover entertainment stories. A little bribery goes a long way with hotel staff, especially at a dump like that. I needed to get them alone after the hotel tossed this whole clown car of weirdoes out."

"What was that about, anyway? Why were they thrown out of the hotel?"

"What have they told you?" she asked.

"Nothing."

She nodded with a secretive smile. “I . . . think I’ll plead the fifth right now.”

“Pleading the fifth is to keep from incriminating yourself,” I retorted. Gilda was annoying the heck out of me.

“Whatever.” She yawned and stretched.

“I have a room for you, but I haven’t made it up yet. We expected you in the morning.”

“I was not going to stay in that death trap hotel another night. I don’t care if the bed is made up or not. Whatever it is, I’ve slept in worse.” She rose and stretched.

I picked up her damp sweater and led her back to the great hall, where she retrieved her suitcase and laptop case. We headed upstairs to her room, one of the smaller single ones. I got sheets from the linen closet and made up her bed while she hung up her clothes. There was a little desk by the window; she unpacked her laptop, setting it up to charge along with her cellphone.

I finished making up her bed and turned. “Sorry, no chocolate on your pillow.”

She smiled as she glanced around at the room. “This place is nice. Thank you so much for finding a spot for me!”

I smiled back, charmed out of my bad mood. “Thanks. I do love my castle. Get some sleep, Gilda, and I’ll see you in a few hours.”

• • •

Five hours later I was again in my kitchen, wiping sleep grit out of my eyes and prepping the breakfast buffet, while responding to a flurry of texts from Janice, Patricia, Virgil, and assorted other folk. Lachlan came breezing into the kitchen, wearing shorts and a windbreaker despite the blustery day.

“Aye, a bonny lass in the kitchen,” he said. “What a sight to warm the cockles of my heart.” He had a towel around his neck. “I’ve been for a run, and now I’m hungry as a bear. Is there breakfast to be had?”

“Five minutes,” I said through gritted teeth.

“Then I’ll shower and greet the day I pop this contest in the bag.” He strode out of the kitchen.

Why do morning people make me so weary? I mean, I’m a morning person to some extent; I don’t actually bite people’s heads off before seven, though I may be tempted. But I *do* require a half hour to wake up before a cheery Scot comes breezing in with a "bonny lass" and a "cockles of my heart." Pish joined me and we worked together. We lined the buffet in the breakfast room with the warming trays to hold breakfast, then I scrambled eggs, cooked bacon, sausage and ham, cut muffins and biscuits, stacked dishes, poured milk and cream and made thermal carafes of coffee. While our guests ate we set up the craft services table in the dining room, firing up the sixty-cup coffee urn and provisioning it with everything we currently had before the troops arrived.

I worked solid for three hours, cooking, replenishing the buffet, making coffee and tea, and clearing dirty dishes, putting the dishwasher on yet again to chug away. I finally crashed at around ten thirty and sat for half an hour staring into space wishing coffee was available in intravenous form. Lynn was upstairs helping the wardrobe/makeup mistress get everyone ready for the interview shoots. I didn't understand exactly what that was, and Anne Parkinson was too busy to explain. Once I finally emerged from my stupor I spotted Sparrow idling at the craft services table in the great hall, where I had a second smaller coffee urn set up.

I asked how it was going, then said, "So what are you going to interview the contestants about today? I'm not sure I understand."

Sparrow gulped a cup of black coffee and smiled slyly, her narrow face shadowed in the dim light. "I'm conducting interviews, but when it's cut and edited you won't hear my voice, you'll hear the contestants' responses. It'll sound . . . mmm . . . confessional," she said, her voice an echoey whisper.

"I don't think I understand."

"Like, I'll ask Darcie, *What do you think of Brontay Bellini?* and she may say that Brontay is talented for her age and a nice kid, blah blah blah." Sparrow rolled her eyes. Kindness was boring, she implied with that look. "So *I'll* ask, *but she's really young and a little flaky, right? How do you feel about that*? If I ask the right way I'll catch her off guard, and she'll tell me what she *really* thinks." She put one hand over her mouth and, eyes wide and filled with glee, snickered. She dropped her hand and continued, "When we edit it we'll toss all that first careful stuff and all you'll hear is Darcie saying *Brontay is an immature little twit.*"

It gave me a distasteful look at the inner workings of the competition. "You mean you'll deliberately warp the contestants' responses?" I asked, keeping my tone neutral despite my revulsion.

"Oh, no," she said, straightening, her eyes wide. "Not at *all*. We won't be *inventing* what people say. How could we? Everything we show will be in the contestants' own words."

I eyed her, catching the implication and the evasion. "But you *will* incite them to say nasty things. You'll encourage spite and gossip?"

Her gleeful smile slowly faded and she eyed me with squint-eyed suspicion. "You're taking this the wrong way. It's all legit, you know, part of the entertainment value. We can't have them saying sweet things and being all lovey-dovey toward each other. *No* one wants to see *that*." She whirled and stomped away, pushing open the dining room door to shouted remonstrance.

I poured tea into a thermal mug, wrapped myself in a heavy cape I kept on a hook by the front door and wandered out, knowing I'd have to clean the ashtrays in the smoking area on the terrace, and not looking forward to it. I was waiting for the text from Patricia that she and Janice were on their way from Costco, but in the meantime I'd take a break.

Accompanied by Becket, I went out the front door, waved to Dani and Brad, who were moving their ladder to another set of gothic windows adorning the turret breakfast room and bedroom above, and circled to the terrace off the ballroom. At the end was the smoking area. Darcie Austin paced and smoked and shivered, her eyes squinting off into the distance.

"Is everything all right?" I asked, cradling my tea.

She whirled, tossed her cigarette onto the flagstone, putting it out with the toe of her boot, and lighting another. "I don't know what I expected from this . . . this bunch of weirdoes, from Primeau the prima donna to Lachlan the Lach-less Monster."

I smiled. "That's funny." I pointedly picked up her dead cigarette butt and put it in the ashtray I had provided.

"Sorry," she growled. "I'm just . . . angry."

"Why?"

"Men!" she spat.

"Men?"

She shook her head and took a deep breath. "Ignore that. It's the competition . . . *Opera DivaNation*. I'm not sure this is for me. I'm freaking out." She stopped and stared into my eyes. "Have I made a mistake?"

"I can vouch for the quality of the judges and mentors; there are excellent opera singers involved."

"What if I don't *want* to be an opera singer? Is this going to funnel me in one direction?"

"Isn't it a little late to be thinking that? Shouldn't you have considered that before entering?"

She sighed, paced away, and then turned back, the blustery wind tossing her blond hair. She pulled it back with her free hand and tucked it in the collar of her shirt. "Who knew this was the one show I'd get? Do you know how many video entries I've done for reality performance shows? *Dozens*: home reno; self-help; talent; dating; singing shows. Who knew the one I'd get would be an *opera* show?"

Who knew there were so many types of reality TV shows? "Darcie, there's only one thing that matters: what do you want to do with your life?"

She didn't answer for a long minute. Arms crossed, smoldering cigarette between two fingers, smoke curling up into the fresh autumn air, she glared off into the distance, toward the arborvitae and beyond that, the forest where the performing arts theater would be built. "Do you know what it's like to grow up ignored? Like you aren't even there? All my life I've tried to make an impact, get noticed."

"I understand that," I said, feeling a kinship. Until I was in my twenties and figured out where I belonged—sort of—I felt the same way.

She pierced me with her cold stare. "What do I want? I want to be famous. I want people to know me, to recognize me. I want *followers*. And I want to be rich. I'll do whatever it takes to get there despite *these* people and . . ." She stopped and shook her head. I wondered what she *wasn't* saying. "This could be my stepping-stone to something wonderful," she said softly. "I have to figure out how to *use* it right."

Sir Daffyd Rhys appeared from the concealment of the arborvitae hedge that hid the parking lot as he strolled the path from Liliana's house toward the castle, his long cerulean silk scarf tossed over his shoulder with splendid insouciance. His white hair fluffed in the breeze, and even at a distance I could feel his magnetic attraction. Darcie straightened her shoulders, throwing down her cigarette again and crushing it beneath her heel.

"Sir Daffyd," she said, her clear bell-like voice carrying in the breeze. "How *lovely* to see you! I'll walk in with you, if you don't mind."

"How could I mind if such a beautiful young lady wishes to accompany me?" he said with a brilliant smile. "Come, my dear, let us walk and talk."

She skipped lightly to his side and threaded her arm through his, leaning in to him and whispering something that made him laugh. Chatting and flirting, her tinkling laughter carrying on the breeze, they moved past the window washers' ladder and around the corner. I followed, watching them, my thoughts zipping around as I conjectured what they might be to each other. There was a closeness beyond flirtation between those two, it seemed to me, an artificiality in their public interaction that made me think in private they would be far different, more intimate, more . . . I watched as they passed by the front door and continued around the other turret room toward the dining room terrace.

"Isn't *that* interesting?"

I whirled to find Gilda Greenwald, garbed in a navy peacoat and jeans, approaching from the path that led from the parking lot, her gaze avid, watching as I did as Darcie and Daffyd disappeared around the corner. "Where did *you* come from?" I blurted out.

"I took a walk around the property. Very impressive, Ms. Wynter!" she said, rubbing her hands together and tucking them into her pockets. "You fell into the lap of luxury, didn't you, when you inherited this place?"

"It wasn't luxurious when I arrived three years ago, let me tell you," I snapped. I headed back to the ballroom terrace, circling the big ladder carefully—Dani and Brad must be having a break—and retreating to the smoking area. I picked up Darcie's second cigarette butt and deposited it in the receptacle. Gilda had followed, watching with a slight smile. I straightened. "The place inside was a wreck: peeling wallpaper, outdated electrical and plumbing. And the property was an open field," I said, flapping my hand to indicate the whole vast acreage. I could see Gordy in the distance on the lawn tractor, dutifully mowing, as he had told Virgil he would. I turned back to the writer. "With the help of Pish and friends we've transformed it."

"So defensive," the journalist said. "I'm not here to do a slash piece on you. But I *have* read a few archived newspaper pieces. It hasn't all been smooth sailing, has it?"

I eyed her warily. "What pieces did you read?" There were interviews with New York arts magazines about our plans for Wynter Castle, but there had been several local papers that had covered in avid detail our troubles with various maleficent murderers in the last three years.

Gilda smiled and turned away, heading back toward the front of the castle. "I'm curious as to where that pair is going. I heard what Darcie said, about being willing to do anything to win. I wonder what all that covers?" She looked over her shoulder at me and her eyes behind her big glasses widened as she grinned. "I smell scandal in the breeze, and a little scandal sells stories like samples sell food."

Eight

I watched her walk away and hasten her step as she rounded the turret. I followed and she, too, passed by the front door, trailing the flirtatious pair. I wondered anew what she had stayed in Rochester to investigate, and how much dirt she had dug up. Her expression had been positively gleeful as she spoke of scandal. Roma exited the front door in time to see the writer slink along the castle wall and circle the turret.

"Greenwald is on the hunt?"

"She is."

She met my gaze. "How much do you know about her?"

"Almost nothing," I said. "Is there anything *to* know?"

"She has a reputation for digging deep to get dirt."

"She swore she wasn't doing a hack job on the competition."

"And you believed her. Of all the things I thought you were, naïve wasn't one of them."

Irritated, I sighed but didn't respond.

"I've always wondered what she does with all the other crap she digs up, stuff she doesn't publish. I've heard rumors . . ." She glanced at me and looked away, finishing the sentence with that lingering invitation to ply her with questions.

I bit my tongue, defying my curiosity, holding back inquiries.

"Fine, *don't* ask," she said, crossing her silk-clad arms and tucking her fingers in her armpits to keep them warm. "If you don't want to know what's going on beneath your nose and behind your back, then that's great."

"I'm trying to keep my nose out of it," I said.

"And I thought you were supposed to be a natural detective. Pish says that all the time."

"I'm busy enough right now *without* poking my nose into other people's business."

She nodded, mollified. "I hope you're right. I hope she's *not* doing a hack job on *Opera DivaNation*. I've heard stuff that makes me uneasy, though," she admitted. "About the contestants, I mean. One of the singers is using steroids."

"Steroids? Why?" Becket wound around my feet and I stooped to pet him, but kept my gaze on Roma.

She shrugged. "For the same reason athletes take them; steroids help the voice recover from trauma."

"Trauma? Like, an accident?"

Roma sighed and rolled her eyes. I tensed, waiting for her to dismiss my question, or argue. Instead she said, "You know I've had my vocal troubles. This is an *extremely* demanding competition, despite how easy they make it sound. To get through, a performer might use steroids for the short term instead of vocal rest to recover. If administered by a doctor they can be safe and effective . . . *in the short term*."

"You said short term twice, Roma. And mentioned being under a doctor's care. What if someone uses steroids on their own and long term?"

Her expression was filled with sadness. She rubbed her arms and puffed out a steamy sigh. "If you use steroids the wrong way or for too long," she said, "you can destroy your voice."

Anne Parkinson stepped out the front door and spotted us. "Roma, you're wanted for an interview. Sparrow will be waiting for you in the Rose Parlor."

Roma trotted away before I had a chance to ask which singer was using steroids, if she even knew, and if it was true. Anne took a deep breath of the brisk air and rolled her shoulders. "Everything going okay?" I asked.

She glanced toward me, and her eyes lit up when she saw Becket. "Oh, my God, he's *beautiful*! I love cats." She moved gracefully toward me and knelt to pet Becket, who flopped on his side to allow belly rubs, unusual behavior for a cat who is preternaturally dignified. But he clearly knew what *she* needed. "I miss mine," she said, ruffling his tummy fur and cooing at him. "My husband and I have two Birman boys."

I watched her get lost in petting my cat, observing that though she usually looked intense and focused, in that moment she appeared relaxed. Cats were her sedative, I suspected. "This can't be an easy job, producing and directing these kinds of shows. Why do you do it when it takes you away from home?"

She rose, wincing as her knee joints creaked and popped. "Good question, but easily answered. It's where the work is. And it happens to use my skill set, that of directing nonprofessionals so that they appear more professional on camera. I'm also organized, focused, and my ego isn't especially big." She shrugged and smiled. "When you're dealing with big personalities like our judges, that, and a sense of humor, will get you through most days."

I smiled. "I don't think the big personalities are confined to the judges. It seems to me that the contestants are larger than life too."

"You can't *possibly* be saying that Alain, Lachlan, and Darcie are egotistical, demanding and pushy?"

I laughed, enjoying the sarcasm in her comment. "What about the others?" I said, curious about how she chose those three from the rest as the biggest personalities. "I find Kamile mysterious . . . like her interior life is very different from her exterior life."

She nodded, appraising me. "Kamile is a mystery to *most* of us. She is so striking, and supremely talented, careful in interviews, with nary a nasty word for the other contestants no matter how much Sparrow pushes and prods. I would say there isn't an honest bone in her body. I don't know what she's *really* like and I probably never will. She is so guarded as to appear a cipher."

"Can she win and still be that cipher? Won't the judges want to see depth and honest emotion from her?"

"She has an uphill battle, but the one place her emotion comes out is in her singing performances. You *must* watch her; it's remarkable." She glanced at her phone. "I'd better get in there. The owner of this dump has said we only have so many days, and days are dollars." She smiled to show me she was joking, and entered.

And . . . my break was over. My phone pinged with a text. Janice and Patricia were turning onto the road to the castle. When they arrived, I roped in HHN crew members to unload the van using their dolly carts, finding storage space in unlikely places and constructing a rudimentary inventory list so I could keep track of what we would need in the coming days. In the kitchen Janice started prepping, singing "Je Veux Vivre" from Gounod's *Romeo and Juliet,* as she cut vegetables for a crudités platter. It's a lovely dancey tune, and she swayed in waltz time as she sang.

Patricia, making batter for a delicious Victoria sponge, which she would fill with her own raspberry compote made in the summer and a mascarpone-sweetened cream, put in earbuds with her favorite Motown on her phone. Her movements to the unheard beat were undulating and rhythmic. It was a musical kitchen.

With such expert and reliable help I was free to wander and snuck into the dining room to listen to rehearsals. It was revelatory. Lachlan, singing when I entered, was competent and emotive, good eye contact, and he seemed supremely confident, but his performance of "Lonely House" from the American opera *Street Scene*—a heartbreaking song lyrically—left me cold. I heard a faint thread of strain in his rich voice, though he swiftly defeated it.

Alain Primeau was up next, singing "Je Crois Entendre Encore" from Bizet's *The Pearl Fishers* to great effect. He was confident, talented, and his lilting voice suited the strong, subtle and soaring piece.

Then Zeb Wolfe was up, and he sang "Somewhere" from *West Side Story*, usually sung by a woman but transformed into a male song. It was . . . breathtaking. I got goosebumps and teared up. I can't explain it, but he transformed the love song lyrics into an expression of yearning for a place where we can find forgiveness, an openhearted plea for love and peace for all. Tears welled in my eyes. Brontay was watching him and she, too, teared up, hands wrung together, spellbound admiration in her gaze. Zeb was a natural, and belonged on Broadway. I wiped tears from my eyes and took a deep, shaky breath to steady myself.

Brontay, her mother pacing behind the cameras, which were recording the practices for editing later, was up next. I think the emotion of Zeb's performance actually helped the teen. She sang Puccini's "O mio babbino caro"—"O my dear papa" in English—a song to a beloved father begging for him to help her marry the singer's lover. Light, sweet, and with a delicious vibrato, Brontay was a revelation. I shared an astonished look with Pam Bellini, who for once was not on her phone but watching her daughter with rapt attention, one gloating glance cast my way.

Darcie had broken away from sending Daffyd flirty winks and glances long enough to perform, and I was amazed, *astonished*, even; I was astonished that she was in this competition at all, given her stark lack of ability. She sang "Je Veux Vivre," which I had heard Janice sing in the kitchen. Darcie could carry a tune, trill a lyric and hold a note, and she was (mostly) on key, but it was all delivered with the lackluster ability of a beauty contestant who must come up with a "talent" in a short amount of time and thought *anyone* could sing opera. She was south of ordinary. She was right when she said that this competition was not for her.

So why was she still in it? I glanced over at Daffyd, who smiled and nodded encouragingly as she arduously made her way through the song. Janice sang it better, with more emotion and control and fluidity. Once done, Darcie was clearly unhappy with her performance, but she pasted a smile on her face for the cameras, and spared one flirtatious glance for the judges.

On to the next performer.

Given the praise I had heard, I was sure my expectations of Kamile Markunis would be too high, but no overblown expectations could have prepared me for her version of Mozart's "Voi che sapete." Pish had just entered and stood, awestruck, listening and watching. She was gifted, and the winner, if the competition was based purely on talent.

While I was so taken in by Kamile's performance a coterie of admirers had appeared. Zeb had stayed and watched with wide eyes. Brontay watched, hands clasped in front of her. Gilda was there too, solely focused on Kamile. She jotted something on a pad of paper, her gaze avid. The woman knew something about the singer; dirt, maybe? Something personal, judging by her expression. I have been told it is my one talent, to winkle out from an expression how that person feels about whatever they regard. Gilda was looking at Kamile as if the singer was her bread and butter, her next big break, her windfall. But as a journalist, or as something else?

The cameras were off and the production team was consulting with the judges, so it was safe to speak. I moved over to stand by Pish. "What did you think of Kamile?" I whispered.

"She is sublime. Completely magnificent."

"I'm glad I watched." I returned to the kitchen to help my helpers. There was a lot of other work to be done, though. With this many guests around, I needed to do a daily inspection of the castle and grounds to be sure it stayed in tip-top condition for the coming shoots, which I could not afford to have delayed or canceled.

So . . . donning my cloak again, I headed outside. The window cleaners were done with the turret windows and were moving their gear around to the ballroom side. They worked as one, like, in the old cliché, a well-oiled machine, but Dani saw me and said something to her workmate, Brad. She came toward me, a serious expression on her freckled face. She wore a heavy nylon jumpsuit over a teal windbreaker with the Batavia Sparkle Clean logo on the breast, and a harness, with carabiners at strategic spots, over everything. Her hair was tightly tied back; this woman was all business, but something was wrong, I could tell from her expression.

I braced myself. What now?

"Ms. Wynter, may I speak with you?"

I wrapped my cloak around me. "What's up? Any problems?"

"Well, yes. We didn't expect to work in this chaos, of course," she said, waving one hand toward the HHN vans, which against my strict instructions had again gathered in the limestone graveled circle in front of the castle, ". . . but we can work around that. Our real concern is that someone is rifling through our van and taking stuff."

That *was* a problem. I frowned and glanced toward the HHN vans and a technician, who retrieved a device and carried it into the castle. "Do you have any idea who?"

She shook her head. "It must have happened while we were out of sight of the vehicle. We arranged with the production crew to let us know when they were taking a break so we could start work on the gothic windows on the dining room side. They were taking a break, so we hustled to get those done while they weren't filming. We're doing our best to work *with* them because we know they can't have us working on those windows while they're filming or we'll be in the shots." Her voice held the aggrieved tone of one who was being taken advantage of while trying to cooperate.

"I appreciate that," I said. "I know this is not ideal for anyone." I got her point; while they were cleaning the windows along the dining room side, someone must have taken items from their van. However . . . "Wasn't your van locked?"

She flushed a rosy pink and shifted from foot to foot. Her gaze slipped away to stare into the distance. "Uh, well, the lock on the back door is broken and we don't have time to get it fixed. We didn't think we'd need to worry about it here," she said defensively, meeting my eyes. "And at night it's locked in a secure facility."

"I can speak to the HHN crew about it."

"We'd appreciate it," she said, her color ebbing. "I tried but they deny it."

"I'm sorry about this. Give me a list of what you're missing, and I'll be sure that HHN either returns the items—the best scenario, of course—or reimburses you for them."

Dani nodded. "Okay. That's great." Her mood had improved. "We understand that this was unexpected for you, too, and that this is time-sensitive, but we have another job lined up immediately after this and need to hustle."

"Are any of the items you're missing irreplaceable?"

"No, we have replacements."

"Thanks for the heads-up; I'll take care of it. You're doing a great job, and we appreciate it."

She flashed a wide toothy smile and said, "No problem. Back to work!"

"For me, too." I headed back in and, in light of this new information, began an inspection tour of the castle. Would I even know if something of ours was missing? I spoke to Pish about it, and he told me he'd get the list of missing items from Brad and Dani and take care of it. This was his responsibility, since he had agreed to the HHN shoot.

But I was still going to examine the guest rooms and make sure everything was in place.

I checked the wardrobe and makeup rooms first, but they were bustling with HHN staffers who were professional and tidy. Lynn waved to me but was too busy to talk. I went next to the contestant bedrooms. You can tell a lot about a person by observing how they live. I'm not the neatest person in the world, but *total* chaos drives me bananas. There were a couple of slobs among the competitors and a couple of neatniks.

Brontay and Pam's room was moderately messy, but not alarmingly so. Everything seemed intact. Kamile's side of her shared room with Darcie was militarily tidy. It made her roommate's side look messy, but Darcie's clutter wasn't as bad as Zeb, Lachlan, and Alain's room, which looked like a tornado had zoomed through, wreaking havoc. Only one of the male roommates had any order, and I suspected it was Lachlan, judging from the notebook on his bedside table, which was open to display a rigorous workout schedule. He was disciplined and focused, attributes I respect. The only sign that his tidy-up was hasty was his toiletries case still open, tall bottles of product sticking out of the top, and a suitcase shoved halfway under his bed with a blue jacket zipper hanging out of the closed edge. Nothing that belonged to the castle appeared to be missing from the room.

I heard raised voices nearby; what was going on? I exited to the shadowy gallery and followed the sounds of an argument to outside of Moze's small room, where I discovered Gilda, listening in. I watched her for a moment; she was intensely focused, her ear to the crack of the door. The uncle's voice boomed and carried; he said Kamile needing to keep to herself while Moze was gone, that she must maintain that separation.

I frowned; why was she not allowed to mingle with the others? Was he afraid she would lose focus, or did he worry that she would make friends? Was he concerned that she would fall for one of the fellows? Many a promising opera career has been derailed by an ill-fated love affair. I stepped wrong and brushed past a hall table, rattling a decorative urn. Gilda reared back from the door.

"Oh, it's you," she hissed. "Go away, will you?" She flapped her hands in my direction.

Annoyed at being ordered about in my own home, I said, in my normal voice, "I will *not* go away, Gilda. This is, after all, my home."

The voices in the other room stopped and Gilda sent me a poisonous glare, her eyes glinting in the light from a sconce. "You don't even live here. I know where you live: that ugly house near the woods."

"It's not ugly, it's Craftsman. And that doesn't change the fact that *this* is my home too. I own it."

Kamile Markunis burst from her uncle's room and whipped past us, her face oddly composed for the flurry of her movement. Moze came to the door of his room and observed us both, but his gaze settled on Gilda. "Miss Greenwald, were you eavesdropping on my conversation with my niece?" he asked, his oily tone underlain with a threatening timber.

"Your . . . niece?" Gilda said, with an odd pause.

I thought back to Lachlan's insinuations that there was more between the pair than a family connection.

"My niece," he bellowed. "My sister's child. *Yes.*"

There was a moment of glowering wrath between them, but Gilda backed down, turning and scuttling off, muttering under her breath. It sounded like she was saying she'd discover what was going on if it was the last thing she did.

I should warn her against tempting fate at Wynter Castle, I thought.

Moze watched her go, then turned to me. With a courtly bow, he said, his tone silky, "Madam, I will be leaving this evening. I will make sure the room is neat in case you need to use it."

"Will you be rejoining us?"

"If you don't mind, yes. I will return within the week for the last day of judging. Then I will take my niece to New York to celebrate her triumph."

I marveled at his sureness. I *wasn't* so sure. Lizzie kept me up to date on numerous reality shows she and her friends watched and none of them, in her estimation, were won by the person whose talent merited it. "The room will still be available when you return, if you should need it."

Nine

Having heard her clatter downstairs, I decided to check Gilda's room for missing items. She had notes scattered all over the desk, and her laptop was open. I jarred the desk "accidentally" and the mouse moved, awakening her laptop. It opened to a page of notes and I just *happened* to scan them.

Okay, I'll admit it: I'm nosy and wanted to know what she was working on.

Her notes were jumbled, typos everywhere, obviously hastily typed; a great many exclamation points and question marks were scattered over the page like raindrops.

Kamile/Moze . . . neese??? Lover, maybe? Or . . . something else??? Chek Lith contact.

Lachlan . . . boybland . . . bad bloof . . . troubel?? Call Colin?

Primo . . . asking wierd questions ab/t Reece . . . Y? Stories ab/t Reece at hotel . . . whutz going on?

Darcee . . . sneeky in rooms, spying?? Ask B whutz up.

Deciphering, I saw that she was indeed questioning the relationship between Moze and Kamile and intended to contact someone in Lithuania, perhaps. She was investigating Lachlan's departure from the Scottish Tenors; was Colin another member of the group, I wondered, someone she intended to interview about Lachlan's past? And as far as I could interpret from her atrocious spelling, Alain Primeau had been asking questions about Daffyd Rhys and his behavior, possibly at the hotel in Rochester. The bit about Darcie made no sense to me, but maybe she had been caught spying on someone, or sneaking into other singers' rooms? Sabotage, perhaps? I still hadn't gotten a solid answer about why they were kicked out. Maybe I could find a hotel biz contact who would know more.

There was more, and I was about to continue reading the notes, but I heard the door open and hurriedly turned. When Gilda entered, I was *apparently* just coming out of the bathroom. However, the eagle-eyed reporter spied the lighted laptop screen.

"What are you doing in here?" she asked, squinting at me, her voice laden with suspicion.

"Checking each room. Yours is the last."

"Did that include turning on my laptop?"

"I jostled the desk and it came on." I paused, but seeing no need to hide that I had read the notes, I said, "Gilda, do you think there's something fishy about Moze and Kamile's relationship?"

She marched over to the laptop and slapped down the cover. "Maybe." She tilted her chin up. "Whatever it is, I'll get to the bottom of it."

"And about Lachlan . . . is there trouble with his old band?"

Her brow wrinkled. "I don't know what to think. I'm waiting for a phone call from one of his former band members."

That must be Colin, I thought.

"There are conflicting accounts out there of why he left," she continued. "He says he wanted to be more than one of a group, but there are rumors . . ." She shook her head. "Anyway, look, I'd appreciate it if you'd stay quiet about what you read."

I nodded.

"I may be zipping in and out of here once or twice. I have to go back to Rochester soon. Can I leave my stuff here?" She gave me a look. "And trust that it will be here when I get back?"

I was about to retort with a snide remark, but she did have a point, with the items missing from the window washer's van, though she presumably didn't know about that. "There are keys for each of these doors. I didn't think it was necessary for anyone to lock up, but maybe there is. I'll make sure you have a key to your door." I paused on my way out of the room and met her steady gaze with my own. "I have the master key to all of these rooms, and it is *my* place. You can trust me not to abuse that fact, and I won't discuss what your notes said. Do you have everything you need, Gilda?"

She relaxed, her shoulders visibly sagging. "I do. The room is lovely, and the castle is absolutely amazing." She paused, then said earnestly, "I don't mean to be a pain, Merry. This article is important to my career." She stared at me, her eyes large behind the glasses. "I want to write true crime."

Caught off guard, I gaped, then found my voice. *"True crime?* What does that have to do with this? I thought your article was supposed to be about the competition show?"

"Yeah, of course, the article for *Modern Entertainment*. The competitors *are* the show, you know? So I need to find out everything I can about them. And I think I'm on to a couple of other stories—maybe even three—nice *juicy* ones. I'm gathering enough material to pitch a more serious piece to another paper or magazine that might pave my way."

"Is that . . . is that ethical? I mean, whatever you're investigating, it might derail the opera competition if there is a criminal story."

She laughed, a short sharp bark. "Are you kidding? Scandal is meat to reality TV fans. They'll eat it up."

Conflicted, I watched her a moment. "Should I be worried? I mean . . . criminal activity?"

"Nothing to concern yourself over. Trust me . . . I have a nose for this kind of stuff, and it will all be okay."

As I left the room, I couldn't help but wonder, if there was criminal activity involved, shouldn't she report it?

• • •

I was back in the kitchen still trying to get organized, and hoping this little detour from sanity known as the *Opera DivaNation* singing competition wouldn't last any longer than Anne claimed. I sat at the trestle table organizing the inventory list on a spreadsheet and deciding what else we'd need as Patricia baked. Janice was taking a break in the dining room, watching more of the rehearsals.

Sparrow Summers came in once and clutched the back of a chair, breathing through a panic attack. Poor girl . . . I felt for her. She did not seem to be cut out for this. The second time she came into the kitchen I asked if she needed anything, and she said no. The third time she came in she was weeping, disconsolately, and shivering, collapsing to huddle on a stool by the fireplace.

I thrust a handful of tissues at her and watched for a moment. "Sparrow, I'm worried, I have to say," I said, sitting on the wing chair in front of her. "You're having a rough day. Not every person is suited to every job, you know. You can say it."

She mopped her eyes, took a deep breath and shook her head. "It's okay. It's my process," she said, her voice breaking.

I frowned and stared at her. She was a complicated young woman. Her cold, calculated pleasure at tricking the contestants into saying horrific things, balanced by this weepy over-the-top drama was puzzling. "Have you worked on other reality shows?"

"Oh, sure," she said, perking up. She unwound herself from her ball-of-nerves attitude and came to join me, sitting beside me on the other wing chair. "After I left my job—I was a writer, once upon a time—I worked on a junior talent show." She shuddered. "I *hate* kids; they're the worst. I swear they're little beasts; any sign of weakness and they pounce. I assistant produced a modeling show. I even worked on a prison lockdown show!" Her eyes took on a vacant look, as if she was returning to the past, and sighed.

"How did that turn out? It must have been . . . scary?"

She shook her head and frowned. "Not really. I mean, we were well protected." She twisted a ring on her finger. "Some of the prisoners were nice. One in particular . . ." She shook herself. "I'd better get back to work." She bounced up and trotted off.

I got up and returned to the table to continue my work. Patricia, who for once did not have her earbuds in, turned from her work and gave me a look. *"Some of the prisoners were nice?"* she mimicked, goggling. "You *know* she's that girl, the one who falls in love with serial killers and writes them mash notes."

"Mash notes?"

"You know . . . *lurv* letters."

I laughed and went back to work.

A half hour later Patricia said, "Merry, where is the bottle of red wine I had in the cupboard for that red wine cherry compote I'm making to go over ice cream?" Hands on her hips, she stared up into the cupboard by the giant fridge.

I looked up from finalizing the next Costco list. "I don't know. Are you sure it was there?"

"I put it there first thing this morning knowing I was going to need it."

Sparrow ambled back into the kitchen, giggling and hiccupping. She sat—fell—into the chair beside me. "You should've seen her face! That Darcie, whata bitch. So smug. She's gonna be so disha . . . disappointed how she looks after final edit." She giggled and hiccupped again.

Sitting across from her I could smell the booze on her breath. Patricia and I shared a look and I nodded. Patricia sighed. She'd have to find another bottle of red. With all the wine we had available, Sparrow had to drink the one Patricia was planning to use!

"So . . . what's so funny?" I asked. Stress drinking; I had seen too many who moved from stress drinking to all-the-time drinking.

"Least I don't hafta worry about these guys asking for help escaping," she said, apropos of nothing. I assumed she was referring back to her time on a prison lockdown show.

"How is it going?"

She doubled over laughing. "Just interviewed that witch Darcie. Ho, boy, she's gonna be sorry, flirty little wench."

I waited.

Sparrow leaned across the table, her eyes trying to focus—she must have drunk the whole bottle in a short time, because her eyes were doing a jitterbug—and said, "Jus' finished Darcie's interview. Asked her about each o' the cast members. 'Bout Zeb she said she'd never date anyone like *him*."

Wise to her methods now, I asked, "How did you get her to say that?"

She winked and leaned over toward me. "He bites his nails. *That's* why she finds him nasty, would never date someone *like him*." She threw her head back laughing. "When we're done she's gonna come across as the worst kinda racist."

Stunned and revolted, I did not join her laughter. Patricia, her face red, picked up a rolling pin, but I put up one hand. I had to think about this and consult Pish; was this something we wanted our castle and future performing arts center to be involved with? How would our beautiful castle and welcoming performing arts center look, once this show was broadcast?

Patricia, her expression grim, brought over a cup of coffee and Sparrow drank it. I went back to my work as she slowly sobered. Tears ran down her face. "You know, I try to stay out of this stuff, but this business . . . it'll hammer you if you're not careful. I *have* to create drama. It's what they hired me for, so Anne doesn't have to get her soft white hands dirty with the crap I do." She peeped up at me. "You won't tell anyone, will you?"

"Tell anyone what?" I asked carefully, watching her.

She held her head, looking wretched. "What I said about making Darcie look like a racist witch."

I caught a glimpse of someone at the door; it was Gilda, and she was jotting notes.

Sparrow saw the direction of my gaze and whirled, seeing Gilda. She jumped to her feet and went two steps, then said, "Gilda, did you sign that NDA I sent you?"

Gilda smiled a Cheshire cat grin. "Sparrow, come on. Who ever heard of a journalist signing a non-disclosure agreement?" She dropped a wink and slipped away.

• • •

For the rest of the afternoon Sparrow, after sobering, did interviews in the Rose Parlor. Despite my intention to stay out of the whole affair so they could do what they were there for and leave, I had begun to care about a few of the contestants. I cornered Pish in the library and shared my concern.

"My darling, I wish I could say I was surprised," he said, looking weary. "I thought this would be easy. It's not. Giu has shared things with me—"

"What things?"

He shook his head and sighed. "I'm sorry I got us into this."

"What things, Pish? What did Giu mean?"

"He didn't explain, but he said he was dismayed by the behavior of some associated with the show."

"What are we going to do about it? About what Sparrow is doing, I mean."

"Merry, if there's funny business, it is *their* funny business, not ours. They are renting our facility. I don't see how we can oversee every aspect of their production."

I knew he was right. "But still—"

"Think about it this way: if we rent out the castle for a wedding, are we responsible if the father of the bride tells a racy joke, or if someone drinks too much and offends another guest?"

I wasn't sure I completely agreed with the metaphor, but was willing to play along. "Think about it *this* way: if a guest gets drunk in our facility and goes out on the road and kills someone, we *do* bear responsibility."

"It's not the same thing."

"We have had our problems over the years, Pish," I said, mulish anger rising in my heart. I didn't see how he could be so cavalier about it. "I don't think we—*I*—can look the other way. Not now that I know about how they are going to portray those poor kids."

"However, remember this: I intend for them to be gone one week from today so we can proceed with our plans. Until they leave there will be *no* peace in the castle. If we raise a ruckus . . . if we cause a fuss . . ." He shrugged. "We could extend the process if we complain enough to change things."

Self-respect warred with self-interest. I paced in front of the big desk, then retreated to a window overlooking the front terrace. Moze Markunis was smoking and shouting into his cell phone as he paced on the drive. He marred the view, but I ignored him. It was such a pretty view, with the new fountain and graveled drive, and the distant trees almost bare of leaves, with a few in mellow shades of yellow and ochre clinging. As challenging as the last three years have been, I love my castle. Inheriting it and moving here, with Pish and Shilo, has changed my life. I've found true friends and a husband I love to the depths of my heart.

I couldn't let it be tainted. I turned back to Pish and explained what Sparrow had told me about her methods. "I'm uncomfortable with how this is being done, how the singers are being treated. Sparrow as good as said that how they warp their words may destroy their lives. It seems to be less about presenting a singing competition and more about drama and turmoil. I won't put up with it, Pish. I won't allow them to ruin young lives for entertainment."

He smiled up at me. "Have I told you how much I love you? You're right. Do whatever you need to do, my dear. I'll back you to the limit."

I marched off to the Rose Parlor. They refused to let me sit in, saying the place was too crowded and they needed to control the sound, so I set up a laptop desk outside the parlor door. I was going to document what was going on and confront the producers if I continued to feel uneasy. I was certainly going to raise, with Anne, my concerns about the Darcie incident. This was my home and I would not allow it to be tainted by such destructive nonsense. I caught glimpses as the door opened on occasion, and could see Sparrow busily writing notes as she interviewed the subjects.

Lachlan entered first, and when he came out he was smirking.

"What did she ask you?" I said as he passed.

He paused, smiled and chuckled. "Sparrow needled me, asked how did it feel to be a failure since I left the Scottish Tenors? How did I like being a has-been . . . or a never-was? I'm too canny for that. Tryin' to trap me, she was, into saying something daft. I talked about what I wanted to talk about. Cut it up as they will, they'll no' trap me with their little ways. Say little, and say it with a smile . . . that's me."

I applauded him for that. He was too wily a fish to be caught in their net.

Darcie loudly demanded a redo of her interview. I heard her complaining to Anne that Sparrow had been "staggering drunk" in her first one. Good for her, standing up for herself. Triumphantly, Darcie sailed back into the Rose Parlor for her redo, and stormed out twenty minutes later, snorting fire.

"What happened?" I asked.

She whirled and glared at me through the gloom. "That . . . that . . ." Darcie made an incoherent sound in the back of her throat. "She implied that I was . . . was using *sex* to get through the competition. I mean, is she kidding? Has she ever *seen* an opera? Of course I'm sexy. Operas are all *about* sex."

"Being sexy is a little different from flirting your way through with the male judges, though, isn't it?" Gilda, suddenly in the hall with us, asked from the shadows.

Darcie whirled and stormed off, incandescent with rage. Gilda smiled—again that Cheshire grin—and let herself into the Rose Parlor.

Next to storm out was Alain, who hauled a soundman with him, hollering a string of what I would later learn was joual, the dialect of French spoken by Quebecois. It was unintelligible at first, but as Alain calmed, he switched to imperfect English. "*Tabarnak!* What does she mean to say, that bird girl, that I am jealous of Zeb and Lachlan, hein?" he shouted at the bemused headphone-wearing soundman, who waited amiably for Alain to lose steam so he could return to his soundboard. "It makes not sense when I am the better singer. *And* better-looking." He calmed more and took in a deep audible breath. "*En tout co*, is no big deal." The soundman took that moment to duck away. Alain turned and saw me in the shadows. He smiled. "Pretty lady, do you have better coffee than that *marde* on the craft table."

"That *marde* – I'm assuming that is similar to *merde,* a word in French I do understand – is decent coffee, even if you think otherwise. However, come to the kitchen." It was impossible not to be charmed by Alain. His rapid recovery from annoyance to sunny smiles was remarkable. It did make me think, though: why was flirting so bad when Darcie did it, and so charming when Alain did it? Double standard in full force. Janice was in the kitchen wrapping muffins for the craft services table and again singing a snatch of "Je Veux Vivre."

"Oh, lala, c'est beautiful, madame, your *voice*! You put the competition ladies to shame," he said as I poured him a cup of coffee.

He caught Janice by the waist and twirled her away from the counter, waltzing her across the floor with surprising grace. She is an accomplished dancer. To finish, he dipped her and kissed her cheek. She is a big woman, and his shoulders beneath the silk shirt he wore bulged, his musculature well developed, better than I would have supposed considering how slim he was.

And . . . he was gone with his cup of coffee, retreating upstairs, he said, to study his next piece. He left Janice red-faced, laughing and entirely pleased with her life.

Ten

Lizzie, who had barely taken a moment's rest since arriving early, joined me in the kitchen and slumped down in a wingchair, slinging one leg over the arm and scrolling through the pictures on her digital camera.

"How is it going?" I asked.

"Interesting," she said, looking up. "Can I hide out here for a minute?"

"Sure. What's up?"

"That kid, Brontay . . . she's following me *every*where. I don't know if she's bored or what, but she won't leave me alone. She keeps asking questions."

"About . . . ?"

Lizzie shrugged. She sat up in the chair, set her camera down and pulled a scrunchie off her wrist and confined her wild mop of hair. She wore, as usual, a racer-back tee in camo, her newish tattoo—of a camera taking wing—exposed on her scapula, and jeans with hiking boots. "She talks nonstop. Finally I asked her, didn't opera singers need vocal rest? But she didn't get it. She asks about me, about my photography, about you, Pish, the castle . . . *every*thing!" She threw her hands up in the air. "I've never met anyone who could talk so much."

"How did you handle it? How did you answer?"

She stared at me. I waited. She *still* stared and I got it. Of *course*; Lizzie can be maddeningly silent when she wants to be. Other people's expectations mean nothing to her. I admire that.

"How did you escape?"

"I left her talking to Gilda." She smirked. "That woman can talk too, so the two of them ought to have a war of the words. I think Brontay's next up to go into the Inquisition."

"Inquisition?" I didn't know enough history to know if she had used the reference justly, how Sparrow was conducting a cruel inquiry, but Lizzie shrugged, so I let it go.

She may be a teenager—eighteen now, fifteen when first I met her—but Lizzie has a remarkable view of the world, one she has developed by eyeing it for three years through the lens of a camera. Her photos display that intense view, especially her portraits. She catches the most revealing expressions on occasion. "Lizzie, you've been observing for a while; what do you think of this show? I mean, the people, and their talents and their participation?"

She picked up her camera and fiddled with it for a long silent moment. That was what she did while contemplating. "There's something wrong," Lizzie said finally, looking up with a clouded gaze.

"Wrong how?"

She flexed her shoulders, always an indication she couldn't explain what she meant. "Just . . . *wrong*. I don't know how else to say it." She gazed at me helplessly. "It's a feeling I have, like everyone is fuzzy, out of focus. I mean, I know there are a couple of people who are a pain in the neck."

"Like Sparrow."

She nodded. "And Lachlan; he's *so* full of himself."

"So are Alain and Darcie, don't you think?"

"Well, yeah, but not in the same way. And there is something up with Kamile Markunis."

"Do you think it has to do with her uncle? Once he leaves we may see a different woman."

"Maybe," Lizzie said, drawing it out slowly. "She's . . ." She sighed in frustration, shaking her head. "I don't know. And Gilda; *that* chick is a piece of work."

"How so?"

"She's everywhere. I mean, *ev-ery-where*! Around every corner, behind every door, in every shadow. Poking, prodding, asking, sneaking, questioning, watching . . . and waiting."

"Waiting?"

"Waiting . . . for something."

"She *is* a journalist. That's what they do."

"Maybe."

I thought over what Lizzie said as she bounced off, saying she was going outside to escape for a while and take photos of the continuing work on the houses. I yelled after her not to bug our tenants if they were there, but she was already gone. I returned to my post outside of the examination room . . . er, Rose Parlor.

Zeb slumped out a few moments later, slamming the door behind him.

"What's up?" I asked.

"I'm such an *idiot*." He made a guttural growl of frustration. "I got mad. Got loud. I *know* better."

His staccato utterances indicated his tension. "What do you mean?"

He gazed at me for a moment, then said, his tone calmer, "The way Sparrow asks questions . . ." He shook his head. "In my rational mind I can see that she's doing her best to elicit a certain response, but after a few minutes of crap I got irritated. Some of the things I said . . . *how* I said them . . . I *know* they're going to twist it. *Damn!*" He gritted his teeth and grimaced. "I'm so *angry* at myself right now. She got under my skin and that's dangerous, especially for me."

"Especially for you? What do you mean?"

He examined my face and looked undecided whether to explain, but then said, "When a Black person asserts their rights on reality TV it gets edited to look like the angry Black person stereotype. If we get passionate or intense . . ." He shook his head. "It's mostly Black women, but men too. I'm going to come off spiteful and violent and . . ." He sighed gloomily, crossing his arms over his chest, like he was hugging himself. "Dangerous Black man goes *off;* film at eleven."

"No one who knows you could think that," I said. Of all of them—other than Kamile—Zeb had seemed the most even-tempered, the most gracious, the quietest and calmest.

"But America *doesn't* know me. All they'll know is what the producers choose to show."

He was right, of course. His fear added to my unease about the whole contest. "What did she ask in particular that upset you?"

He frowned. "I can't even remember exactly *what* she said. It was *how* she said it."

"Hasn't she been doing this all along? You've had these 'Diary Room' entries for a while, right? Throughout the competition?"

He frowned and bit his fingernails as he considered. "It's *different* now . . . Sparrow's questions are different now."

"How?"

"She's asking more personal questions, digging deeper. It all feels more intense. Maybe because we're almost at the end."

"Maybe."

He dropped his hand from his mouth, took in a long breath and let it out, the tension draining from his whole body as he centered himself. He tugged at his close-fitting sweater and pulled down the sleeves. "She held back at first, didn't want to show her cards," he said, nodding as he worked it out. "She didn't want to alienate us at first, but now she wants to ratchet up the drama, maybe start feuds. You'd think after a lifetime of being the only Black kid in a class on opera and classical music I'd be immune to the jabs and digs," he said. "But she got under my skin. She's *real* good at it."

I debated for a moment, but then felt compelled to say, "I should warn you, since you won't see the rough cuts, I've had it straight from the horse's mouth that Sparrow is going to make it look like Darcie has racist tendencies. She said something completely innocuous, but they're going to cut and paste it to make it look like Darcie is a bigot." I told him what Sparrow had said.

"Thanks for the warning. I'll talk to Darcie . . . let her know, too." He paced back and forth, scrubbing his cropped hair with both hands. Finally he stopped and met my sympathetic gaze. "I talked to Alain," he said. "They did a number on him, pulled every string, made him dance like a marionette. He's worried now he may have said something in the heat of the moment that'll make him look bad. Post-production will make us all over into typical reality TV tropes: mindless bigoted flirty party girl; oversensitive or angry Black person; conceited calculating diva; childish teen girl; petulant foreigner. I'm beginning to regret joining up for this."

My heart hurt for him. I put my hand on his arm and felt the tense muscles under his skin. "You'll be okay, you know."

He shrugged.

"You will. You have a rare gift, a voice that conveys emotion beautifully. When you sang 'Somewhere,' I melted into tears. You *belong* on the stage. Don't let the doubters get you down."

Moisture glistened in the corners of his dark eyes and he nodded. "Can I hug you?"

I opened my arms and we hugged. He was strong and warm and smelled good. "If there's anything I can do to help—with this or anything else—let me know." I squeezed and released him.

He nodded, then gave me a smile that flickered to life, transforming his expression with warmth and light. "Thanks. I needed that right this minute." He took a deep breath. "Okay. All right. I can take it. I can weather the storm." He shook his arms, releasing the tension once more. "It's nothing I haven't faced before. Next time, I won't let them see me crack. I'll smile through it."

His courage in the face of adversity should have cheered me, but as I watched him stride away, all I felt was sad. I shook off the gloom. Zeb was strong; he'd find a way. I considered his last words, that next time he'd find a way to smile through the verbal assaults. He hinted that he had done that many times over the years. And it made me think: what emotions, resentments, worries, or tensions were the others hiding? Most involved in this production were likely monitoring their own behavior, being cautious, being deceitful even, to appear in a more sympathetic light. Kamile had been damned as too careful, but it was like a tightrope act; too emotional and she would be condemned as flighty, too calm and she was condemned as cold. Finding the balance must be virtually impossible.

A few moments after Zeb headed back to the dining room to rehearse, Kamile bolted out of the Rose Parlor. Her cheeks were flame red but she didn't pause long enough for me to engage her; she raced past me and clumped up the stairs in an unusually graceless exit. Brontay, on her way in, paused a second, then entered the lion's den with a worried frown and her mother in tow.

I finalized my Costco list, texted it to Janice and Patricia for the next day, closed my laptop and considered checking the craft services table in the dining room. Brontay stormed out of the parlor weeping loudly and bolted past me toward the kitchen. Before the door completely closed I heard screaming in the Rose Parlor, Pam Bellini's voice shrill and at top volume as she accused Sparrow of bullying. I followed Brontay to the kitchen, where she had collapsed in one of the wing chairs. I sat down in the other and let her cry, handing her a handful of tissues.

"Brontay, what's going on?" I finally asked when the worst of the storm was over. "What happened in there?"

"She called me fa-at!" she wailed.

I stiffened. "Who did? Sparrow?"

She nodded, sniffing. Her weeping stopped, leaving her red face blotchy and tearstained.

Pam stomped into the kitchen and, hands on her hips, confronted her daughter. "Brontay, what the hell were you thinking, storming out of there like that?"

I gawped at her, knowing that she had stayed behind to scream at Sparrow. Why was she now laying into her daughter?

"Mom, she asked me how much I weigh, and said did I think my weight would stand in the way of w-winning!"

I was appalled.

"You behaved like a spoiled brat. If you'd kept your cool and answered her, you'd get more air time. This way there isn't even any film they'll be able to use and you'll have to do it over again."

"No way. I'm quitting! I'm not gonna do that again, she can go f—"

"Brontay, stop acting like a baby!"

The girl stiffened and glared up at her mother.

Janice, face pink with anger, drifted over and said, her tone filled with urgency, "I don't mean to interfere." She dried her hands on her apron. "But I'm a mom. It breaks my heart to hear this. As her mother it's your *job* to defend your little girl. I know how it feels to be . . . to be bullied for being . . . for being a little on the bigger size, you know, as a kid. It's not right. You've *got* to support her."

I didn't know what to say because I knew that Pam *did* stand up to Sparrow, but how to enter that into the conversation?

"Look, I don't mean to be rude," Pam said to Janice, putting out one hand to halt her. Her pixie face was set in an expression of mulish determination. "But this is none of *your* business." She looked Janice up and down, taking in the wooly tunic sweater and leggings. "*You* can look however you want, but once you're on camera, it's different."

"Talent doesn't need a look, it needs a chance," I said as Janice retreated, miffed and upset.

Pam gave me a withering look. "How naïve *are* you? No offense—I know you used to be one of those plus-sized models—but you're not anyone important now and won't be ever again. You are, at best, a *used*-to-be. Brontay's best chance in this competition and her chosen field is to lose weight and be groomed by a stylist."

Lynn had entered the kitchen and caught what Pam said. "You don't know a thing," she said loudly, approaching, bony fists balled at her sides. "Merry Wynter is not a used-to-be, she's a still-is. She saved my life, and I won't let you or anyone talk to her like that."

Pam looked conflicted. She knew Lynn as Leatrice Pugeot, world-famous supermodel, and now stylist on *Opera DivaNation*. To alienate the stylist on *any* shoot is a big mistake. "I'm sorry," she said in full retreat. "I was upset."

"Brontay, for what it's worth, I heard what went on after you left the Rose Parlor," I said. "Your mom *did* stand up for you to Sparrow."

Pam's ever-present phone rang that moment and she nodded and walked away.

"Don't listen to anyone, Brontay," Lynn said, tears welling in her eyes. She put her hands on the girl's shoulders and stared into her eyes. "You are *beautiful*. Enjoy what you have while you're young: beautiful brown skin, glowing brown eyes, gorgeous hair." She took the girl's hand and tugged her toward the door. "Come upstairs and I'll show you the outfit you'll be wearing for the production video shoot. You're going to look beautiful."

Eleven

After a late lunch all of the judges and mentors were now in the dining room. Before they started shooting I had a chance to look over the performance area close up. It was a lovely scene, with the autumnal woods in the background, viewed through the sparkling diamond-paned gothic windows, Pish's beautiful piano and the fireplace dressed to impress. The layered Turkish patterned area rugs that concealed the wires and flooring gave added warmth to the scene where the contestants would be filmed singing. The crew had set up movable frames holding midnight-blue spangled curtains about twenty or more feet long that ended in a wide curve to give a good solid backdrop for the three director's chairs emblazoned with the *Opera DivaNation* logo, a treble clef and the title, and each of their names. Rhys's chair said *Sir Daffyd*. He was going to let no one forget his knight bachelorhood given to him ten years ago for services to the entertainment industry.

Giuseppe Plano, a singer whose actual résumé greatly outclassed Rhys's, had simply *Giu* on his chair despite the honors he had been given in his homeland—he had been awarded the title of *commendatore* several years ago, Pish had whispered—while Anokhi also had her name on the back, with no embellishment. The mentors—Carlyle, Liliana and Roma—were placed off to the side, observing and coaching, their chairs nestled in the curve of the curtained backdrop.

There was a hum of intensity among the crew, twenty or so altogether. They were for the most part youngish, except for a few senior crew members managing the chaos. Anne (who was the director in addition to her producing duties; at HHN staffers filled many roles simultaneously), Sparrow, and a couple of technicians sat at a bank of tables. The producers had tablets and clipboards, while the technicians sat in command of the monitors, soundboards and various other pieces of equipment I could not identify. There were two boom mics and two steadycam operators, and a lighting supervisor who set and tested the lighting for every shot. A young PA—she couldn't have been more than twenty—held the digital clapperboard and watched Anne anxiously. Between shots she updated the shot log.

I had never seen a reality show shot before—you can't count our ghost-hunting crew experience, short-lived and tragic as it was—and watched with great interest from the back near the craft services section. As with all TV and film shoots, there was endless repetition, and before every shot someone would shout "Quiet!" I'd practically hold my breath. The singers had to repeat their "rehearsal" a dozen times, and the mentors had to give the same advice over and over until Anne and the technicians were satisfied.

The judges were filmed having discussions after each rehearsal about who was doing well, who was tanking. Moze Markunis lurked in the background watching, occasionally speaking with Anne or Kamile, his gaze stolid and somber. Pam was in and out, mostly on her phone texting. There was bickering, especially about Pam's restless presence and her chiming phone, but the person I noticed most was Gilda; she was there through it all, watching, listening, noticing, and scribbling notes in a loopy slanted hand.

Darcie was up; looking nervous, she started her practice session. She looked lovely, dressed in a filmy silk blouse and cream wool trousers with black and gold stilettos. Rhys stared at his phone during her practice session. When she was done she stormed off behind the cameras and held a whispered conference with Anne. The producer motioned for her to join her outside of the doors and—I'll confess I've become hyper-aware of anything shady going on in my castle—I followed, stealthily. Slipping out the closing door and lurking in the shadows, I listened in.

"Darcie, you've got to calm down," Anne muttered. "If you don't, you're going to self-destruct."

"What's the point?" the singer hissed. "Daffyd didn't even look up *once* while I was singing, not one *single* time. He's tired of me already."

"What do you mean, *tired of you*? Darcie, that sounds like you have a personal relationship, and you *know* that's strictly against the rules," Anne said, her tone laden with warning. "*Don't* tell me," she said, half raising one hand. "I don't want to have to eliminate you, not at this stage."

"Oh, come on, Anne, don't pretend you don't know all the crap that went on in Rochester."

Anne shook her head and didn't answer.

"And why do you let Gilda sit in on the shoots? I told you I don't trust her. She's going to be trouble."

"Stop, just *stop*. Gilda is a vital part of our promotion. How did you get to a point where you feel you can tell us what to do? Huh? *Tell* me!"

Darcie crossed her arms over her chest. From my vantage point, I saw moisture glisten at the corner of her eye. She was under a great deal of pressure, nearly to the breaking point.

"You do want this production to go well, don't you?" Anne said, her tone softer. "I shouldn't have to babysit you, Darcie. For heaven's sake, Brontay is only fifteen and she's behaving like a pro."

"Don't you dare—"

"Don't *you* dare. Don't threaten me, Darcie," Anne said, her voice a growl. She poked the younger woman in the chest and said, "I've had it up to my eyebrows. At this point I am *willing* our way to the end so I can finish this tragicomic circus and get home to my husband and my cats." The producer sounded angry and weary in the way any woman trying to herd a group of insecure, emotional, high-strung performers does after working a long day managing egos and hissy fits. Having worked in the modeling industry, I felt for her.

"That's fine for *you*, Anne. But this is my *career*. Daffyd promised I'd be at the top. He *promised*!"

My eyes wide, I put one hand over my mouth. Could she not shut up? It seemed like career suicide for Darcie to so openly say that a judge had promised her a certain outcome. And it could be damaging to Daffyd, too; it surely went against everything he stood for as a top-notch professional in his field.

"If that's true—and I'm not admitting it, Darcie, that's just your word—then Sir Daffyd was out of line," Anne said stiffly. "The winner will be chosen by the judging panel after consultation with the mentors and producers. There are no guarantees ahead of time."

"In other words you'll choose whoever fits your idea of what will excite the public most. It'll be that little twerp, Brontay, or that cipher wrapped in an enigma, Kamile. I warn you, Anne, I *won't* be kicked around." Her voice rose in a frenzied fit of anxious anger. "I will *not* be ignored. I will tell Gilda every single *dirty* little secret I know and tear this contest down!"

"Shut up, Darcie, just *shut up*," Anne muttered in a furious undertone, looking around the great hall. She moved forward and thrust her face into the singer's. "I won't be bullied, not by anyone, and least of all by a whiny little two-bit—"

Anne stopped abruptly at a faint noise in the shadows by the door. Unnoticed by me or the two combatants, Gilda had crept out too. She stood scratching notes on her notepad. Anne whirled and herded Darcie back into the dining room. Gilda smiled at me and waggled her eyebrows, then slipped away. She caught up with Brontay, who was heading toward the big double doors, and exited with her.

I was with Lizzie on one thing: something was wrong behind the scenes of this show, and I didn't like it one bit. Anne's normally calm demeanor had become menacing and cold, like she was willing to throttle Darcie for blabbing contest secrets. I wanted to see how things were going. I was torn, though, wondering what Gilda would have to say to Brontay. But in the end curiosity about the proceedings in the dining room led me back to the production. Anne, looking tired and distraught, had returned to the control table to observe. She whispered to Sparrow, who nodded and rolled her eyes.

Alain sang. Extraordinarily, he went from flirtatious bubblehead—flattering and flirting with every female in sight, including Anokhi, who stolidly ignored him, Liliana, who merely smiled, and Roma, who rolled her eyes and sighed—transforming when performance time came into a serious and able opera star as Carlyle gave him guidance. He was young yet, but I could see Giuseppe Plano paying close attention and nodding along with him, in approval, when he sang snatches of his performance piece. I was impressed with his ability and consistency. Primeau was the real deal.

When he was done and the technicians were setting up for the next singer he came to me and leaned over my chair. "Beautiful one, you stay to watch me. I am good, yes?"

Torn between laughter and irritation, I said, "Yes, you are good." I pointedly turned my attention back to the next singer, Kamile Markunis.

She was fabulous and beautiful, dressed simply in a skirt topped by a tunic sweater. Her performance was haunting. I'd remember it long after I forgot many more famous singers. She had smiled faintly after the judges' comments and glided away. Rhys slipped from his director's chair and followed her to the sidelines, speaking to her in hushed tones, grabbing her arm. She pulled away from him. Moze stormed over and grabbed the tenor by the collar of his jacket.

"Stay you away from my niece," Moze growled in an unmistakably possessive rage. "I told you in Rochester and I will tell you again, I will squeeze your throat and make sure you never sing again if you so much as *look* at Kamile."

"Uncle Moze," the young woman cried, her tone low as she wrung her hands in anguish. "*Please,* let it go."

"I will *not*! This man—"

He was interrupted by Anne, who hurried to quell the dispute. She held Moze off, one hand on his barrel chest, and ordered Daffyd back to his chair. She then spoke to the Lithuanian in a soothing murmur, giving Kamile a moment to escape. The singer fled, gliding out the doors. I followed her out to the hall but she was gone, clattering up the stairs.

When I returned to the dining room the room had filled with tension. Plano was lecturing Rhys, his round face red with anger. Anokhi intervened between the two singers. As a conductor she had experience with quelling disputes, no doubt.

I slipped away to start dinner. Whatever else happened, there would be food. It was lovely working with Patricia and Janice. Janice had been in the dining room and witnessed much that I did. We discussed (gossiped about) the events as she chopped vegetables and I put together two antipasti platters to precede the spaghetti Bolognese that was dinner for those staying at the castle. Patricia, making a lovely savory ricotta, olive and sundried tomato "cake," listened in.

"I'm not sure I understand the relationship between Moze and Kamile," I mused, rolling prosciutto slices around locally made pickled asparagus spears.

"He's a bully and she's afraid of him," Janice stated, rapidly chopping onions for the Bolognese.

"That may be true, but there's something else." I was silent for a moment. "She's so self-contained, so . . . what did Darcie call her? An enigma wrapped in a puzzle, or something like that."

Patricia said, "Sounds like that quotation from Churchill, about Russia. He called that country a riddle wrapped in a mystery inside an enigma. Or a puzzle . . . I've heard the quote both ways."

We stared at her and she smiled.

"I was a history major in college."

"I can't imagine Darcie Austin knowing a Churchill quote," I said dryly.

"Don't underestimate anyone," Patricia said. "You're surprised *I* know it."

"True. Anyway, back to Kamile—"

That moment Lizzie trudged in from the back door and butler's pantry hall, trailed by a chattering Brontay, who was trailed by a burr-covered Becket.

"—and didyouknow, Sparrow's crazy in love with one of the guys . . . guess which one?"

"I don't *want* to guess which one," Lizzie said grumpily. She was beyond her tolerance level for other humans.

"Darn it, Becket, come here," I said and grabbed my cat, carrying him over to the chairs and pulling burrs off him as Lizzie slumped into the other chair and gloomily clicked through her camera, looking at shots. Becket wriggled and growled, but I was not going to let him trail burrs through the place.

"Come on, *guess*!" Brontay demanded, standing in front of her chair.

"I'm not gonna guess, Brontay!"

At that moment Sparrow popped her head into the kitchen. "Oh, there you are, Brontay! We've been looking all over for you. Get upstairs now so Lynn can style you for the cameras . . . rehearsal shoot clothes and hair, okay?" She eyed the girl critically. "Good lord, you look like you've been pulled through a bush backward. Go *now*!"

Brontay sulkily exited, followed by a chattering Sparrow, exhorting her to stay closer to the castle in future, or carry her phone.

"Well, at least she recovered from when I last saw her," I said, pulling the last burr out of Becket's fur. He swiped at me, but I evaded the claws of doom and let him jump down to sit on the hearth and sulk while he cleaned himself up. I turned to Lizzie, biting my lip to keep from laughing at her forlorn expression. "How long has Brontay been following you around?"

"Gawd, an hour? Two? Three? I don't know; seems like forever."

"It can't be *that* long. I saw her leave and it was about an hour ago. What was she saying about Sparrow?"

Lizzie rolled her eyes and set the camera aside. "That kid does nothing but gossip. Honestly, was I ever that bad?"

Janice, still chopping onions, cackled. We'd all witnessed Lizzie's tumultuous transformation from feckless adolescent to almost-adult with a purpose.

"She says that Sparrow is crazy in love with one of the guys and she wanted me to guess which one."

"I *heard* that part. You didn't get her to tell you who. Now I need to know."

"I was not going to go through the guys' names with her holding the answer out like a prize. I don't give a hoot one way or the other."

I sighed. I am insatiably curious about other people; one of my many failings, or strengths, depending on how you look at it, I guess. Since Daffyd was a star, I'd guess he was the guy Sparrow was crazy about, but I'd probably never know. Perhaps it was one of the contestants. "What else did she have to say?" I asked.

"All kinds of random crap. I was trying to take pictures, but she kept yammering."

"About *what*?" I said. With Lizzie—especially when she's in a bad mood—you have to keep prying until she gives you what you want.

She sighed. "Uh, her mom is a pain in the neck ever since her dad died. She likes chocolate ice cream. She won't wear a push-up bra—"

"Lizzie, I meant about the contestants and others!" She knew that's what I meant, she just enjoys the torment.

"Alain is a perv; he's always trying to ogle the girls, *any* girls. Darcie is a stuck-up witch, except when she's not."

"What does *that* mean?"

Lizzie was silent for a long moment. She had taken a great shot of Brontay by the woods; the teen singer was standing on a stump with her hands raised to the sky. "Brontay says that when she relaxes, Darcie is nice. She talks to Brontay about boys, makeup, and living in the city. Darcie is the only one Brontay has been able to talk to about singing and what it means to her. Her mother is all business, the producers are too busy, and Kamile is . . . Kamile."

"What does *that* mean?"

"She says that she's tried talking to Kamile, but the woman seems standoffish, you know? Like she's too good for everyone else."

I didn't get that impression of Kamile, that she was superior, but there was certainly a mystery. I did not like her uncle at *all*. I shivered.

"Did you talk about Gilda at any point?" I asked, remembering Gilda and Brontay heading outside together.

Lizzie twisted her lips. "That is weird. I asked her about Gilda because I saw the two of them talking around the corner from the front door, on the terrace. Look."

She showed me her earlier pictures, taken from across the open expanse, of Gilda bent toward Brontay. The younger girl had her hands shoved in her pockets but she did not look sullen, or bored. She looked . . . engaged, animated, chatty. Maybe Gilda was getting info for her article.

Or maybe their conversation was about something else entirely.

"Do you think they'd let me in to listen to Brontay?" Lizzie asked suddenly.

I knew then that she liked the kid, and that the exasperated demeanor was my young friend's usual curmudgeonly put-on. "Why wouldn't they? Aren't you supposed to be an intern?"

"Yeah. I guess. They won't let me do much but clean up and get them coffee," she groused.

"Welcome to the world of interning."

• • •

An hour and a half later the day's taping finally wound down. Anne Parkinson had gathered everyone together and decreed that they would all have the evening off.

Liliana majestically sailed to the front to take over from the producer. "You are all doing dazzling work," she said kindly to the contestants. "Use this evening to relax, sleep, read, listen to music . . . let your soul roam free so you can recharge. You're within sight of your goal." She smiled graciously, and turned to the judges and mentors. "I'll expect you all at my home in one hour for dinner. We have much to discuss."

"I'll look forward to it," Anne said with a smile.

Liliana turned and stared at her, her gaze level, her dark eyes unreadable. "I'm sorry, Anne; you misunderstood. The dinner party is for judges and mentors only. I am unable to invite you and Sparrow. We require time to discuss the singers, their futures, and their place in the contest."

"But we film your discussions so that—"

"No. You *film* the discussions we have planned with you. But this, we do alone. These young people have futures to consider and we will let no one"—she paused, and steadily stared at Daffyd—"*no one* tell us who to choose. The judges and mentors are unanimous in that. Is that not true, Sir Daffyd Rhys?" The Welshman inclined his head to her in gracious assent.

Pish hid a smile as he stood with me, watching Liliana's majestic command performance; how to control television people in one easy step. With her in the lead, the professionals donned their coats, cloaks and capes and trooped out of the castle, headed to their billets at the two houses on the edge of the open area of the property. Huddled in my heavy sweater, I exited the castle and watched them circle the parking area in the autumnal gloom, disappear and then reemerge, following the path beyond the veil of the arborvitae. They disappeared into the darkness.

Brad and Dani, the window washers, were packing up for the day, the clunk and thunk of equipment hitting the metal floor of the van echoing in the evening stillness. They both looked bone-tired . . . gray and wan and cold. I had a sense that this was a bigger job than they had anticipated. They had made real progress, Dani said, as Brad climbed in the driver's side and revved the van; they were almost caught up from the hours they had lost when the drone operator displaced them. I lost sight of her as she circled to the passenger side of the van, but I heard the heavy slam of the van door. I waved goodbye as their vehicle chugged down the lane, the throb of the heavy motor echoing and then fading. I sighed, glanced around to make sure the front terrace was tidy, and returned inside to finish dinner preparations.

Twelve

As a representative of the castle Pish had been invited by Liliana herself to attend the dinner, he informed me. He had said no; he would stay behind and help me. I assured him I could look after dinner for the contestants and producers, so he called Liliana to accept her invitation. He came back down to the kitchen looking handsome in a cranberry rolled collar sweater, hand-knit for him by Patricia, and an autumn gold silk scarf, with charcoal dress slacks.

"Wow . . . hubba hubba," I said as he kissed my cheek. "You look marvelous and smell even better. So handsome!" He smiled and donned his Burberry trench coat. We strolled arm in arm through the great hall and I followed him out onto the flagstone terrace and watched as he walked away into the gloom. The sun had already sunk below the horizon, turning the sky purple and golden. A cold wind built vigor, sweeping across the graveled drive.

I was about to reenter when the door opened and the technical crew, the last to leave, trudged out, heading wordlessly to their vehicles, which were scattered between the gravel drive and the hidden parking lot. There were more of them than I had even realized: sound engineers, the lighting tech, boom operator, videographers, technical assistants, gaffers, grips and more. The slamming of the van doors and revving engines echoed in the chilly night air, and eventually the caravan of vans and trucks wound around the arborvitae and headed out and away, down the sloping curved lane toward the road, windows flashing, reflecting the last threads of light, and taillights bouncing and bobbing. Their evening, from what I overheard as they tramped away, would consist of fast food, whiskey, weed and poker.

Becket, having forgiven me for the de-burring, rubbed against my legs and purred. "It's been a long *long* day, fella," I said softly, listening to the wind whisper through the trees, a rattle of dry leaves that danced across the flagstone. I pulled my sweater close around me, shivering. "And we're not done yet. Dinner with these kooks, cleanup, and then bed. Virgil will be back tomorrow, if I'm lucky." My phone pinged. He must have been reading my yearning mind and body; it was a text from my husband. He and Dewayne had succeeded in their quest to follow up on a cold case and would indeed be back around midday tomorrow. I called him, we had an intimate conversation I cannot repeat as I paced to the limits of the terrace, and I signed off for the night.

I could avoid it no longer; it was time to get dinner ready. "*Once more unto the breach,* Becket." Where did I get that quote? I had no idea. And it wasn't just once more; I had signed up to provide meals for the duration, just a few more days. I sighed. My cat followed me in and went off to find a quiet place to sleep.

Patricia had already tidied her work area and headed back to Autumn Vale, giving Lizzie a lift. My young friend was helping Hannah at the library the next day. A new shipment of books had been delivered, and with her inability to unload heavy boxes she had two willing helpers in Isadore and Lizzie. Janice, however, I had invited to stay for the meal, ostensibly to help me, but also because I knew she would enjoy talking opera.

Dinner was again served in the breakfast room. The group was subdued at first, contrary to my anticipation. I think everyone was tired; I know I was. Anne was interested in my collection of teapots, and talked about her own collection. Brontay was sullen and appeared bored, while her mother spent every moment on her phone.

Gilda, however, though she appeared weary, was full of questions. As I served the antipasti platters the writer had parked herself in a chair next to Kamile and was questioning her. Kamile, who ate little, appeared to be biding her time until she could slip away. Tension radiated from her in waves as the journalist invaded her space.

"What was life like as a little girl in Lithuania?"

Kamile murmured something about school and that her youth was mostly spent taking music lessons.

"Surely you had boyfriends?"

"I was raised strictly; there was no time for friends between school and music."

"What about your parents? Are they happy with what you're doing?"

The poor woman looked the soul of misery, her gaze darting about the room. She didn't answer.

"Where is your Uncle Moze?" I asked, retrieving a picked-over antipasto tray. "Doesn't he want dinner?"

"My uncle is finishing his packing," she said. "He leaves tonight. He has a business meeting in the morning in Buffalo."

"Business meeting," Gilda said. "What *is* your uncle's business? No one seems to know."

"He is an importer."

"Of what?"

Kamile shook her head. Sparrow watched her closely, frowning. Lachlan grabbed the last prosciutto-wrapped asparagus spears from the platter in my hand. Gathering everyone's attention, he said, "I propose more general conversation. Gentlemen, I propose we each take a moment to confess our most feminine qualities. For instance, Alain, sharing space with you I have noticed that you have more skin products than all the ladies here combined."

Primeau answered good-naturedly, "I must keep this handsome face looking good, yes?"

Zeb smiled. "I likely have more hair product than is warranted by how short my hair is."

"And I . . . my weakness is long, *looong* bubble baths." Lachlan raised one eyebrow.

"I've noticed your bottles of bubble bath. They are huge!" Zeb said. "I don't like baths. Who wants to soak in their own body water?"

"I do," Lachlan said with a grin. "And unfortunately our bathroom doesn't have a tub, so I have to use the communal bathroom in the hallway, which, I have discovered, has a *glorious* soaker tub. It's big enough I can do laps."

He might have his peculiarities, but he knew how to get a crowd laughing and talking. Zeb ribbed him and even Kamile smiled. The only sour face was Darcie's. She glared at him as he bit into his hors d'oeuvre. "I hope 'long' doesn't mean all evening, like it did last night. You were in there forever!"

"You could always join me, Darcie; there's room for two." He waggled his eyebrows.

I laughed. It was a joke, after all, suggestive but harmless enough, but Darcie's pale face turned crimson.

"Don't flatter yourself," she retorted.

I wondered, had Lachlan meant it as an innocent naughty joke, or did he know how to get under her skin? These competitors had been doing this for a couple of months now. There were tensions and undercurrents I was not aware of.

"Not every woman wants to have it off with you, Lachlan," Gilda said, observing him closely. "Or weren't you aware of that?"

Brontay watched, her gaze flicking back and forth between the adults while her mother texted. Zeb frowned, Kamile ignored them, and Alain looked perplexed. Janice was avidly paying attention between bites of roasted red peppers and Genoa salami.

"Maybe I pay closer attention to those who rebuff me, trying to win them over," he said with a droll wink. "I'm intolerably self-absorbed," he said, rolling his *r*s comically, "and convinced of my ain charm. Or weren't you aware of that?"

As entertaining as the pre dinner conversation was, it was time to serve. Most of them enjoyed the spaghetti Bolognese and wedges of Patricia's marvelous savory cake, especially Brontay, who ate enthusiastically, muttering about how good it all was after the hotel's less-than-stellar fare. I served, to those who wished it, a nice Sicilian red wine and a light Californian zinfandel for those who preferred a lighter beverage, which was definitely Anne. The chatter became more general, and finally they drifted out of the breakfast room, heading toward the stairs. In the great hall Moze gave his niece a brief hug and departed, suitcase in hand. Kamile followed the others upstairs.

Janice offered to stay and help with the cleanup, but my darling friend looked completely worn out. "No, I need you fresh as a daisy for tomorrow," I said, giving her a push toward the door. "I can take care of this. Lynn promised to help." Lynn had again not eaten with us, but had promised to help with cleanup.

Finally, they were all upstairs. The castle was quiet. Becket was curled up in a wing chair in the kitchen. I organized the dirty dishes, then drank a cup of tea while making a to-do list for the next day. My phone rang. It was Pish.

"Is Daffyd there?" he asked.

"No. Isn't he there? I saw him walking in the direction of Liliana's place behind the rest of them."

"He was here at first at dinner. We are having drinks and Liliana said she wanted to speak with him. I said I'd find him, but he has disappeared and now is nowhere to be found."

"That's odd."

"Maybe he went for a walk. I'm sure he'll show up." He hung up.

Lynn descended from her lair and took direction, loading the dishwasher while I filled the sink with the things I could not put in the dishwasher: china, crystal, real silver, platters . . . I sighed. I was tired and did not whistle while I worked. Instead I grumbled while I worked, slamming cupboard doors and drawers as I searched for misplaced items. My kitchen did not feel like my kitchen. Inevitably, with two other cooks around, things went missing, or rather, were mislaid. I groused through rearranging mugs, glasses, and trays, and carped while searching for missing knives, spoons, dishwashing detergent and rubber gloves.

I was *really* peeved by the missing gloves. I'm not overly precious about my physical appearance but I *do* wash many muffin pans by hand, so I use rubber gloves, and my favorite pair were gone. I have big hands and long fingers (for a woman), so there is only one pair that fits well. "Where could they be?" I said. "I wonder if Janice used them; she has big hands too. But where would she put them?" I got down on my haunches and looked into the bowels of the bottom cupboards. Nothing but unused pots, cat bowls, dishwasher detergent and dust there. I grabbed the dishwashing detergent.

"Well, they didn't just grow legs and walk out of here," Lynn said, and I laughed as I clambered back up to my feet. "What?" she said, cocking her head to one side.

"That was my grandmother's favorite phrase when I was missing something." I gave her a side hug, squirted dish detergent into the water, then plunged my ungloved hands in. "Thanks for the laugh. I needed it."

"I think I got the phrase from *my* mother," she said.

We finished cleaning up and putting things away. "Where is my cat?" I said as I turned off the lights. He was no longer on the wing chair.

She gave me a guilty side glance. "Becket scooted out the back door a few minutes ago when I took a bag of garbage out to the lockbox."

Darn cat! He is a crafty opportunist who has a second sense about when people are going to open a door. I went to the back door and called, but he did not come. I wasn't going to wait up for him. He knew where there was shelter, and even had a cozy outdoor retreat at Virgil and my house on the edge of the far woods. However . . . I knew I'd still worry about the little dude. It was getting cold at night and was set to plunge into the thirties.

It was about ten thirty. Done, with all the lights turned out but for the one over the sink, which I left on for Pish when he got home, I wearily ascended, arm in arm with Lynn. Who would have thought that after years of fury at her, we would become friends? Almost more than friends; she was family, in a sense, a part of my life before Autumn Vale.

As Lynn retreated to her bedroom I checked in with the contestants. Brontay was practicing tone placement and vibrato, Pam explained to me as I stood in the doorway. Vibrato, she said, was achieved when a singer learned the correct tone placement and how to manipulate their voice. It would then come naturally rather than be manually forced. The teen rolled her eyes as her mother spoke over her practice—which she was recording on her cellphone using a recording app—and I stepped back out, smothering a smile.

Moze Markunis was gone, of course, his room empty and unlocked. Gilda's door was closed and locked, as was Roma's; I knew my least favorite opera singer was not back from the party yet, and might not be until the early hours of the morning. Anne and Sparrow were both done with their ablutions and answered my tap at their door with a duet of "come in," but I said goodnight from the doorway. Anne sighed, tipsy and tired. She was taking a pill and would be asleep in ten minutes, she said, while Sparrow, heavy-lidded, simply waved.

In the men's bedroom Zeb was in his pajamas—a T-shirt and plaid flannel pants—and Alain was emerging from the shower. He wore only a towel wrapped around his waist, and I was taken aback at the etched musculature of his torso, eight-pack and all. He caught me ogling and grinned, but I put up one hand. "Don't even *try* to flirt, Alain, or I will have my big, tough former cop husband have a stern talk with you."

He winked and ruffled his wet hair, spraying droplets of water around him. "Bien. I saw him. He is handsome, your husband. I might enjoy a talk with him. You could come too. We could all talk togeder," he said, his delightful accent broad, his wink and smile lascivious.

I blushed, surprised by his statement and its implications, that he was fond of the attentions of both men and women. I smiled and laughed though; it was hard not to be charmed by his open confidence and joyful sexual energy. "Monsieur Primeau, *tais toi et bon nuit.*"

"Hein, Parisian schoolgirl French. Okay. I will shut up . . . for now."

"Where is Lachlan?" I asked Zeb, who had been listening in, amused.

"In the tub," both men said.

I exited their room and visited the last room, the ladies', tapping on the door. Kamile was in bed, earbuds in, eyes closed. Darcie, still dressed, was pacing. She whirled and glared at me. "Did you know that Lachlan has been in that bath for a half hour. A *half hour*! What does he *do* in there?"

"I don't think I want to know," I said.

She did not smile. "I want you to go bang on that bathroom door and—"

"And what? Demand he come out?"

"Well, yeah," she said, hands on hips.

"There's no timer on the bathroom. Next time, you'll have to nab it first."

"I was going to but he beat me to it."

"Do you have an appointment you'll miss if you don't get in the tub by a certain time?"

She stiffened and glared.

I sighed. "Darcie, I sympathize. I'll have a talk with him tomorrow and ask if he'll let you have first dibs at the tub. Maybe you can take turns. But tonight I am *not* going to go banging on the door and demand he come out. I'm just *not*. Good night."

I did pause at the door of the bathroom and listen for a moment. There was a soft splash, and I could hear Lachlan's voice, humming. He said something, and it suddenly occurred to me that he had a girlfriend and was engaging in a little online sexting, maybe by video chat! I flushed red again, and retired to my lovely bedroom to long for Virgil, and count the hours until this lunatic crew vacated my castle.

Thirteen

Country road between Wynter Castle and Autumn Vale
10:47 p.m.

A woman drove her Wrangler along the dark backroad. Worried, she drove slowly, window down with the chill autumn wind pouring in. She scanned the brush at the edge of the woods, squinting and trying to see. A movement caught her eye. She stopped the car and clambered out, carrying a leash and jingling it. "Laddy! Laddy, where are you, boy?"

No welcome bark or yip. She shivered and glanced around, pulling her parka close around her and feeling lonely. This was like the beginning of every horror story she had ever read. It was so *very* dark and getting colder. An hour earlier she had been coming in from the barn after feeding the sheep when Laddy, her rough collie, bolted out the door of her farmhouse and escaped into the woods. She had called and waited, but he hadn't responded, so she had gotten in the Wrangler and started a slow canvass of the country roads near her home. She had passed a gated lane that she knew she had seen before, so she hadn't come far, probably not more than a mile or so.

She shivered and held back a sob. Laddy was her baby, her best friend, her *life;* where could he have gone? "Laddy, come on, boy, *please* come to Mama!" She jingled his leash and stared through the gloom and shadows. There, in the depths, a flash of white! Was that Laddy's white ruff of fur? She edged down the graveled sloping shoulder to try to get a closer look, her heel skidding and sending gravel flying with a rattle into the leaf-strewn gully. She held up her cellphone with the screen set to the flashlight app and scanned the woods, which were almost denuded of leaves.

Her heart thudded; there was movement, and was that a flash of white? Who knew what kind of creature it could be. There were all manner of predatory animals in Western New York: bobcats, coyotes, even bears! And her Laddy was out there alone.

"La-ddy! Come on, boy, come to Mama!"

Another flash of white . . . wait, what was that? A falling, shuddering screech echoed out of the woods. Woman in distress? Or eastern screech owl, which *sounded* like a woman in distress? "Hello? Is anyone there? Do you need help?"

Two unblinking lights glared out of the bush; she trained the cell phone screen at it, only to see a big ginger cat staring at her from the edge of the woods.

She put one hand over her thudding heart and sighed. "Okay, well, whoever *you* are, I know for sure Laddy's not here or he'd be chasing you," she said out loud.

She hesitated, but then, feeling a little foolish, she cupped her hands around her mouth and said, "Hey, whoever is there, if you're looking for your orange cat he's here, near the road. He looks fine; I wouldn't worry about it!"

Relieved at the mundane sight of a house cat on the prowl, hoping his owner would find him, she got back in the Wrangler and drove on, still searching. After an hour she finally headed home, where she found Laddy on her porch waiting for her. Happy to see him, she threw her arms around his neck and wept. This would make a good story at the coffee shop in the morning when she went in to work.

• • •

Back street in Autumn Vale
11:06 p.m.

Not much crime in Autumn Vale, William Wilson thought, tap-tap-tapping his way along the deserted back street in the dark. He was late; he *never* missed his wife Sally's bedtime at Golden Acres, his last visit of the day, but he had fallen asleep in front of an old *Matlock* episode, and had woke up with a start. It was past visiting hours but Gogi Grace, the owner, was a sweetie pie who allowed spouses and children to come in at any hour. Through their whole long marriage he always sang to Sally at bedtime: old standards, a little Frank Sinatra, even the Beatles from that time in their life when they were happiest, raising their kids who were *crazy* for the Fab Four. Until this last year it had been in their own home, but his Sally was failing and had needed round-the-clock nursing care. She didn't have long; he knew it. She barely knew he was there, now, just a shell of who she once was, but still . . . he would not miss a single bedtime song.

Tonight he would sing "Yesterday," and she would close her eyes, not able to see his tears at the mournful words. It made a good lullaby if you discounted the sadness threaded through it.

Gosh, he was late! His big dial watch with the light-up face that his kids gave him showed the time, and he was l-a-t-e *late!* Maybe a shortcut was warranted. He stopped at a little alley not many knew about, a few houses long, no sidewalks. It was named Chandler Lane, and cut two minutes off his walking time to Golden Acres. Making a quick decision—nothing wrong with his brain, even if his hip joints weren't so good!—he cut down the alley. The single streetlight was out, darn it! He'd report it in the morning. Or tell Gogi, who had the ear of the town council. But he knew the way, and his cane would support him as long as he was careful not to stumble on a piece of loose asphalt or gravel.

A car pulled into the alley, headlights off, and William moved into the shadows, not wishing to stop and talk if it was someone he knew, and aware he'd make an easy target if it was a hoodlum. But the car simply glided to a stop. A man got out, beeped the lock, then, in an odd gesture, leaned back to the car, thrust his arm in through the open window and tossed something inside. It gave him an odd feeling in the pit of his stomach. What was going on?

The man—*was* it a man? It was someone tall, for sure—then slipped away, hurriedly, shiftily, stealthily, disappearing into the gloom. A dog barked. A security light flashed on. Someone shouted. Another light came on. William stayed in the shadows a moment, but the fellow was gone. He moved on, but as he passed the car he bent over and glared at the license plate, shining his watch face at it for a trickle of light. Hmph. Not local; he could tell by the letters. He examined the car further and saw the telltale barcode in the window; could be a toll or parking sticker, or it could be a rental car. He shrugged. The person's behavior was peculiar, but William was late.

He filed the incident in the back of his mind and ran through the lyrics for "Yesterday," so he could get it right to sing to his Sally.

• • •

Autumn Vale
11:09

Damn security light, going on again! John got up to see what critter had triggered it and spotted a leg . . . or what *looked* like a leg of someone climbing his fence. Moving swiftly, he limped out onto the back porch in time to hear a rustle of brush and a muffled expletive as someone tripped in his neighbor's yard and fell into the honey locust hedge, thick with thorns, *his* motion detector light also going off, and then the one in the *next* yard, like a goldarned string of timed lighting on a runway. That was the problem with living along Chandler Lane . . . too damn dark!

"Hey, who's there?" he yelled. "Get offa my property!" A dog started barking.

Damn nasty kids, cutting through his yard *again*. John called the police and then, phone in hand, checked his security camera for footage of the intruder. Ah, there it was! He babbled to the police dispatcher that he had sighted an intruder in his yard but the culprit had escaped and had cut through other yards.

"Did he break into your home or car, sir?"

"Well, no," John admitted.

"So, he or she cut through your yard but didn't do any damage?"

"Well, I don't know unless I go out and take a look, do I? But I'm not about to march out there and have a look at eleven oh dark at night, am I? What kinda fool you think I am?"

There was silence for a long moment, then the police dispatcher said in that patronizing voice John recognized from a hundred other calls, "Sir, I don't think our officer can come out at this moment for a simple trespass when the trespasser has already left. We have no way of knowing—"

"But I have video footage!"

"Okay, sir; have you looked at it?"

"Yes."

"Can you see the trespasser's face?"

"Well, no."

"Any identifying marks? Tattoos? Piercing?"

"It's too far away and too dark, but the fellow is—"

"So it *is* a man?"

"Well, I don't know. Damn kids all wear hoodies and jeans. It could be anyone!"

There was silence on the other end, and then a sigh.

"Forget it, just *forget* it!" John shrieked into the telephone, and slammed the receiver down. What did he pay taxes for, if no one was going to take his calls seriously? He'd called seven times in the last month and the cops hadn't come out for a single one of the calls.

Time for Leno . . . no, wait . . . Leno wasn't on anymore. Time for whatever late-night idiot was on TV and another shot of the best friend a man could have, Jim Beam.

Fourteen

The day had been too long, too busy, and I could *not* sleep. About eleven thirty I rose and headed downstairs, planning to go through the kitchen and to the back door to call Becket, but instead, in the great hall, I surprised Pam Bellini coming in, still dressed. I tried not to react as irritated as I was—I don't like the guests wandering about the property at all hours, but we *had* told them where to find the key to make sure to lock up after themselves—and simply said hello. She murmured that she hadn't been able to sleep and was out for a walk, then slipped past me, heading upstairs.

A walk in the freezing cold and with nowhere to go. Hmm. She smelled like tobacco. I pulled my housecoat more tightly around myself and tied it at the waist, then went out to the front terrace to call Becket. Nada. When I returned upstairs I heard footsteps and a door close; if that was Pam she sure had taken her time getting to her room. One of the guests could have used the hall bathroom, I supposed, though why they would when all the rooms I'd given them have washrooms I couldn't fathom. Or was someone room hopping? I smiled in the dark, picturing Alain sneaking in to see Darcie, or Lachlan creeping around to meet with Gilda.

I tried to sleep in my pretty turret room, like a princess with no crown, but couldn't and finally ended up scrolling through texts on my phone, sending a late-night kissy text to Virgil, and a note to a friend in the city. I got up again at one and sat in my comfy chair by the window in my room. It looks toward the forest, and I watched out the window for a while in case the moonlight showed me a glimpse of Becket. I thought I saw movement at one point along the forest edge; it may have been Becket, but it was more likely another nocturnal animal wandering. We have coyotes and other critters all around us.

I then entertained myself with going through pictures on my phone, but finally got bored. The further sleep fled, the more I worried about being exhausted the next day, which led to more wakefulness and a bout of worrying about the Wynter Woods project. I needed tea, and a full carafe was in the kitchen for that reason. I padded downstairs again. Pish came in the front door and followed me to the kitchen. "Hey, you," I whispered. I don't know why, but when it's dark and the house is quiet, I always whisper.

"What are you doing up, dear heart?" he said and hugged me.

He smelled deliciously of cigar smoke and wine. I explained about Becket, and missing Virgil, and my insomnia. "Did you have a good time?" I asked as I poured a steaming cup from the carafe of tea. He had that relaxed happily inebriated look in his eyes.

"I had a delightful time." He sighed. "I'm so happy that we have the houses there now . . . it's not so lonely."

I smiled. "You should not have walked home alone, though, my dear. Not drunk, anyway." If he had stumbled or hurt himself . . . I sighed. I worry too much. "Did you see anyone out and about?"

He hung up his coat on a hook and turned back to me. "I *felt* like there was someone nearby, but I didn't *see* a soul."

I heard a door close and headed out to the great hall in time to see a flash of white at the top of the stairs. Someone else coming in? What were we, Grand Central? I ascended with Pish, we kissed goodnight and I headed to my room to sip tea, scroll through more texts, and try to sleep.

I tossed and turned and got up again about two or three. I descended, paced the kitchen, got a book from the library, called the cat, then went back to bed. As I closed my door I heard a bang and jumped, running out to the hall, but saw nothing and no one. My sleeplessness was probably caused by multiple events all at once, first, my cat. Becket had been out all night before, though seldom in the last year or so. He was probably fine; *I* was the wreck. This is, after all, the cat who spent an entire year living in the wild, and yet I worry about him as if he's a dewy-eyed kitten. Then there was sleeping in the castle when I had become accustomed to my house by the woods, with Virgil's protective arm flung over me. Then there was a castle full of people I wasn't sure I liked all that much. It was too much all at once.

I willed myself to sleep for a few hours. Sheer exhaustion proved the final antidote to insomnia. I rose bleary-eyed at six and slumped at the trestle table sipping strong coffee, hoping caffeine would carry me through the day. I started a to-do list but got no further than labeling it *To Do* before pausing, tapping the pen against my lower lip and staring into space. I flexed my shoulders, trying to ease the tension that was building between my shoulder blades. I was still troubled by Lizzie's gloomy assertion that *something* was wrong. Too much had gone horribly in the last three years, and even recently, to take her feelings lightly. My lingering sense of doom was probably exacerbated by the restless, weary night.

Lynn and I put together the breakfast buffet and I spent a couple of hours replenishing the warming trays and making more coffee. People drifted in and out over breakfast, wan and weary. It looked like no one had slept well except for Alain Primeau, who was full of sparkling energy, and Lachlan, who came back from a run sweaty and energetic, with a big smile.

Janice brought Lizzie to the castle, telling me that Patricia was doing the Costco run alone in her SUV because there wasn't nearly as much stuff to pick up this time. Lizzie immediately joined the camera crew to shadow them in her official gofer intern position. The morning wore on. Pish, sleepy after an evening of rare indulgence, drifted into the kitchen midmorning. He noticed my worried expression as he made his coffee. "What is wrong, my darling?"

"Becket is still not back!" That worry morphed into me fretting out loud about Lizzie's assertion that something indefinable that had not happened yet was wrong on this shoot.

"What does she think is wrong?"

"I don't know. Something feels off, but it's so vague that—"

Anne bustled in, much more wide awake than she had been first thing, and clutching what I suspected was her fourth or fifth coffee. "Has anyone seen Gilda? She was supposed to be doing interviews today of the last remaining contestants. And she was *also* supposed to clear preliminary text with me concerning her article."

"I haven't seen her this morning. Have you checked her room? She had already gone to bed when I checked last night."

"She's not answering when I knock, and her door is locked."

I felt that familiar quiver in my belly and could not ignore it. I shook my head at myself; I was being an alarmist. "She must have overslept," I said confidently. "It seemed like everyone in the castle was up and about all night and maybe she was as restless as I was. I'll run up and open the door so we can get her up." Anne and Pish followed me. I rattled the key in the lock, dreading what I'd find, but it was most definitely anticlimactic. Her bed was made up, her purse and laptop were gone, though her suitcase remained, and the room was neat. All evidence pointed to a woman who had departed, though not in haste.

"What's going on?" Anne said, scanning the room, hands on hips.

"She told me she'd be coming and going . . . that she'd have to go back to Rochester," I said, turning to face the producer.

"She wasn't supposed to go until tonight or tomorrow," Anne said with a frown, plucking at the bedcover.

"I would bet that she got a hot tip and scooted off to follow up. Is her rental car still here?"

Anne's eyes lit up. "Good thought! We'll check that and I'll text her, too." She bustled away, already thumbing a text to the writer.

While I was upstairs, I checked in at the styling and wardrobe rooms. Lynn was busy, so I curled up in a chair to watch for a few minutes. She had arranged the larger room with two distinct dressing areas created with movable screens, men's clothes on one side, women's on the other. It had been impractical to have separate rooms for men and women, she explained, because she could not be in two places at once. As a former model Lynn was in her element, surrounded by racks and racks of clothes and accessories. She had discovered within herself a talent for choosing the exact right outfit to suit not just the person, but the situation they were going to be in.

Darcie's video was to be shot by the piano, so Lynn chose for her informal shoot a pretty cocktail-length dress that floated around the lovely young woman like a dream, exposing her slim white arms. Pearls adorned her décolletage and her blonde fluffy hair. Darcie whirled in front of the mirror, hugged Lynn, and headed downstairs.

Primeau emerged from behind the dressing screen in a dark silk suit with a dashing silk scarf, similar in style to the one Daffyd Rhys perpetually wore. Lynn shook her head. "Too elegant. We'll save this suit for the next more formal shoot. Go back and change into this," she said, handing him a hanger with a trucker jacket in brown faux suede and a pair of slim-cut caramel chinos. When he came back out she nodded and looped a muted plaid wool scarf around his neck, adjusting it and finally smiling.

"Mademoiselle, you are a genius," he said, admiring himself in the full-length mirror. He looked into it, then caught my eye and winked.

I smiled. It was good to see this aspect of the competition going so well, at least. In each case I thought Lynn found the right extra touches. I had brought Lynn tea, which we shared. She seemed contented but subdued. Maybe she was as tired as I was.

• • •

The morning dragged on. Sparrow, dark circles under her eyes, slouched at the trestle table at times, so bleary she was either drunk again or exhausted. I was thankful to Janice and Patricia; with those two women in the kitchen I was able to take care of myriad other tasks that continually occurred to me. My list of daily duties was lengthening. About noon I mounted the stairs and was about to start a survey of the rooms and bathrooms to make sure they were all clean when I heard screaming in the wardrobe room. I followed the noise to find Lynn and Pam having it out, while Brontay watched avidly from the sidelines, dressed in a springy blouse and cool jeans.

Pam, holding a hanger with a filmy dress, shook it and said, "I want her dressed like a star, not a tot."

"Pam, Brontay is fifteen, not twenty-five, and the show is going to be on in spring. That dress is clingy and too old for her. And this is the informal shoot . . . it's going to be done outside the dining room windows. She'd look like an *idiot* in that dress."

Anne, looking frazzled and worried, was finally summoned. She supported Lynn's judgment and had the final say.

I stayed out of it and it was soon over. As Anne passed, I asked, "So did you find out, is Gilda's car gone from the parking lot?" She nodded, fidgeting with her phone. "Then Gilda probably forgot she was supposed to do interviews today, or had an emergency she had to take care of, right?"

"I wish she'd told me, or that she'd answer my messages," Anne groused. "The phone is going straight to voice mail, and now even her voice mail is full."

I got busy and the day wore on. During a lull I reviewed what Patricia had brought from Costco, checking it against my inventory and requirements spreadsheet. We decided that we probably had enough of the drygoods if the shoot lasted only as long as the producers said it would. There would be supplies arriving from Binny's and the butcher, which Janice would be there to accept and sign for.

Pish and I had business that did not involve the current crew, so we holed up in his office for a while, composing press statements for the ground-breaking ceremony we were going to hold the week before Thanksgiving while we had Liliana and the rest of the LSO and LOC folks available. We were planning to capitalize on the growing popularity of the video Lizzie had uploaded before its viral nature was cured, so to speak, so in two weeks while we had folks gathered for the groundbreaking, we were holding a quickly organized charity benefit ball in the castle ballroom to help fund renovations of the carriage house, which would become a residence. It was an enormous project to put together quickly, but we could do it. Wynter Castle was made for large gatherings.

Pish and I finally descended about two thirty in the afternoon to the discordant sounds of an argument in the great hall. Lachlan and Darcie were standing face-to-face shouting. Something about bathing, and being inconsiderate, and other garbled rudenesses.

"What's going on?" I asked, stepping between the two combatants. Lachlan merely looked irritated, but Darcie was red-faced and furious. "What are you two fighting about now?"

"The same thing!" he said, throwing up his hands. "She's frayed to bits because I was using the bathtub."

"It's so rude and he's laughing it off," she cried. "Like it's not a big—"

"Because it is *not* a big deal and you're being a doss radgepacket." He turned to me, his face drawn with an irritated scowl. "She's pure skyrocket," he said, descending into Scottish slang so obscure I had no clue what he meant.

"I don't know what *any* of that means," I said. "Explain!"

"It means she's pure evil and crazy."

Tears stood in her eyes. "You took *hours*!"

"I did *not*! Stop lying, Darcie. When I came to find you to tell you the tub was free you were nowhere to be found and your roommate was fast asleep. Sparrow says you went out. Where the hell were you?"

Darcie's face turned an interesting array of colors, starting with pasty pale beige and then flushing with a dark red, just on the cheekbones, then settling on a pink midway between. "I was . . . having a cig on the terrace."

"In the dark. In the middle of the night. In the freezing cold."

"It's none of your business where I was, Lachlan."

"It is if you're going to accuse me of ridiculous things like taking hours in a bath."

"It wasn't the middle of the night, it was—"

"Come on, Darcie, where *were* you?"

"*Enough*, children!" Pish said, putting up both hands. They stopped.

"I cannot believe you two are fighting over a *bathtub* like a pair of spoiled toddlers," I said. Perhaps it was the tension of the competition that was getting to them.

"Darcie, you may use *my* bathtub tonight, if you wish." Pish then turned to Lachlan. "But that doesn't absolve you. I *know* you were in there a rather long time—" He stopped and held up one hand as Lachlan sputtered. "And you've been rude to this young lady. This is our home," he said, including me in his warm look. "Here, we value consideration and courtesy. I would appreciate it if you would give Darcie her time in the bath tonight. Will you do that?" He said it much better than I would have, a born diplomat.

Lachlan, with a chagrined look, nodded and gave a little bow. "Thank you, Mr. Lincoln, for a salutary lesson in courtesy." He turned to his fellow contestant, hands clasped in front of him in a prayerful attitude. "Darcie, lass, I *humbly* apologize. Tonight, the bath is yours." He smiled, but there was a wicked gleam in his eyes. "And it's none o' *my* affair where you were in the wee hours o' the night. In the freezing cold. Alone?"

I shot him an annoyed look. His humility was staged, his apology insincere, and that last bit unnecessary. I glanced over at Darcie. Her impotent rage was still apparent, and I'll confess I did wonder . . . where *had* she been? Was she the flash of white I saw in the early hours? Or the thud I heard another time? We're in the middle of nowhere; where could she have been?

In that moment, though, my unease and fretfulness melted away as my darling Virgil entered on a blast of cold November wind, trailed by a ruffled and unrepentant Becket. I wasn't sure who to make the most fuss over, and finally picked up the cat and hugged my husband, as Becket squirmed and growled. "Where *were* you!" I said, setting him down on the floor. The cat, not my husband.

"You know where I was; Rochester."

"Not you, *him*," I said, laughing and flapping my hand at the cat, who was stalking toward the kitchen, throwing perturbed looks over his shoulder at me. "He scooted out last night and hasn't been home since. He doesn't do that often anymore and it worried me."

Becket didn't answer my question. He's funny that way. He simply retreated to the warmth of the kitchen. Janice fussed over him and fed him a bowl full of turkey and chicken scraps. When he was done eating and Virgil, too, had been properly spoiled and fed by my opera-loving zaftig friend, we drove back to our house to have a proper welcome home, just my husband and me, carrying Becket, who was clearly as tired as I was. On the way I saw our friend Gordy Shute, who was steadily working on the fall cleanup of the property. He had his uncle's tractor and was mowing the edge of the woods. We waved and continued on our way.

After some lovin', a nap and a shower, I had to get back to the castle to start dinner preparations, as well as the interview Sparrow and Anne wanted to do with me as owner of the castle. I did a proper blow-out of my hair—that takes a while; it's long and thick—and dressed carefully in a long skirt, a tunic sweater belted at the waist, with black ankle boots.

I ducked my head in the office before heading back out. "Virgil, I'm going back to the castle to make sure the heathens get their dinner. You know where to find me."

He smiled and nodded, then picked up his phone. He had a lot of business to catch up on. I slipped out the front door, not noticing that Becket had escaped until I saw him loping across the grassy expanse like a cheetah, toward the arboretum woods that lines my property along the road. "Becket . . . *Becket!* Damn cat," I muttered, then shouted, "I won't be staying up tonight worrying about you!" *What is wrong with him?* I wondered. Normally after a night out he sleeps all day. "And stay away from the tractor!" I yelled again, waving at Gordy, who was now clearing brush.

My first task was the Rose Parlor interview with Sparrow. It was supposed to be about my delight in opera and how welcome the *Opera DivaNation* competition was to Wynter Castle, as well as promo for our future ventures, but Sparrow had discovered online news pieces about the murders on my property, especially the one a few years back during a Halloween party, and grilled me on that more than anything. I kept my cool and answered in monosyllables, leaving with a rigid smile on my face.

I thought back to what she had drunkenly confessed about tricking people into saying unfortunate things. Surely the point, though, was not to alert them to what she was up to *while* she was doing it? Her questioning seemed clumsy to me, as I recalled how upset so many of the contestants had been after her maladroit interviewing. Was she *trying* to upset the contest?

I entered the dining room, intent on complaining to Anne. They were in the middle of a technical furor; something was not working as it should. The only contestant there was Kamile, who was awaiting her turn. She was wearing, as usual, a lovely dress that she was in danger of ruining by holding my big ginger cat on her lap. So Becket hadn't gone far this time and had returned to the castle; what a relief! I sat in the chair next to her and we talked.

After chatting, I glanced over at her. She seemed so relaxed, with Becket lolling on his back on her lap. "Do you have any pets?"

"No. I have no time, and no home."

That sounded so sad. "Maybe you will soon? Are you staying in America?"

She shrugged. "Whatever Uncle will want, I suppose."

"Kamile, you have a choice, surely. You're old enough now to take control of your career."

She flicked a glance my way then shook her head. "It's not so easy as that. Uncle Moze has always guided my career and we are too . . . entangled."

Entangled. What did that mean? I opened my mouth to ask, but then she picked up something from her lap and held it up for Becket to bat at. "What is that?"

"A bow," Kamile said, holding it out to me.

"Where did you get it?"

"Your cat brought it to me and dropped it at my feet."

A trophy, then; I know my cat. Sometimes it was a dead thing, sometimes a leaf, sometimes a found object. I took it from her and turned it over in my hand. It was black ribbon shaped in a bow, and glittered. Also, it was fastened tightly to a hair clip that still held a clutch of wiry hairs coiled around the clip. I had seen it recently holding back the curly mane on Gilda's head.

Had she dropped it as she departed? I rubbed it with my thumb and mud crumbled and dropped off. Odd.

Anne approached, motioning Kamile to return to the staging area while she spoke on the phone. "No, I told you, I don't know where she is and . . . what do you mean, what did *I* do with her? *Nothing!* . . . No, I can't help you. We had a day of interviews and she . . . what? . . . She was supposed to check in with you?" Anne listened, as Kamile glided over to the staging area and took her spot by the fireplace hearth. I met the producer's gaze and she shrugged as she listened. "Look, I don't know what to tell you. Gilda was here until she wasn't. As far as I know she left last night, driving her rental car, with her purse and her laptop and her notes . . . no, she didn't say a word to *anyone*." She tapped the Hang Up button on her phone screen and sighed.

"What's going on?" I asked.

"That was Gilda's editor at *Modern Entertainment Monthly*. She was supposed to be sending them files with her information—everything she has so far—for fact checking, but she hasn't sent them anything, and she isn't answering their calls. I told her—the editor—that we don't know where she is either. She's not answering calls or texts and I'm getting really *really* cranky. My own crew I expect to have to ride herd on, but not independents." She frowned down at her phone. "It's not like her."

"When did they last hear from her?"

"She talked to her editor yesterday and promised she'd send the files before the end of the day. The editor expected them to come in late last night, Gilda's usual habit. I told her we saw her here until late. But after that she didn't talk to her editor, or send her a note, or call or anything . . . nothing. Zip." She heaved a sigh and trudged off to yell at Lizzie for getting in her way. Lizzie swiftly ducked out of yelling range.

I looked down at the bow in my hands. This was Gilda's hair bow. It had been retrieved by my cat, who had spent the night out, most likely in the woods on our property. He had headed there just an hour before, bringing back this muddy bow. Had he found the bow in the castle?

Or outside somewhere. That was more likely, given the mud.

And . . . where was Gilda?

Fifteen

"Virgil?"

"Yup."

I was reassured by his gruff voice on the other end of the line. "Virgil, we have a problem at the castle. Gilda is missing." I had a knot in the pit of my stomach. I flattened my hand over my belly and swallowed hard, willing myself to calm down. As I explained the circumstances, including the bow I knew was Gilda's, he listened and did not brush aside my concerns.

"Have you checked the whole castle?" he asked.

"Not the *whole* castle . . . not the attic, or the cellar."

"Do it, but take someone with you. I'm on my way. I'll call Dewayne and we'll come and search the grounds. Ask Anokhi, Liliana and the rest if they've seen her . . . discreetly, of course. She may be at one of the houses working, you never know."

"I can get Pish to do that."

"Question: Becket was out all last night. Could he have been in the woods?"

"I'm assuming that's where he was. You know what he's like; he gets these fits where he remembers his life during the year he was lost and he spends a night skulking around in the forest." I hesitated, but I had to know what he was thinking, afraid he was on my wavelength. "Why?"

"I stopped in the coffee shop on my way home and a woman who works in the store was telling a customer about her weird experience, seeing a big ginger cat at the edge of the woods, and hearing what she thought was a woman's scream."

I gulped, and my breathing sped up. This was worse than what I had been thinking. "Was she sure it was a woman's scream?"

"She told the customer that at the time she thought it might be an owl that sounds like a woman . . . I think she said an eastern screech owl. But—"

"It could have been a woman. It *could* have been Gilda."

"Look, it's likely not. She's a journalist; she probably took off on a gossip-finding mission. You know what writers are like . . . flaky."

"Gilda was a dedicated professional, Virgil, not some dippy gossip columnist. I don't like this. I don't like it at *all*."

"Take it easy; we don't know anything yet," he said, then hung up.

I told Pish my worries. Gilda had not gone to the party the night before—which was one possibility, as she *had* been invited—and he hadn't seen her after dinner. Lizzie and I searched the attic first and then the cellar. Gilda was in neither place, nor had Liliana or the others seen her, Pish reported to me when we next met.

I put on a sweater and headed outside. The window cleaners had set up scaffolding and were working on the diamond-paned gothic windows above the double doors, which would take a while. Dani came down the ladder from the scaffold when I beckoned and said she hadn't seen anyone matching Gilda's description.

"While I have you," Dani said as I turned away, "has your partner looked into the missing stuff from our van?"

"You gave him a list?" I said, turning back to her.

"Yeah, but I haven't heard anything." She chafed her red hands, which must have been freezing cold. "Oh, and another thing, someone keeps moving our stuff, and it's getting a little—"

"Look, I don't have time right now," I said, on edge and almost rude.

"Well, neither do I." She looked huffy for a moment, but then examined my expression. What she saw there likely told her I was dealing with more than someone interfering with her property. "Okay. Get back to me about the stuff, if you can. We'll be finishing up tomorrow, I hope."

I returned inside. Pacing in the great hall I eyed Becket, who had a habit of going back to his favorite spots and retrieving trophies. The woman had supposedly seen him on the edge of our forest, by the road. "Sweetie, if only you could talk," I said to the cat. That gave me an idea. I called Virgil—he was on his way out the door—told him what I had learned, and asked him a question. He promised to ask Dewayne, who was more expert in many facets of investigation and surveillance.

"But first," he said, "I'll start looking. Maybe Gordy has seen something. He's still out there finishing up for the day. At the very least I'll rope him in to help search."

Pish joined me in the great hall and stopped me from pacing. Hands on my shoulders, he gazed steadily into my eyes. "My darling, there is no point in worrying until we know more."

Jittery and anxious, I said, "I have a bad feeling, Pish."

"I'm not saying you're wrong, but let's focus all that energy on finding Gilda."

I nodded and took a deep breath. He was right. Even if she was there, in the woods, she *could* still be alive. But my mind turned inevitably to . . . *why* was she out there? It could not be a case of wandering off, since her car and purse and laptop were gone too. I took a deep shaky breath. "I'm changing into jeans and going out to look. Virgil is on his way, and he's getting Gordy to help."

Janice had dinner covered. I took her aside and told her, in confidence, what was going on. I should have spoken to Anne; she knew Gilda far better than I did, after all. But we didn't know *anything* yet. I didn't want the entire crew and cast of the show to be upset if there was no reason. It was still possible that Gilda had driven off after a tip and had not been paying attention to her phone all day.

But that wasn't likely.

I went up to my castle bedroom, changed into jeans, a hoodie, cable-knit cardigan and hiking boots and slipped out to join my husband and Gordy at the edge of the arboretum. I knew those woods as well as anyone and better than most. We began at the path in, where Gordy had already mown the long weeds and cleared the brush. There were many paths and dead ends and I quickly began to doubt myself. Gilda's bow had likely dropped off her head when she was taking a walk, and Becket retrieved it.

We searched for an hour, calling Gilda's name, but we didn't find her, nor did we see any sign of her. We went back to where we started and I sat down on a log at the edge of the woods as my husband glanced at his phone and Gordy went to work clearing more of the sticks, stacking them in a neat pile.

"I called Urquhart," Virgil said. He glanced at the darkening sky, the chill November twilight fast approaching, a purple bruised look to gathering clouds that foretold rain overnight. Shadows loomed and swayed as the treetops tossed on a high wind that we couldn't feel at ground level. "You said the woman was driving a rental car, so I have him checking—informally, of course; it's too early to even call in a missing person report, but he's doing this as a favor to me—with every car rental place in a hundred-mile radius."

An official police request would get a faster response than

anything we could do, and I appreciated it. If Gilda was headed back to Rochester her car wasn't off the road between the castle and Autumn Vale; Janice would have seen it. But if she was headed somewhere else, who knew? It could be in a ditch in the other direction. There were miles of roads that led to New York City and a thousand other places.

Dewayne arrived with his equipment and drove his pickup to where we waited at the forest path entrance. I retrieved my cat from the castle, along with the harness I use when I take him to the vet. I shivered, wishing I had worn a coat, but I didn't want to go back again. Dewayne, sitting on the tailgate of his pickup, clipped a micro camera like the ones they use to track wildlife to the cat harness. I held Becket down and with much fussing and growling on both our parts, I got the harness on him and buckled. If the matter wasn't so serious I would have been laughing at his expression of wounded chagrin. As I expected, as soon as I released him he loped into the woods and away from the weirdoes imprisoning him.

Dewayne brought up the livestreaming camera on his tablet. We were treated to shadowy video, mostly of the ground, as Becket sniffed, then ran, stopping to sniff again and again. He would pause, look around, go a few feet, pause again, pounce, then take off like a shot, running and leaping over dead trees, trying to ditch the harness. He rolled and rubbed, again trying to ditch the harness, but it held fast, though it was sliding sideways. He climbed a stump and sharpened his nails, then backed down the stump and investigated the smells at the base of it, then took off again.

It was late, and the sun was already angling, creating long shadows that cast eerie patterns on the unkempt grass and brush along the edge of the forest. Clouds were gathering and the sky turned lilac, with puffs of gray like dirty cotton balls. The cold was needle sharp, poking icy skeletal fingers through the open weave of my cable-knit sweater. I shivered again and Virgil, my hero, took off his jacket and threw it around my shoulders. I cast him a grateful glance. We all looked over Dewayne's shoulder as he monitored Becket's movements.

"Do you recognize any of this area, Merry?" Dewayne asked.

"Some of it, yes. Look, this is a rise," I said, pointing to the monitor. "The tree he's under is the red oak . . . I can tell by the leaves on the ground. I know where that is." It was a planned forest with a variety of native trees planted as a document of the natural roots of Western New York. With the help of arborists recommended by SUNY and Cornell we had started mapping the arboretum.

I watched the video as Becket continued on. "I know that one!" I cried, pointing to a tree ahead of him. He was going toward the far edge of the forest, near the highway. I looked up at Virgil then to Dewayne; this was most likely the wildest of wild-goose chases but I could *not* let this go. "Can you drive the truck around to the road, while we watch Becket?" I asked Dewayne. "I know where he's headed."

"What are the chances that Becket will find Gilda?" Virgil asked.

"A hundred to one," I admitted. "But there's always that one."

My husband nodded, hugged me, and jumped off the tailgate. He held out his hand. "Keys, Dewayne. I'll drive. You need to keep track of the camera on our critter."

"Look after my baby," his friend said with a wink and tossed him the keys.

Gordy and I scooted behind our friend into the bed of the pickup as the light waned and changed, while Dewayne still sat on the tailgate, legs dangling, holding onto the tablet. We watched over his shoulder as we pitched and bounced our way across the field toward the castle driveway. I looked up and could see, at the castle, a couple of people out on the terrace looking our way. My heart was pounding and I felt sick.

I felt a hand on my shoulder and looked up at Gordy, his sweet, goofy, high-foreheaded narrow face with a serious expression. He nodded and I took a deep breath; it was a reminder not to worry about anything but the task at hand. Virgil carefully drove the truck down the lane, around the twisty corners and through the new stone gate as we watched the video.

I knew where Becket was going. We crept along the darkening road, shaded by the forest wall on one side and a rock face on the other, until I thought we were at the right place. I scootched back and banged on the back window of the truck; Virgil pulled to a stop. He got out of the truck and joined us at the back. Dewayne leaned over and with one hand unlatched a kit box in the bed of the truck. He rustled around and tossed me three headbands, all equipped with headlamps. "You're going to need them," he said, indicating how dark the screen was getting, the weak light from the camera almost completely faded as the battery conserved energy to stream video.

Gordy, Virgil and I donned the headlamps and turned them on. I hunted along the edge of the graveled shoulder, directing the beam of light until I found what I was looking for. "There," I said to my husband, as I scanned about ten or twelve feet ahead of where we had stopped the truck. "This is likely where the woman looking for her dog scaled down the slope to see Becket."

There were heel marks in the gravel, and a slide spot where she had likely slipped, and skid marks where her car had taken off, spraying gravel. I started forward, but he put out one arm to stop me.

"You may be right, but those skid marks could be something else," Virgil said grimly. "There was no reason for her to gun her engine to leave."

I felt a chill down my backbone as I met his steady, sober gaze. He was right. My husband was a cop for many years and he thought about things I hadn't considered. "We need to protect that spot . . . leave that area undisturbed," I said, my voice a ghostly whisper.

"Let's approach the woods from another entry. Gordy, you coming with us?" He clapped our friend on the shoulder and gazed at him steadily.

"Yes, sir," Gordy said, and nodded.

"Hey, Merry, come here!" Dewayne yelled.

I carefully circled off the gravel onto the paved road and went to the back of the pickup. "What's up?"

Dewayne pointed to where Becket and the camera had stopped. Becket was sniffing something. It was fuzzy and hard to see; the forest was getting dark. "What is that?" I asked.

Quietly, Dewayne said, "I think it's hair."

I let out a cry that sounded animal; it erupted from my throat and the two guys came running. I clutched on to Virgil's arm as Dewayne pointed to the moving grainy video. "We need to hurry; I think that's Gilda's hair," I said, tugging my husband's arm.

"You can stay here," Virgil said to me.

"No, we need to find her." My voice sounded guttural and strange. "Becket will respond to me. I know what to say, how to get him to answer."

Dewayne handed out larger flashlights. He would monitor the video and call Sheriff Urquhart as we entered the forest. Focusing on the task at hand, I led the way.

I paused once we had made our way in about a hundred or so feet. "Be-cket!" I yelled.

"Hey, you don't want him to come to you!" Virgil warned.

"He'll yowl first . . . then—" We heard the sound, his answer, an unearthly howl, echoed back by another sound. "That's him and . . . something else." The owl . . . it did sound like a scream! Maybe Becket's yowling set it off.

Gordy started off. He was exceptionally good at tracking sound and soon we were following *him*. We heard Becket again, then that weird shriek, and entered a familiar clearing.

"This is it," I said softly. I played the flashlight beam around the darkening forest until I saw the flash of cat eyes reflected, and the orange of my cat. "There!"

We approached and there, slumped over a log, was Gilda, facedown, arms extended, her hair a tangled mess. "No!" I sobbed.

Virgil carefully approached, and I followed, crouching down by the body.

She was sodden after a light rain, her clothes saturated. Around her were a couple of scraps of wet paper and crystal beads from a bracelet. The back of her head was bloody, as was her torso, her kinky hair a tousled matted mess. How had her bow been ripped out of her hair? I tried to focus on anything other than the horrible fact that the poor woman was—

"She's alive!" Virgil shouted, holding a finger to her throat.

I fell to my knees in the soaking leaf-strewn muck and wailed in relief.

Sixteen

The ambulance pulled away into the night, sirens screeching, Anne Parkinson following toward the hospital in Ridley Ridge. Gilda was clinging to life, her temperature low, suffering hypothermia and unconscious. She had been beaten and suffered a knife wound that should have killed her but didn't. Virgil held me in his arms, close to him, as I shivered in the growing chill of an autumn night despite his jacket around my shoulders. Urquhart was taking statements, the blue and white lights on top of his car reflected in a pattern on the wall of forest and opposing wall of rock on our narrow road.

I explained from the beginning. Urquhart was puzzled why I jumped to the conclusion, as he put it, that Gilda was in the woods. I stiffened, then, as Virgil hugged me, I relaxed. Urquhart was doing his job. I would ignore the sheriff's insinuation that I magically guessed her fate.

"Gilda is a professional, Sheriff; she has a reputation for being fierce and hard-nosed, and I know from speaking with her that she is ambitious. She promised her editor notes for the fact checker and she did not turn them in. She was scheduled to do interviews today, and she was nowhere to be found. Then Becket came in with her hair bow—"

"Was there something special about the hair bow? I mean, it's just a black hair bow."

I sighed, but again heeded Virgil's quick side hug. "Sheriff, trust me, hair bows, despite their current popularity among prepubescent girls, are *not* a popular hair ornament. A woman is more likely to use a claw clip or barrette, but not a bow. I had noticed it when Gilda used it. And it had curly hair in it; I *knew* it was hers. For Becket, trophies are things he has brought in from outdoors, usually a dead mouse or vole, but sometimes a found object."

He nodded.

"Taken together, and with my knowledge of my cat's tendency to go wild in the woods once in a while and his overnight absence, I thought there was a good possibility that's where the woman was." Tears welled up and, choking back a sob, I said, "I can't prove it, but I'd bet he stayed with her all night."

He nodded and jotted notes. Then he looked up, his gaze serious, as always. "Merry, you probably saved her life. With temperatures going down to forty and rain expected, she would have died of exposure, especially since she lost a lot of blood." He glanced over at his sergeant, who was speaking with two constables. They would guard the area until daylight allowed a better search. He looked to me and leaned forward. "Don't say I told you, but the car rental agency in Batavia got back to me immediately," he said in a low tone. "Her car was turned in late last night or early this morning, before opening."

"How is that possible when she was here, unconscious?"

He shrugged, tight-lipped, his eyebrows raised. The car was obviously not turned in by Gilda.

"Come on, buddy, who turned in the car?" Virgil asked.

"We don't know. But there is security cam footage we'll be going over," he muttered, glancing over at his deputies, a woman and a man. "The car was parked on the lot and the key put in the locked drop box." I opened my mouth, but he held up one hand. "I can't tell you more. We don't know what time yet or what the video shows."

"One more question," I said. "Were her laptop and purse in the car?"

He paused, meeting my gaze. He was thinking it over and finally, reluctantly, he shook his head. "We have not yet found those items."

"I'm pretty sure they aren't in the castle, but I haven't searched everyone's rooms yet."

"They're being searched right now during dinner."

"That's going to go over well," I remarked dryly. I picked up Becket, who had been freed from his camera halter. I gave him a smooch and murmured that he was a hero and had saved a life. I leaned against Virgil. "Can everyone continue? The singing contest, I mean?"

He nodded. "And they'll be able to return to their rooms *after* we've done our search."

I turned, ready to return to the castle, and noticed a clutch of contestants standing off to one side, watching. It was a long walk down our lane to the road and along the road, but a few were curious enough to make the trek. Kamile, dressed in leggings, boots, and a long sweater that reached mid-thigh, her long hair tied back, stood by herself, arms crossed over her chest. In the weird light thrown by the police car, flashing blue and white, her jutting cheekbones were in stark relief. She looked distraught. Lachlan and Zeb stood together, while Alain, muttering to himself in joual, turned and headed back to the castle, his long strides demonstrating agitation. I joined the group and suggested we all repair to the castle and let the police do their job.

"Is Gilda dead?" Zeb asked anxiously.

"Of course she's not dead, eedjit," Lachlan said acerbically. "They wouldne scream off in an ambulance with the siren goin' if she was."

Zeb glared at the older man with a clear expression of dislike.

"There's no need to be rude, Lachlan," I said. Virgil took Becket from me—the cat is heavy—and took my arm, murmuring that we should return to the castle and maybe the others would follow.

"Aren't we *all* a wee bit upset at this?" Lachlan said, his forehead wrinkled, his voice tight with anxiety. "You canna tell me she just wandered into the woods and fell. She was not a woodsy lass. *Someone* hurt her and left her for dead."

I took a deep breath. I didn't need the contestants cycling into hysteria. "Our police are looking into it, and besides, you'll be safe in the castle."

"Like Gilda was?" he muttered, turning away.

• • •

"I'm staying here with you tonight," Virgil said, leaning back on the bed in my room in the castle, arms behind his head as he watched me change.

"Are you sure? I don't want you to be uncomfortable." My phone, tossed on the bed, kept pinging, more messages from my Autumn Vale friends, no doubt.

"I've been on surveillance in a ratty car for forty-eight hours with a pop bottle for a urinal. It's cute that you think a night in our luxurious bed in the castle will be uncomfortable."

In a Lane Bryant wide-legged ribbed sleep pant (deep wine, if you care about the color) and gold-lace-edged tunic, I dropped down onto the bed beside him and he enfolded me in his arms. I sighed. "I'm so lucky," I whispered against his whiskery chin. "I hope I never take it for granted." We lay like that for a long minute. Then, reluctantly, I heaved myself off the bed and stood, looking down at him. "Pish is waiting in his office. We need to get in front of this and coordinate our response before this gets out to the media. Maybe with luck we can—"

PingPingPing . . . my phone blew up (not literally, but constant pinging, you know) and I picked it up. The news of Gilda's near-death had already been shared on social media and was zooming around the world. Friends of mine in NYC were texting me and asking about it. I sighed. "Too late."

Virgil got up and sat on the edge of the bed, pulling me down to sit next to him. "Ignore them for now." He rubbed my thigh, kissed my cheek. "I hate to say it, but you do get that Lachlan is right? Someone here, in this castle, is likely responsible for Gilda's attack."

To think we were again sharing space with a would-be killer was chilling. I considered my top list of suspects, but was halted by the first name: Moze Markunis. I turned and pulled one leg up under me, facing Virgil. "I've had a hinky feeling in my spine about Moze Markunis. There is something not right about that guy. Poor Kamile freezes up around him. He left last night, but who's to say he really left? He *could* have hung around and lured Gilda out and attacked her, then took her car to Batavia."

"Doing what with *his* car?"

"Maybe he has a confederate."

Virgil nodded, scratching his whiskery chin. "You're right that he can't be counted out just because he left earlier."

"Pish is going to call Gilda's editor in New York in the morning to try to schmooze his way to info. I'll be talking to Sparrow. As associate producer with Anne she ought to know more than we do. I think I'll go into town in the morning and talk to Hannah." Hannah Moore, our local librarian, is the best person I know for doing research and collating the results. Like most librarians she has an insatiable desire for knowledge, a deep understanding of research techniques, and a world-class ability to focus. If anyone could find out more about these people, it would be her.

"I should be talking you out of this," my husband said, with a half smile turning one corner of his mouth up.

"But you're not."

"Nope. Waste of effort. The quickest way to a resolution is if we all tackle this from different aspects. Promise me you won't get in Urquhart's way."

"I solemnly promise that I won't *deliberately* get in his way."

He gave me a narrowed-eyed look.

"What? I won't intentionally get in his way; that's the best I can do." I kissed him, then stood. "Gordy was a real help," I said as he pulled me between his knees and laid his face against my stomach. I threaded my fingers through his thick hair.

"He's a good kid," he murmured. "We've all been tiptoeing around him since the cult camp problems, and it makes him withdraw even further when we do that. So I decided to do my best to treat him normal."

"You make him sound like a teenager. He's thirty, Virgil." I twirled a dark lock of hair around one finger, noticing with pleasure a couple of strands of silver. "You're not that much older." My husband is a little younger than I.

He looked up at me, loosening his hold. "They all seem like children to me: Gordy, Zeke, Hannah. Is that wrong? I've known them since they were little kids, when I was a teenager."

And I knew my husband had matured early; even as a teen he could be counted on in a pinch, his mom had told me. It's what drew him to law enforcement, that need to help in times of trouble, and it's what had made him an effective and competent sheriff. He is one of the good guys. As is Urquhart, I admitted to myself.

There was a tap at my door. "Come in," I called out, moving out of my husband's arms.

Pish entered, looking tired. "I called the hospital and got an update."

"How did you do that when Gilda is not family?"

He flushed pink. "I *may* have gone out once or twice with one of the hospital administrators."

I stared at him. "You sneaky devil. You didn't tell me you were dating. Who is he? What's he like? When do you see him again?"

Pish, looking somber, said, "We only went out twice. I don't think it's going to work out. He's a little younger than I am."

Hand on Virgil's shoulder, I said, "That didn't stop us."

"I don't think a relationship is in our future. *Anyway* . . . Gilda is in critical but stable condition. She's in a coma right now, and they're doing a CT scan and blood tests."

Sobered by the seriousness of the situation, I said, "Thanks, Pish.

I'm going down now and calling a meeting with the contestants. Is Anne back, or is she staying with Gilda?"

"She's staying at the hospital until Gilda's mother can fly in tomorrow."

"Are the police still here?"

"They're still searching the rooms. They asked all the contestants to stay downstairs."

We followed Pish out. I nodded to the police officers—two women and one man—conducting the search as they moved on to the men's room. The male officer, one of the two left from Virgil's time on the force, stiffened and almost saluted, but my husband waved the young fellow off and smiled, telling him to go ahead with our room whenever they needed to.

Downstairs in the dining room I found that the contestants had been joined by technicians who had stayed late to work on the setups for the next day, as well as the judges and mentors, who sat together at a big table in the center. Kamile appeared tearful, eyes watering, while Darcie shivered, standing alone against the wall with her arms crossed. Alain and Zeb sat together, near Lachlan. Pam stood with her arms around her daughter; Brontay was crying into her mom's shoulder. Roma was ghostly pale and grave. Pish went and stood with her, his arm around her shoulders. Giu joined them and linked arms with Pish.

Sparrow asked, her voice trembling, her gaze darting and fearful, "Is Gilda going to be okay?"

I shared a look with Pish and he nodded. "I have unofficial confirmation that she is in critical but stable condition. She's in a coma and they're doing tests. That is literally all we know. Anne is with her until family arrives."

I scanned the room, and the thought that one of these people was a wannabe killer churned in my stomach. I hoped that the police were guarding Gilda well, and I was deeply curious about what she would have to say when she awoke. *If* she awoke.

"You found her, though; how was that possible?" Kamile, her voice sounding strained and weary, watched me with fear in her eyes.

"I'm not going to go into that right now. As the police say, it is an ongoing investigation. We were fortunate to find her."

Lachlan looked disturbed and mistrustful. "I still don't understand how you did it. Did you know she was gone? Were you wandering the woods looking for her? Why didn't you ask us if *we* knew where she was?"

"*Did* you know?" He shook his head. "Any of you?" I scanned the others.

All shook their heads.

"Enough." Pish disengaged himself from his friends. He turned to gaze at the gathered group. "The police have said that you can all go on with the contest, but I think we're done for the evening. It's upsetting, I know. But gossip and speculation are not going to get us anywhere."

Lynn, who had been hanging back, her eyes huge with alarm, put one hand up, and I smiled at her. "If . . . if anyone is particularly upset by this, I know a local therapist who is good. Just . . ." Her voice faded away. But then she took a deep breath and stiffened her backbone. "In case you need help, you know? There is no shame in needing help."

The judges and mentors began to disperse, but Pish took Daffyd Rhys aside, then beckoned me to join them. We moved to a corner, Rhys with a puzzled expression.

"What's up?" I said after greeting Rhys.

"I was thinking about poor Gilda," Pish said with an expressive look at me. "She was invited to the dinner last night but didn't come, as far as we know. Did you see her, Daffyd?"

"No, not at all." The handsome tenor stared at Pish, his expression perplexed. "Why do you ask?"

"You disappeared for a time during the evening, and I thought you might have taken a walk and saw her. Or spoke to her?"

I examined the Welshman carefully. He appeared concerned but not worried. "You're mistaken, Pish. I was there all evening."

"Are you sure?" I said. "Maybe you stepped out to take a call, or for a walk, or . . . are you absolutely *sure* you didn't leave the house for a time?"

He had stiffened and glared at me with a haughty glare. "What precisely are you suggesting, Miss Wynter?"

"I'm not suggesting anything, I'm *saying* you were missing from the party. No one knew where you were."

He stiffened and drew himself up, tossing one end of his perpetual silk scarf over his shoulder. "I resent your insinuation, young lady."

"Hey, now, my mistake," Pish said, with an affable smile and a clap on the tenor's back. Rhys shrugged Pish's hand off and stalked away.

"Why is he so angry?"

"You were a little confrontational, Merry. Don't read guilt into his resentment. He's a star and not accustomed to people questioning him."

"Hmmm. Well, I'll definitely be telling Urquhart about that," I said, watching him go. "Did anyone else miss him last evening?"

"I know Liliana did. And Giu asked if I had seen him. They were supposed to be talking about the judging but I don't think that happened."

"But he must have come back, right?"

Pish nodded. "He did. I saw him later, but . . ." He shrugged. "I had a little too much to drink, as you know, and my memory is foggy."

I thought for a moment, but then shook my head, thinking of my promise to Virgil. "Let's let Urquhart take care of that." The judges and mentors were allowed to retreat to their homes, but told that they should stay together and that an officer would accompany them. Two officers were still searching the castle rooms, so I suggested to the gathered contestants that they retire to the library, where there were sofas and I could bring refreshments. Pish led the way, promising to make them comfortable.

Janice, Lizzie and Patricia had gone home, leaving the kitchen pristine. While I fed Beckett, boiled the kettle and put together a tray of goodies, I considered what I knew. I had checked on my guests at bedtime. Darcie was there, but Lachlan said she was *not* there when he got out of the bath. She disputed that, but if he was right, where was she? Anne and Sparrow were together in their room. Zeb and Alain were in *their* room, Lachlan in the bath, Kamile in bed with her earbuds in, and Pam had Brontay practicing. I suspected, now that I knew more, that Gilda was already gone and perhaps in trouble.

I lined up two trays and filled platters with goodies. By Pish's report, Daffyd Rhys was missing from the party. I was beginning to fear that he was involved in Gilda's attack. It was difficult to put the two together, urbane talented Sir Daffyd Rhys and the brutal attack on Gilda Greenwald, but attractive, talented, bright people could have hidden dark depths. Who else could it be? Was anyone else missing from Liliana's? Had anyone seen him leave the house party? And when did he reenter? How had he been: distressed, upset, disheveled, or just normal? So many questions and no way to ask them. But I would certainly be telling Urquhart all my thoughts.

I stood at the counter for a long moment staring out into the darkness, facing the far woods on the other side of the castle, toward the houses. There *must* be other possibilities among the contestants, producers, judges and mentors. Moze Markunis was certainly on my list; Urquhart, with his arsenal of police tools, was best suited to find out about his movements. As had been pointed out to me, he would have needed an accomplice, and as much as I hated to think it, Kamile was the best bet for that. She was a bundle of nerves tied with a tight cord. Motive? Keeping concealed whatever it was that Moze and Kamile were hiding. Gilda was a journalist and seemed drawn to the two of them, curious about their relationship. I shuddered to think what secrets she may have uncovered.

I had been up and down all night, worried about Becket, and I did see some of the contestants, but I also heard other sounds—closing doors, footsteps—and saw fleeting figures. I drummed my fingers on the countertop; had I been up two or three times? Three, I thought. The first time I had seen Pam, who had been oddly off-kilter when she came in, saying she had been smoking. Why? It was a harmless enough activity. However, I suspected she didn't want her daughter knowing she smoked. I couldn't imagine she was involved in the attack on Gilda. Of all of them Pam and Brontay seemed the most transparent and open of the group.

Not like Darcie, who was most certainly flirting, and possibly more, with Rhys. Or Kamile, who I was sure had secrets that might be worth killing to keep. Beyond that, what did I know about the rest? Who needed Gilda gone, or who was angry enough at her that they attacked her? A journalist makes enemies. I thought back to the notes I had seen on her laptop screen. Could I recall them with any accuracy?

I plopped teabags in the giant tea urn, and while waiting for the kettle to boil I got a notepad out of one of the drawers and tried to reconstruct the notes; she had questioned Kamile and Moze's relationship, and there was a note to check what I assumed was a

Lithuanian contact. Maybe he wasn't her uncle at all, but if he wasn't, why hide it? Perhaps their "relationship" had started when Kamile was underage. Kamile had mentioned not seeing her mother very often.

There was also something about Alain Primeau asking too many questions about . . . someone or other. I wished I could remember . . . oh! Gilda's lousy spelling reminded me: she said Primeau was asking questions about Daffyd Rhys, which she had spelled Reece. What was there between Alain and Daffyd? I wondered.

And there was something else . . . I tapped the pencil on the notebook. Bad blood between Lachlan and other members of the Scottish Tenors, and a name; Colin, that was it! Maybe he was another member of the Scottish Tenors, one who would talk to a journalist, reveal dirty secrets.

I suddenly thought . . . in Gilda's determination to uncover information for her articles, was she using contestants as sources? There had to be a reason why she would leave the castle on foot, and one possibility was to speak in confidence with a source, away from other listeners. So, had she met her attacker down near the woods? Or was she dragged so far? *That* was not likely. She was tall and would not have gone without a fight. She *must* have been lured out of the castle.

Did she know who she was meeting, or had she been tricked? That was the question.

Seventeen

I had been away from the others too long. Lynn came to find me and I gave her the lighter tray holding two platters of sweets and savories, and carried the heavier tray holding a teapot and coffeepot into the library. Pish, a talented raconteur, was in the middle of telling how I inherited the castle and invited Shilo and him to live here. Lynn set down the tray with a clatter and drifted off, uneasy and a little defensive, as she still was when the tale of my flight from New York was spoken of. Virgil took pity and engaged her in conversation. She shied away from him much of the time, but he has his own way of putting people at ease.

As Pish finished the story and my guests helped themselves to cups of tea and coffee and munchies I had provided, I drifted from group to group. Sparrow, sitting by herself, looked weary and wary, her gaze darting about the room. She glared at an oblivious Darcie; why? I wondered. Kamile also sat by herself staring into the shadows, a worried look on her face. I joined the most equable of groups, comprised of the male contestants.

"Interesting to lairn how you came about living here, Merry, lass. We've haird the tales, suitable to any opera, they are," Lachlan said, smiling at me and winking. "You've had your share of drama and *murder most foul* here at the castle."

Brontay, sitting at the library table with her mother and Pish, swiveled, her eyes wide. "Murder?" she squeaked, staring at me. "Why haven't I heard?"

"You're too young. It'll give you nightmares," Lachlan replied with a chuckle.

I eyed him with dislike, but what could I say? It was true. I *had* once found a murder victim in the half bath off the butler's pantry hall. And one in a hole in my yard. And one in a casket on the terrace after a Halloween party.

"I don't think we're going to speak of that tonight," Pish said quickly, before Lachlan continued to razz Brontay. "Why don't we sing?" He had rescued a small piano from one of the houses we moved onto our property and had it refinished, tuned and placed in the library. He moved to it and began playing show tunes.

I eyed the Scots tenor, who joined in with the singing readily enough and sang a sentimental and melodic version of "Danny Boy." Was there more to him than a cheerful flirt and tormentor? I noticed his voice cracking, and a momentary look of discomfort; was he having vocal problems? That was unfortunate timing, if so, so close to the end of the competition.

As the others crowded around the piano with Pish, whose magnetism made him the perfect spontaneous party host, I noticed those who did not partake. Pam was on her phone. She was in charge of Brontay's social media accounts and promoted her daughter relentlessly. I wondered if she would use this latest drama to her benefit. Darcie paced and stared out the window into the darkness. I observed her for a long minute, wondering if there was something in particular about Gilda's attack that had her uneasy. Lachlan's assertion that she had been nowhere to be found when he came out of the bath was worrying.

Kamile still sat alone, curled up in the corner of a sofa with a book, which I learned, peeping at the cover, was one of Pish's, a social history of the opera. I hesitated; the woman was so self-contained that I was loath to disturb her, and yet, with Moze not there I wanted to get to know her a little. I sat down near her on the sofa and she looked up.

"There's tea and coffee if you like."

"No, thank you."

"You know, you playing with that hair bow with Becket probably saved Gilda's life. If I hadn't seen that . . . the sheriff says she would not have survived another night out in the open."

Silence. She cast a glance down at her book. I know what it's like to want privacy, but I had a right to engage a guest in my home in conversation. Wasn't that the polite thing to do? "Do you miss Lithuania, Kamile?"

She hesitated, then said, "I did not feel any more at home there than anywhere else. I miss my family, but I do not miss my country."

"Your family; are your parents still there?" She hadn't answered last time I probed; I wondered if she would now.

"My mother still lives in Jonava," she said.

"My knowledge of Lithuania is abysmal. Is that a big city?"

"Thirty thousand or so, that's all."

Encouraged by her engagement, I said, "Moze is your uncle and you have the same last name, so he's your father's brother?" She nodded, but her gaze became shuttered, like opaque drapes drawn across a window. Whenever I touched too closely on her and Moze's relationship she withdrew. "He believes in your talent. That's wonderful. Not many uncles and nieces are so close." Again, silence. "So, why did you enter this contest, Kamile?"

"My uncle wished it."

"But you didn't?"

She hesitated, frowned, and picked at an imaginary piece of lint on her long sweater. "I wish to sing. My uncle wishes me to sing. He is helping me to find my way."

"You do have the most lovely voice. Were you raised to sing, or is it your choice?"

She hesitated once again, but her voice was warmer when she said, "I was raised to music, yes, but I *do* love singing more than anything in the world. I get lost in it, in the music." Her large expressive eyes were liquid and glowing. "I *dream* of the stage, of the lights, of the audience. I dream . . ." Her words drifted off to a whisper.

"You don't need this competition for your dream to come true," I said, watching her soulful eyes and remembering her voice. "I don't say this lightly; I can see you as the next great star, performing Carmen and Lucia."

Oddly, her expression sobered, but she nodded, almost grimacing. "Perhaps. Though I have worked years with little progress. The mentors . . . they mention every time that I create a distance between me and the audience and I know not how to bridge it."

"In my experience the best performers have an authenticity to them, an unspoken connection to the audience that comes from their soul. If you open your heart, I'm sure you can do it."

"Open my heart? It sounds painful." I smiled at the jest. "Do you think they're done upstairs yet?" she asked as Urquhart entered the library.

Our friendly (or not) local sheriff said, "Thank you, folks. We're done, though we're still finishing up in the victim's room, which will be sealed until further notice. We have taken a few items, which we are in the process of documenting. We will give receipts to the owners for each item."

There was grumbling and eye rolling, and suspicious glances at Urquhart, which he stolidly ignored. He glanced around at the group, then flicked his gaze down to the paper he held. "I'd like a brief word with Ms. Darcie Austin, Mr. Lachlan McDermott, Ms. Kamile Markunis and Ms. Pam Bellini. The rest of you can go back to your rooms."

Everyone got up and trooped out, eager to end the long evening of forced conviviality, while the four named followed Urquhart to the great hall. I watched them go. Both Kamile and Darcie appeared alarmed. I thought that items were probably removed from those four's rooms and they needed to be informed and receive receipts. I followed them out into the hall, but Urquhart had drawn them away and spoke too softly for me to hear.

It was now one in the morning and I was relieved to drop into bed with Virgil. Surprisingly, since I thought after the trauma and activity of the night I'd be awake for a while, I fell fast asleep and did not awaken until early the next morning. Virgil was already gone, leaving me a text saying he'd be back, that he had to follow up on business with Dewayne and Sheriff Baxter.

• • •

With the cold-blooded efficiency of any show business event, *Opera DivaNation* was back in business the next day. The crew showed up. The window cleaners showed up. The show—and everything else—must go on. Midmorning Anne returned, looking wan and weary. Gilda was still in a coma, she whispered to me as we stood in the great hall. Her mother was with her, and her sister was arriving that afternoon.

"Did her mother say anything? Had she heard from Gilda recently?" I asked as I walked with her upstairs, toward her room. She was going to shower and sleep for a couple of hours, since Sparrow had everything under control.

Anne frowned and paused at the top of the stairs, then walked on. "It's odd. Gilda was writing her mother a text, and it got sent, but only a few words made sense about some problems with her article, and her determination to get to the bottom of something. There were scrambled letters, then nothing. But it *was* sent. Gilda was different from many young women, her mother said; every text she wrote was in full sentences and full words, with punctuation. No 'R U' for 'are you,' no phonetic spellings or run-on sentences for her."

"What time was that sent?"

"She got it in the morning. It worried her and she wrote back to Gilda, but never received an answer. Now we know why."

"But what time was it *sent*?" I repeated.

"I don't know. I didn't ask. Is it important?"

I shrugged, but my mind sped through possibilities. It could be that she was meeting her attacker and texting while waiting. Maybe she didn't get a chance to finish the text and it got sent accidently. If so, the time stamp would give a good indication of when the attack occurred. As soon as I left Anne I texted Urquhart with the possibility, as well as a separate lengthy text about Daffyd Rhys. Pish's information about the singer being absent for a time from the party was alarming. How long would it take to attack Gilda and drag her into the woods?

But . . . what could Rhys have to do with Gilda Greenwald? There was the note concerning him on her laptop, but looking into allegations was not necessarily damning. So much still needed to be discovered, but with Gilda in a coma we had to proceed without her input.

I changed into a denim shirtwaist dress with rust leather boots and a shawl over a coat and headed to Autumn Vale, leaving the food and craft services in the able hands of Patricia and Janice. I stopped first at Golden Acres—I had muffins for them—and checked in with my mother-in-law, then found my great-uncle's best friend and the grandfather I never had, Doc English.

He was in his own room, sitting in a recliner reading a large-print book by the bright daylight of his window. As always, he was overjoyed to see me. I hugged him, then sat on the edge of his bed and we talked.

"That gaggle o' opera singers you got there is quite the talk in town," he said, peering at me through his perpetually smudged glasses.

"Nobody's even seen them!" I said, gently taking his glasses and cleaning them with a tissue. "How can they be the talk of the town?"

He gave me a look of withering contempt, and I laughed. "You got

Janice Grover working for you," he growled. "That woman never met a rumor she couldn't pass on, and never heard a voice she liked so well as her own."

"True. But I do love her." I appreciated his humor, but my long night and my sorrow over Gilda's near-murder had left me shaken. I gently placed his glasses back on his spotty nose, making sure the arms were over his pendulous ears, and told him the tale. I smiled over Becket's part in the story . . . our feline hero! Without him, we may have been too late for Gilda. I also shared with him my prime suspects.

"What was the writer woman doing out at that time o' the night?" he asked, having realized, as I did, that there was no way anyone could have dragged Gilda out of the castle without being noticed.

I pondered that question, one that nagged at me. "That's what I can't figure out. I think she might have a mole in the crew or contestants. Maybe one of the crew was meeting her there to share info?"

"Or someone was pretending to be the mole to get her out of the castle?"

"But why? I mean, if it *was* the mole, they could surely arrange to meet her to pass on information, and if it was someone *pretending* to be the mole . . . wait . . ." I thought about it. "It wasn't necessarily someone pretending to be the mole, though. Gilda was always on the lookout for a good story, and she had aspirations to be more than an entertainment reporter, and hinted that she had another article in the works beyond the *Opera DivaNation* story."

"Yeah? So?"

"She was ambitious. If someone said they had a good story on one of the contestants, or even one of the judges or mentors, she would have met them anywhere to get the information."

"I guess that's possible," Doc said grudgingly.

"Anyway, I'm going to enlist Hannah's help with research. Based on the notes I saw on Gilda's laptop, there are mysteries in the background of more than a couple of that group."

"Say, talkin' 'bout mysteries, you'll like this." He planted his elbows on the arms of his chair and hoisted himself forward. "I got a friend, an' he told me a funny story this mornin'. Said the other night when he was coming to sing his wife to sleep—he does it every night without fail; really good guy—he saw somethin' strange. Seems he was in a hurry and ducked down an unlit alley—not wise to do at his age, even in Autumn Vale, I tole him—and saw this guy park a car in the alley, then toss the keys through the window onto the front seat."

"A little odd, but maybe the guy was leaving the car for somebody?"

Doc shrugged and made a face. "Made William feel weird, you know that feeling, like the Tingler is crawling up your backbone? The guy was skulking . . . that's what William called it . . . skulking. He thinks the feller hopped a fence and took off through backyards. When William went back that way a half hour later, the car had been moved."

"Okay. Are you implying it's connected to what's happened to Gilda?"

"Well, I dunno. But two weird things in one night . . . could be, right?"

Gilda's car had been turned in to the rental place in Batavia, so it was unlikely to be on a backstreet in Autumn Vale. However, it wasn't impossible. An idea teased at the back of my mind. "I'll mention it to Virgil, and he'll pass it on to Urquhart. Do you think William would mind being interviewed by the police if it turns out that it's important?"

"You kidding? He'll dine off it for days. He'll tell that story at the Legion, the Brotherhood of Falcons hall, and here, if anyone can hear him."

I laughed, then kissed him on the cheek. I paused at the door; he had already gone back to reading an old Zane Grey, his comfort reading he said, from when he was a kid listening to the old radio westerns and dreaming of being a cowpoke on the lone prairie. I watched him for a moment, then headed out to the library.

At one time people had to leave Autumn Vale if they wanted to go to the library. Hannah Moore changed all that by starting her own community library, an amazing accomplishment for anybody. She's a remarkable young woman. The large print Doc was reading likely came from an interlibrary loan via the Autumn Vale Community Library, a poky little cement block hole-in-the-wall place on a side street, lit by overhead fluorescents and high windows.

Lined with bookshelves, and with tables down the center, it is rapidly becoming too small for the book collection Hannah is patiently gathering from handouts, estates and gifts, and buying using donor money. I had donated my grandmother's pristine Agatha Christie and Dorothy L. Sayers collection.

I entered to find our local hermitess, Isadore Openshaw, seated at one of the tables eating an apple and reading. She nodded, then returned to her book. Hannah was at her desk at the far end of the library with a stack of books and a cup of tea. I hugged her, then sat down. We chatted for a moment. Of course she was curious about what was going on at the castle with the attack on Gilda, but in general about the show, as well. I invited her out to watch a taping, but she reluctantly had to decline as she had an out-of-town expert who was helping her start a Friends of the Library foundation to fund her ongoing expenses and expansion plans. It was something she could not and would not shirk.

She offered me one of her home-baked cookies—of course I took it; I'm no fool and her macadamia nut cookies are delicious—and watched me for a moment, then slyly said, "Why do I have the feeling you have research you need done?"

I smiled. "You have my number, don't you? I need it done quickly and discreetly, and there is no one better than you."

"No need for flattery," she said, her head tilted to one side. "I do like helping you, and I love research. Two birds, one little stone . . . *c'est moi.*" She made an elegant flourish with her small beringed hand, a fairy flutter of a gesture.

As I explained what I needed to know, she started researching, tapping away with her indefatigable slim white fingers. Looking up the Scottish Tenors was easy; the first incarnation was Lachlan, James, Ian and Colin. First, we looked at the polished bio of the singing group, how the lads were in school, a Scottish technical college for electrical engineering, accounting, woodworking, and upholstery. We waded through ten years of information, how the group was formed, their tours, gossip about one of the members, who married, became embroiled in a nasty three-way love affair, then a public and acrimonious divorce. That wasn't Lachlan. Neither was it Lachlan who was behind the wheel of a car that was involved in a tragic accident, in which someone died. Nor was it Lachlan who had gotten a groupie pregnant and abandoned her. Side note: who knew opera singers could have groupies?

Gossip-filled and scandalous were the lives of the Scottish Tenors gentlemen, though it all seemed to happen in the beginning, when they were in their early twenties. Lately the fellows had settled down to touring, marrying and having babies, as wild young men are wont to do in their more sober thirties. Lachlan had never married, though he had been publicly linked to a member of a Gaelic women's group. He seemed to be the most abstemious and careful of the foursome. I looked up the young woman on social media and put in a friend request. I wanted an independent evaluation of Lachlan's character from someone outside of the opera contest. I wrote her a brief message, explaining who I was and saying I'd like to have a chat, if it was possible.

"So . . . why *did* he leave the group?"

She tapped in the question, but all we found were the publicist-framed press releases quoting "unnamed sources," who speculated based on "inside knowledge" about "artistic differences" and diverging visions for the future. Publicity babble at its finest.

"He claims to want a solo career, something meatier and with more potential for growth than being with a touring tenors group. I wonder how much of that is true?"

"Why don't you write down what you need and I'll do the research between other tasks?" she asked, her gaze going to a patron who entered the library. She nodded to the woman and held up one finger.

"Are you sure I'm not taking you away from work?"

"Merry, I am a woman," she said, her gaze flicking back to me. "That means I am capable of doing at least three things at once, and doing them all well."

I chuckled at her optimistic confidence and applauded it. She manipulated the joystick of her mobility chair, the soft hum of the motor a warm burst of sound as she wheeled around the desk toward her patron. I took her notepad and wrote down Lachlan's name and Colin's, underlining it. That was the name in Gilda's notes, and I assumed he might be her contact regarding information about Lachlan's days in the group. I then wrote *a little on each contestant, please,* jotting their names, with what I knew about each to help her along. In particular Kamile and Moze Markunis, in whom Gilda had expressed such an interest, and the town of Jonava, Lithuania; were they or were they *not* uncle and niece?

But beyond the contestants, I was painfully interested in the talented, ineffably good-looking Sir Daffyd Rhys. He was a big personality, a playboy in the old-fashioned sense; irresistible to many women, and insatiable when it came to sex, according to the press coverage. As Darcie had pointed out, most operas were all about sex; why shouldn't the singers' lives be as consumed with it? But was there a more unsavory side to the Welshman? Were there any scandals that a reporter could dig into, explore, maybe . . . threaten to reveal?

Hannah came back to the desk and picked up the notepad. I capped the pen and pointed to his name. "I don't think you'll find anything there," I said about Rhys. "But he does show up in Gilda's notes." And he was missing, for a time, from the party at Liliana's.

I bid her farewell, but paused on my way through the library to say hello to Isadore. "Say, *you* work at the coffee shop," I said, sitting in the empty chair next to her. "Virgil overheard a woman there talking about seeing a cat in the woods . . . that—and him bringing in Gilda's black bow—is what convinced me it was Becket she saw. Did you overhear anything else she said about the experience?"

"She said she saw a woman."

"I heard she thought she heard a woman scream, but that it may have been an owl."

"No, not heard, *saw*! She said she *thinks* she saw a woman . . . something about a flash of white."

"Gilda?" The journalist had been wearing a white blouse; it could be her.

Isadore shrugged.

"Maybe you can ask her about it when you go back this afternoon?" Isadore worked as a dishwasher and busperson in the coffeeshop, a split shift to cover the morning and lunch, and then the dinner runs.

Her eyes widened and she shook her head. Her chronic shyness and dislike of talking to people for more than a word or two made her an excellent employee for Mabel, the coffee shop manager, who saw chat with customers as wasted time, but it meant she was unlikely to agree to my request.

"Please try? Here," I said, handing her a card with the castle's monogram. "Give her my number. I'll do the talking."

"Uh, okay, maybe."

I had to be satisfied with that, and returned to the castle. It had already been a long, difficult day, and it was about to get longer and more difficult.

Eighteen

I returned to find a standoff between a furious Anne Parkinson and a stolid and unmovable Sheriff Urquhart.

"What's going on?" I said, closing the big double doors behind me. Becket brushed up against my legs and meowed. I bent to pet him, then approached the fractious duo.

"He wants to interview all of the cast and crew," the producer said, throwing her hands up in the air.

"Well, of *course* he does," I said, glancing from one to the other. "Anne, Sheriff Urquhart is here to find out what happened to Gilda. It's a crime. He's a police officer. He's doing his job." Her round face set in a mulish frown and she crossed her arms over her sweater-clad bosom. "I'd think you'd want that too," I said. "You do not want this hanging over the contest; think of the negative publicity."

"It would slow things down. *You're* the one who was adamant we be out of the castle in X number of days."

"That was before a woman was attacked and left for dead in my woods!" I took in a long breath, releasing my fingers from the crabbed fists they had balled into. "Anne, *you* are the one who assured me you'd take five days. Or seven. You can still do that and take a few hours to help the police find out who attacked Gilda Greenwald."

"All right. All *right!*" she said, her tone on the edge of exasperation. "I guess we don't have any choice, do we?"

I gave her a look and her expression softened.

"I want to find out who did this to Gilda; of *course* I do!" she exclaimed. "But don't blame me if this slows things down."

Urquhart turned to me. "Merry, we'll need a place to interview. I'd suggest your library."

"The library is yours, Sheriff." I turned to the producer and put one hand on her plump shoulder. "It'll be okay. The important thing—"

"I know, I *know;* it's to finish this damn competition and get out of your castle."

I snatched my comforting hand back and sucked in an irritated breath. "The important thing, I was *going* to say, is to find out who attacked Gilda."

She nodded and sighed. "Of course. Excuse me; I'm a little stressed right now. They're all being a pain. Darcie is acting like a diva before she even is one. Alain is coming on to every female within sniffing distance and some of the males, too. And Kamile . . ." She frowned and shook her head.

"What *about* Kamile?" I asked, as Urquhart moved away to make a phone call.

"The wardrobe mistress is complaining about her again. Kamile has always been thorny about fittings. She doesn't like people touching her."

"Why do you think that is?"

"I wish I knew, but I do *not* have time for this. I'm not a baby-sitter." She sounded at the end of her patience.

I know what it is to feel overwhelmed. "Tell you what; I'll do what I can to get Sheriff Urquhart to arrange his interview schedule with yours, as much as possible."

"Thank you." She sighed. "That's all I'm asking, for a little cooperation, but the lug looked at me like I was—"

"Like you were out of your mind. I'm familiar with that look from the sheriff. Don't worry; it's habitual and has nothing to do with you. Let me handle it."

Urquhart was still on the phone. I wanted to talk to him; he covered the phone for one moment when I asked. "We can speak in a few minutes," he murmured. "I have something to ask you, as well."

"Okay. I'll find you in the library." I ran upstairs, with Becket following in a merry chase—or a Merry chase—and found Lynn, first, in the wardrobe room. She was sorting accessories while waiting for one of the contestants. I asked how she was doing and was pleased that she was doing well. "Lynn, I have a question. Have you noticed any problem with Kamile while you were dressing her? Has she been skittish at all?"

Lynn, basket of hair accessories in one hand, frowned and was silent. She set the basket down. "I haven't had any problem with her but I know the wardrobe mistress did. She was trying to measure Kamile when the singer slapped her hand."

"Measure her for what?"

"I don't know. Does it matter?"

"I guess not."

"I've found her perfectly lovely to work with," Lynn said. "We're almost the same height and build. I told her I had a lot of gowns in

New York that she could have if she'd take them. I was hesitant. I didn't want to insult her by offering her clothes, but she didn't take offense."

"That was kind of you, Lynn," I said, touching her arm. "But you know, you *will* still have occasions to wear gowns. We're having that charity fundraiser in a couple of weeks, and there will be more of that in the future."

"I don't know how much of that I'll be participating in."

"As much—or as little—as you want." I gave her a hug, then went to Pish, who was in his sitting room at the computer. He was frowning, which he rarely did because it causes lines. He is not vain, he is committed to staying young, he always says. "What's up?" I asked, sitting down in his guest chair.

"I spoke to a section editor at the magazine where Gilda works."

"*Her* editor?"

"No, a fellow I met a few years ago when I was doing research for one of my books. He is subbing for Gilda's editor, who is in the hospital as of this morning. Nothing serious, he said." He turned in his swivel chair and met my gaze. "There have been whispers for a while at the magazine about Gilda and her sources. She poaches them, for one thing—"

"Poaches?" I was picturing eggs, I'll admit it.

"As in steals, darling; pay attention. Gilda is ambitious—"

"Not a sin, even for a woman."

"But shortsighted when you poach sources from other writers."

"What does that have to do with what happened to her here?"

"A few years ago there was a young writer who worked at another mag where Gilda was also employed as a copywriter. She was working on an important story about Hollywood stars who had gotten their kids into college using less than ethical—and perhaps illegal—methods. Gilda cozied up to the writer and then stole her sources, sold the story to another magazine, and made a huge hit. It gave her a start and is the reason she was hired at another magazine."

I waited. There was bound to be more.

"The young writer Gilda stole from was named Sparrow Summers."

"Oh. *Oh!*"

"My source says that Gilda was eventually found out, lost her job and was blackballed from the industry for a time, but the young writer—Sparrow—had left New York by that point and was no longer writing. Gilda worked her way back up in publishing and is determined to again make her big break."

"It's like the perfect storm, having them both associated with the same project," I said. "Are you saying you think Sparrow is responsible for the attack on Gilda?"

He sighed and swiveled back and forth. "I don't know. It seems unlikely."

"And yet Pish, is it coincidence that finds them here, involved with *Opera DivaNation,* together? I thought you didn't believe in coincidence."

"I'd like to ask around before I jump to any conclusions, see who assigned Gilda to this job, that kind of thing." He jotted down a note on our Wynter Castle stationery. He loves fine stationery and had a professional graphic artist design writing paper, note cards, postcards and business cards using and pen and ink rendition of the castle. It was elegant, like him. We keep a supply in every guest room.

"How angry would Sparrow be after several years? It is years we're talking about, right?" He nodded. "Seems to me if it was important to the former writer to write, she'd still be writing. One stolen story should not stop her forever."

"It's more complicated than that. Messier. Sparrow didn't know her source had been stolen and wrote the piece in good faith, presented it to her editor, but Gilda had gotten there first and had virtually the same wording in her piece, so it looked like *Sparrow* was a plagiarist, not Gilda. It took time to sort out before the truth was revealed. You know what rumor is like . . . if Sparrow had been labeled a plagiarist no one would touch her, and being exonerated might not change that."

I thought of the bundle of nerves that was Sparrow. Was Gilda's presence the real problem? "That's worse, being accused of plagiarism. Sparrow could have it in for Gilda," I mused. "Do you think Gilda recognized her?"

"I don't know. Wouldn't you think she'd remember at least the name—and such an unusual one—of someone she'd wronged?"

The temptation for Sparrow to get back at her could have been strong, but still . . . it didn't seem all that likely. "I don't know, Pish. As a motive for attempted murder it's weak. Sparrow doesn't seem like the type to plan and execute this kind of fiendish plot, which if discovered could ruin her own life. The woman is a nervous wreck."

"Maybe because she was planning a murder."

I shook my head. "I don't see it."

"Just a thought. That's not all I found out today. I called in a favor in Rochester—"

"Someone in Rochester owed you a favor?"

"I provided the testimony in a civil suit that got money back from a con artist for a friend in Rochester once, and his son works in the hotel industry."

I saw where this was going and leaned forward. "Yes?"

"He gave me the scoop on what happened at the hotel that caused them to kick out the entire production of *Opera DivaNation*."

"I'm waiting with bated breath."

"There was so much, I had him send me an email. Here," he said, handing me his laptop. "Read it out loud. And accept my apologies in advance for landing us with this crew."

"Not your fault, Pish; who could have known?" I read aloud:

> *Mr. Lincoln . . . always happy to help a friend of my father's. The service you did him was so important I cannot repay you with a simple list, but I'll try. We at the award-winning Rochester Grand Waterfront Hotel take pride in our service, hospitality and accommodation, and we were excited at the opportunity to host the Opera DivaNation event. We were under the mistaken assumption that a group of opera singers would be staid, elegant, even inspiring. We were wrong. The crew members were, without exception, faultless; it was the cast that was the problem.*

I looked over at Pish. "This doesn't sound good."

"Read on, my darling."

I sighed and looked back to the screen. I skipped down through vague complaints and came to the enumerated list, and read aloud:

> *1 – Room Service staff harassed; I will not get into particulars and will not name names – we don't need a lawsuit on our hands for breaching guest privacy – but suffice it to say, our comelier female maids were not safe with a certain male member of the Opera DivaNation cast.*

"Hmmm . . . Pish, that could mean Alain, Lachlan or even . . ." I hesitated. "Even Sir Daffyd Rhys. He's a womanizer, I've heard."

Pish sighed and nodded. "I'm afraid you're right, but keep reading."

> *2 – Dining room damaged: a prank pulled by one of the contestants resulted in a coffee machine spewing hot oil instead of coffee. We had to send the machine out for cleaning and repair, and explain to the contestant that the "prank" was not funny. The producer paid for the cleaning.*
>
> *3 – Complaints about service; several of the haughtier in the judging/mentor capacity were constantly complaining about our accommodations. It took far too much time to cater to their complaints and make them grudgingly satisfied. We are a midlevel hotel, not the Four Seasons.*
>
> *4 – Several "accidents" happened to the contestants.*

I looked up again. "Accidents? I heard about some of this, but in at least one case – and that was Gilda who told me this – it seems to have been the hotel that was responsible." I looked back down and continued to read from number 4.

> *I had/have deep concerns about a few incidents among the cast. In one case a piece of stair carpet seems to have been deliberately torn, resulting in a fall. In another, there was an electrical incident that we cannot explain. And there was more than one problem with food poisoning that is inconsistent with our top-grade food service.*

Electrical incident . . . "Oh! The electrical accident . . . that happened to Gilda, not one of the cast or crew; she mentioned being almost electrocuted in the shower." I sighed. "I don't know how much of this to credit as the usual problems with hotels, or whether it was caused by the cast."

"I agree. It's concerning."

I read on:

> *But the final straw was a brawl in the barroom between one of the judges and the uncle of one of the contestants.*

"Well, the only uncle is Moze Markunis. Pish, the judge *has* to be Sir Daffyd. They had another confrontation in our dining room."

"I'll look into it."

"None of this is likely to have anything to do with Gilda's attack though."

"I don't imagine."

I sighed.

Pam Bellini burst in, followed by Lizzie. "Where is she?"

I looked to Lizzie, past Pam. "What's going on?"

"We can't find Brontay, and her mom is worried that—"

"That the same person who almost killed Gilda is out to get my daughter!" Pam shrieked, hands balled into fists. "Where is she? I can't find her and she's not answering her phone and that cop is a big, useless hunk of—"

"Okay, stop. We'll find her, Pam," I said, standing. "Lizzie, when did you last see her?"

"She was following me around, and . . . and . . ." She looked guilty.

"Pam, can you go find Anne Parkinson for me?" I said. "Maybe she has an idea where Brontay is." The senior producer kept a pretty close eye on the talent. Pam stormed out of the room but didn't go downstairs, heading instead down the hall toward their room. "Lizzie, what's going on?" I said, my tone hushed.

"I told Brontay to take off," Lizzie said, her eyes clouded. "She's been hanging around and you know how I don't . . ." She shrugged.

My young friend is a loner most of the time. Her friendships are generally with other kids who are also loners and don't cling. "So she had been clinging a little too hard and you told her to take off. How did she react?"

"She was mad . . . stomped off."

"But nothing else?"

Lizzie sat down on the carpeted floor and Becket climbed into her lap and curled up. She scratched his ears, her expression uneasy. "She's been upset all day, but she wouldn't tell me why. I didn't think she was especially close to Gilda. I mean, the woman is just a writer, right?"

"But you had a sense that her being upset was connected to Gilda's attack?"

Lizzie nodded. "I'm almost certain. She kept whining about how Gilda's attack was all her fault, but she wouldn't tell me anything more!"

"Did you tell Urquhart about what Brontay said, that the attack on Gilda was all her fault?"

My young friend got that stubborn look on her face, her eyes dark, her brow furrowed. "No," she said, ruffling Becket's fur in agitated motions. He squawked, glared at her with an injured look, and raced out of the room to sulk.

Lizzie detested Urquhart, and unlike me had not softened her position on him. Regardless, I was not going to let her dislike keep her from doing what needed to be done. "We're going to tell him right now, and then we are going to find her. She's probably sulking." I hoped that was the answer, anyway.

We told Urquhart what was going on; he said to talk to him again if we didn't find her within a reasonable time. We then spoke to the contestants. No one had seen Brontay in the last hour. Janice, though, had seen the teen stomp through the kitchen in a foul temper. She tried to give the kid a snack, but Brontay angrily said according to *some* people she was already too fat and sure didn't need to be eating between meals. After that she flounced down the butler's pantry hall off the kitchen, and presumably out the back door.

Had she come back in, I asked.

No one knew. I wasn't sure whether to be worried or angry. It was likely that Brontay was out tromping around working off her snit. But there was a would-be killer around, and we couldn't be complacent. I have been through enough in the last few years to know that.

Pish headed out to check with the folks at the two occupied houses on our property, while I searched in the basement, then every room of the main floor, and then the second floor, even the locked rooms. Finally, with Lizzie, I climbed the stairs to the attic, where we keep all the extra furniture. There, curled up like a sleepy mouse on a ratty dusty divan, was Brontay.

I was furious by then, tired and upset and angry. But I took one look at the relieved expression on Lizzie's face and decided not to make a big deal out of it. My young friend already felt bad enough; I wouldn't make it worse. I paced away to the stairs and phoned Pish, calling off the search. Then I returned to where Lizzie was waking Brontay up.

The kid was drowsy still, wiping the sleep out of her eyes and looking about ten, her fluffy hair a halo around her round face, which was pouchy from sleep, with lines imprinted on her cheek from where she had rested her face on the upholstery. Brontay sat up and narrowed her eyes, squinting up at us in the dim light. "What's going on?"

"We've been looking for you for hours!" Lizzie said, exaggerating. "Your mom is *frantic*. She thought someone did you in."

The kid smirked and I took in a deep breath, about to go ballistic, when Pam charged into the room and lunged at her child. I was wondering if I'd have to pull her off, but she hugged her baby and rocked back and worth, weeping, like a wren with her cuckoo chick. As much of a stage mother as she occasionally seemed, it was clear that more than anything she loved her child.

"You missed your slot," Pam finally said.

"Oh, gosh!" Brontay said, her expression stricken with guilt. She jumped to her feet. "I didn't mean to. I'm sorry, Mom. Can I still get in?"

"I'll make sure you do. I won't let them sideline you, sweetie." Pam put her arm around her daughter's shoulders. "Let's go and get you ready. Lynn is in the makeup room, so we can kill two birds with one stone, get you dressed and in makeup."

"You're not going to make me wear that gown, are you?"

"You can wear what you want. Let's get it done. The singing is the important part."

Nineteen

Urquhart and Anne worked out a schedule, and interviews went on. I took my turn and told him all I had heard and seen during the night, including Pam coming in at about eleven thirty, the accusation that Darcie was not about when Lachlan got out of the tub—though I didn't know the timing of that—and what I had already told him about Pish noticing Rhys being gone from the party. I told him, as best as I could recollect, about the rest of my restless night: seeing movement near the forest at about one a.m.; how I was downstairs when Pish came in, a while later, and that he had felt someone nearby as he walked home from Liliana's; how at two or three in the morning I heard a loud bang, but did not know the source. It didn't amount to much, related in stark terms. My mind a jumble, I added in Brontay's garbled insistence that Gilda's injury was her fault.

As usual, the man did not share a thing with me, but then, why should he? I had to respect his discretion. However, he did mention one thing, and asked my opinion. He took a plastic bag out of a folder and pushed it across the desk to me. It was a note, waterstained and blurry, with a long tear in it. I examined and read it. *Meet me by the woods usual time,* it said, but there was no signature.

"Do you know the handwriting at all?"

I met his gaze. "I can't say I do. Did you find this near Gilda?"

He didn't answer. That likely meant yes. I examined it again. Dampness had blurred the felt-tip ink. The paper was torn at the bottom, but it looked like there were a few jots right near the tear, a couple of V-shaped marks. Was there another part that had the signature on it that had been torn off and fluttered around in the woods even now? I squinted . . . aha! "This is written on our Wynter Castle stationery," I said triumphantly, pushing the plastic bag across to him and pointing. "There, at the top . . . see that straight line? That's the bottom of the castle image. You'll find the stationery in the desk if you want to compare. So . . . the note was written by someone in the castle."

"Interesting. Thanks, Merry. I appreciate it. You can go."

Dismissed in my own home. I sighed, but obediently departed. I did prep work in the kitchen for dinner. Virgil was back at our house, but he was coming to the castle to help with dinner. He'd grill steaks on the indoor grill for those who wanted them, burgers for those who didn't, and marinated Portobello mushrooms for the vegetarians. We were also doing salads and a baked potato bar with an array of fixings for every taste.

Hannah texted me to call her. I trotted up to my turret room, retrieved my laptop, sat at my dressing table, and put her on video chat. My dainty friend popped onto the screen. She was in the library of her home, where Zeke—my friend and her boyfriend—now lived with her family. He was in the background with a computer, its guts spilled out over a desktop as he fiddled with a hard drive. He waved, then went back to work, new glasses in place, expression of oblivious concentration furrowing his brow.

"What's up?" I asked Hannah. "What did you find out?"

"So much," she said, looking down at her computer keyboard. "Too much to tell you on the phone. I'm sending files to your email, along with links."

"Give me the Cliffs Notes version." Nobody did that better than Hannah. Maybe that's true of librarians in general, the ability to condense a lot of useful information into sound bites for antsy library clients.

"Where should I start?"

"Wherever you want."

Her narrow pixie face took on a sober expression and she consulted a notebook. "Okay, the Cliffs Notes version. Gilda is a story thief. Alain Primeau is up to something opera-related, but I'm not sure what yet. There *is* no Kamile Markunis *anywhere*, though I can find Moze Markunis, and he's involved with shady people, think Lithuanian mobsters. Lachlan is probably lying about why he left the Scottish Tenors. Brontay Bellini was in regular school but was taken out because she was being bullied."

"Wow. That's a lot to unpack, Hannah. How do you do it . . . find so much out in so little time? I will never understand in a million years."

Zeke shouted, "Because she's amazing," and Hannah colored sweetly.

"Now, let's fill in the outlines," she said.

"First off . . . nothing on Darcie?"

"Nope. She is a wannabe actress-slash-singer-slash-reality show babe. She had an agent but was dropped last year. She seems to be who she says she is; no deep dark secrets in her background."

"Okay. Now, as to the rest, I do know some of it. I know that Brontay was bullied in school and is homeschooled. I know that Gilda is a story thief. I'm interested in what you said about Lachlan and why he left the Scottish Tenors. What do you mean, he's lying?"

"He told you he wanted a solo career, right?"

"Yes. He's ambitious, wants bigger roles on stage. Etcetera."

"In most cases artists who are planning a solo career start even before leaving the group they are in. But Lachlan was most definitely voted out of the group. There was a falling out. *Something Happened.*"

By her significant tone I could hear that those two words were capitalized, like in a text, to make it clear that Something Mysterious Was Going On. "What's your take? I'd like ammo when I talk to him next."

"Well, remember that all we found when you were with me in the library were the other members' problems. But I dug and found more, or . . . *didn't* find something is more accurate."

"I don't understand."

"Three years ago, before they broke up, there was, like . . ." She frowned and grimaced. "Like a media blackout from the Scottish Tenors. They all stopped talking simultaneously, it seemed. *The Daily Mail*—that's a British newspaper—even commented on it in their online gossip blog. Something like *ominous presentiment of doom from the Scottish Tenors: silence is not golden?* I've sent you the link. But they didn't exactly break up, they emerged from the media blackout *without* Lachlan and *with* a new singer. Since then they have recorded three albums and done four specials and are more popular than ever."

"Interesting."

"Now, about Gilda—"

"I've already heard the tale, and know about her stealing a story and sources from another writer—"

"And you know who the writer is."

"Yes, Sparrow Summers." We both said the name at the same time and she giggled. "Associate producer on *Opera DivaNation*. I'm wondering if it was a coincidence that Gilda ended up being assigned a story on the production. However, I am *more* curious to know about the other stories. First, what did you mean that Alain Primeau is up to something opera-related?"

She squinched up her face and wriggled her nose. "Interesting stuff. I dug around and found out that Primeau is from a family of singers. His father was a French-Canadian pop singer way back in the seventies. And his aunt was a prominent opera singer; she even sang at the Met."

"And then . . . ?"

"And then something went wrong in a touring company of *Orfeo ed Eurydice*," she said, stumbling over the title. "Primeau's aunt was Eurydice. Want to know who played Orfeo?"

"Tell me."

"Sir Daffyd Rhys."

I was silent.

"She had what was called a breakdown by some, and voice problems by others—it's kind of hard going back that far; this is from a Canadian source, the CBC, their national broadcaster—and left the company and retired, never to sing again," Hannah said.

Never to sing again. And here was Primeau, in a contest being judged by Rhys. "But what does that have to do with Gilda being attacked?"

"Fair question. I don't know," she said with a shrug. "Maybe nothing. But it's something to look into. I mean, Gilda is a journalist and would have done her homework."

I shifted uneasily in my chair. Rhys was mysteriously missing from the party, possibly at the same time that Gilda went missing. It was either an unfortunate coincidence or something darker. Had *he* written the note asking her to meet him? He could easily have purloined some of our notepaper or . . . gosh, *yes*! I had put Wynter Castle notepaper in each welcome basket; I'd forgotten that. I'd have to tell Urquhart. Anyone staying at the houses would have had access to the castle notepaper. I'd have to ask Primeau questions, and Rhys, too. *That* I did not look forward to. To question Rhys about his past behavior would be difficult; I'd have to tiptoe around the topic. He was already angry at me; I didn't want to offend him by insinuating that he had an unsavory past.

That stopped me in my tracks; I was actually *worried* about asking vital questions concerning a violent attack? That was ridiculous. Nothing was more important right now than finding out who had so viciously hurt Gilda on my property. "What about Moze Markunis? No mention of a niece, you say?"

"No mention of a niece in his family biography at all. He *was* married, but is now a widower. More than a decade ago he started promoting Kamile in competitions in Europe. She was in a big competition there and came in third. The videos are on the internet. I've sent you the links."

A decade ago she would have been in her early teens. If Kamile wasn't his niece, then what *was* she to him? "She is so brilliant, a front-runner. And yet she's never won a competition before. I wonder why?"

"The common negative comment from judges was that she 'lacked authenticity,' whatever that means."

"That's what she said," I mused. "What did you say about a Lithuanian mob? Moze is involved in organized crime?"

Hannah twisted her mouth and hummed then spoke. "Mmmmaybe," she said, drawing it out. "Nobody knows. Here's what I learned: Lithuania, Latvia and Estonia make up the Baltic states. Moze Markunis has holdings in all of those countries, involved in oil refineries and banking." Hannah rustled through papers in front of her, notes she had made. "He was born poor, but now he's wealthy, and no one is quite sure how he gained his wealth and got to the point that he could invest so much into those industries except that he has ties in the U.S. with politicians and tech entrepreneurs. He's paid millions to lobbyists in the fuel industry. He's listed as an exporter, but I can't find out what he exports. I'm still digging, but there are vague hints of bribery in being awarded contracts. He spends most of his time in Europe, but a significant amount in the U.S. as well." She looked directly at me. "There are rumors I scouted out; it seems that men who have opposed him have disappeared or turned up dead."

"Well *that's* alarming."

"I know, but Merry, it's conjecture. Who knows if it has anything to do with him? What's that old saying . . . if you swim with sharks, prepare to get bit? Maybe he's only one of many sharks."

"It's all so sketchy. What about his family?"

"He's widowed and has no kids, just this girl, Kamile, his niece, he *says*. I'm still looking into it. I may have more to report later. I have photos of them together at events, her on his arm as if she's his escort."

I pondered that, but I was not willing to jump to conclusions.

Still . . . it was all so vaguely fishy. "I don't think Moze had any interaction with Gilda."

"If he was planning to kill her, wouldn't he make sure *not* to be seen with her?"

"I suppose. He left around dinnertime the night she disappeared, but he *could* have still been close by, I suppose." I sighed. I felt like I was grasping at straws, searching for answers when I wasn't even sure what the question was. I scrubbed at my gritty eyes. It was hard to fathom that this was happening to us again, but we do attract trouble. "I'm hoping that the attack on her had nothing to do with anyone in my castle or on my property. I'd better go. Talk to you soon." I closed my computer and sat in thought for a minute. There was nothing there that I should share with Urquhart. I mean, what *did* I have, vague suspicions and possible problems? Until I learned more, I would keep it to myself.

I returned to the kitchen, finished prepping, let Patricia go, then checked in with Urquhart. He was still in the library making notes, having finished his interviews.

"So . . . make any headway?" I asked.

He merely stared at me with no expression.

I joined Janice and Pish in the dining room to watch the last taping of the day. Anne and Sparrow, watching monitors and wearing headphones, guided the performers through their bits. What that meant in truth was a dozen false starts, with sound levels wrong, lighting wrong, mistakes in singing, chatter in the background, equipment falling over, or any one of a number of problems. Finally, each performer got one take down completely, sung to a simple piano track, then the performance was critiqued by the judges, as the contestant stood in front of them. Janice had been allowed to sit in; she was wide-eyed, thrilled to be there and quiet as a mouse. Pish was serious and interested. Giu looked over and smiled at him, and he gave a little wave back.

Alain was up first. After several stops and starts, he sang a final good version of "Je Crois Entendre Encore." His tone was light but rich. I'm no expert, but he was very *very* good, in my opinion, and I noted Pish nodding along with his performance in approval. I couldn't forget Hannah's revelation concerning the French Canadian. What was Alain up to? He hadn't mentioned his aunt's past as an opera singer, but why should he? And yet . . . Hannah had felt like there was something going on, something to do with Rhys. Did Primeau blame Rhys for his aunt's breakdown? I had an uneasy feeling that there was more to the story, but I had no idea what. I didn't want to upset the delicate balance of the show for the performers, but I *did* want to ask Alain about his aunt's breakdown and whether he blamed Rhys. What that could have to do with Gilda's attack, I could not figure out.

The judges commended him on his excellent performance, dismissed him, then turned to each other and discussed his performance among themselves, with the camera operator using a steady cam right in front of them. Primeau, they agreed, was a magnificent singer, with great promise, after which they proceeded to pick apart his performance in minute detail. He had faltered at one moment, and his vibrato felt forced. He had a minor problem with pacing, and at times appeared distracted, staring toward the judging panel and losing a word here and there. That comment from Anokhi made me think that perhaps the presence of Rhys had thrown him off.

Zeb Wolfe performed next, his silken voice tenderly lingering over the notes of the song "Somewhere (There's a Place for Us)" from *West Side Story*. I had already heard him sing it, but it still moved me, and tears welled in my eyes as I followed his swelling voice, over the hill and down to a whispered, heartbroken valley. It was mesmerizing. I wanted to leap out of my chair and clap and cheer. And yet . . . when it came time for the judging they criticized the light texture of his voice, wobble on the emotional notes, and an overall lack of operatic sensibility. I was miffed and would have protested except I had no business doing that. On sober reflection I got that Zeb was, indeed, less operatic than theatrical, which everyone acknowledged was his forte.

Lachlan was the last male, and he was great . . . at first. Singing "Lonely House" from *Street Scene*, an interesting cross between American musical and opera, he was doing well, but the song climbs . . . and climbs and *climbs*. His voice broke. They tried it again and again until Lachlan began to look panicked, the fear in his eyes sad to witness. I squirmed in my seat. I've always had trouble watching people in pain or being humiliated, and this, to me, was humiliating. I could see Roma at the edge of my sightline, pacing, looking worried. Finally, he made it through the song, but it was evident that he was struggling.

The judges were brutally honest, both to him and with each other. I didn't see any chance for Lachlan in the competition. When they were done eviscerating him, his face flooded with red and he threw down the microphone—it squawked and popped and one of the sound engineers wrenched the headphones off his head with a grimace—and yelled, "You lot are the worst judges I've ever seen, and I've seen too many. Puir lot o' posers, y'are." He stormed from the room, with the camera operator in his wake and Roma following too. Another camera operator documented the looks of shock and irritation on the judges' faces.

"That was unexpected," Anokhi said, a masterful understatement if ever I've heard one.

They then critiqued his performance for final judgment. Giu, ever the diplomat, stated, at the end of it, that anyone could have a bad day, and perhaps the dear boy was coming down with something. Rhys gave an uncharacteristic snort and said he didn't think Lachlan was coming down with anything but hurt pride.

It was the ladies up next. Darcie wended her way through a painful rendition of "Je Veux Vivre." Janice looked smug, and well she might; as I had noted before, my friend's rendition of it is far superior. Darcie *looked* lovely, everyone agreed. Unfortunately they also all agreed that she was getting worse, not better.

Brontay, rested and sparkling, was up next. She sang, with great aplomb, "O mio babbino caro." I was impressed with her light, sweet, flowing high notes and her lively engagement in the piece. I'm not an expert, so I looked to Pish, who is, and saw him smiling his way thought it. The judges enjoyed the performance and congratulated her on taking their advice and making progress. Brontay floated out of the room on wings of praise.

And last was Kamile. I sat closer to the edge of my seat. There was tragedy in her bearing, mystery. I've been on the fringes of the entertainment world for quite a few years and it had always struck me that the best performers were often the most tortured, the most troubled. She sang "Voi che sapete," a lilting, floating, trilling and graceful aria in the "trousers role" tradition. Her bottom notes were throaty and full-bodied. It was a brilliant performance, and watching her I thought for the first time since I had met her she looked, simply, happy. The judges were unstinting in their praise, stating that finally, *finally* they were getting genuineness. Kamile flushed, looking happy and relieved. Whatever else was going on in her life, she did love singing.

Finally, taping was done for the day. The judges returned to their houses, while the crew packed up and wearily drove off into the dark toward the dubious luxury of the motel. I sent an exhausted Janice home, and returned to the kitchen to finish dinner preparations, as Virgil arrived, freshly shaved, showered and far too handsome. He smelled good too, which I had the opportunity to find out when he pulled me onto his lap in the wingchair by the fireplace for a little canoodling.

We were surprised by Kamile, who, when she discovered us, backed off a step, looking flustered and embarrassed. I jumped off my husband's lap and straightened my clothes.

"I'm sorry to interrupt," she said, her throaty voice a murmur. "I wondered if I could help? I helped my mother in the kitchen when I was young, but I'm on the road so much I don't have the chance."

I gave my husband the side-eye. "It's a clear evening so I'm going to do the steaks on the outside grill," he said. "It's got a lot more space on it than the stove grill. I'll go fire it up."

"If you're serious, I could use the help," I said to Kamile, seeing it as an opportunity to get to know her better.

She was tall, towering over me, though she was wearing flats. Her clothes were loose . . . ill-fitting, I would say, a sign to me of someone uncomfortable with their body. My heart ached with concern, but I reminded myself not to jump to conclusions. I set her to the task of chopping green onions for the baked potato fixings. She had large bony hands, suitable to her long-limbed body, but she used them with grace and economy. "I'm out of practice," she said with a husky laugh.

We chatted about nonessentials as the others flitted in and out of the kitchen. Sparrow in particular was annoying, unusually gloomy, perturbed. She lingered, asked me weird questions about the police, about the castle, about past incidents at Wynter Castle. I answered with as much economy as I could and busied her with things that took her out of the kitchen. Finally I banished everyone but Kamile to the breakfast room with trays of hors d'oeuvres. The singer laughed as I sighed in exasperation.

"Try being questioned by Sparrow," the young woman said. "It is torture."

"The point of her questioning, as I understand it, is to evoke an emotional response from you all, and then edit what you have said to fit a narrative they devise. How do you feel about that?"

She paused, her hands resting on the edge of the cutting board. "Perhaps I observe more closely than the others, but I did not let her control the interview. She is clumsy, oafish, even," she said, her faint Euro accent present in her stilted wording. "She is easily manipulated, which is surprising considering she is the one supposed to be manipulating *us*. She tried to trick me into unthinking remarks concerning another contestant, but evading her intent was not difficult."

I eyed her with respect. She was surprisingly savvy. "Who did she ask you about?"

She glanced at me with an assessing, chilly look. "Darcie. Sparrow wished me to make unkind remarks about her. It was cruel, like suggesting I beat an injured animal."

It was an apt description, given Darcie's poor performance. "I can understand. You were not in the room when she sang but trust me . . . Darcie's performance was dreadful. How did she make it so far?"

Kamile shrugged.

After a silent pause, I asked, "Did Gilda interview you all for her article? I know she was on-site, watching the proceedings, but did she have access to you?"

"On occasion. She asked many questions."

"What kind of questions?"

"Oh, just . . . questions."

I watched her for a moment. She was so self-contained that it was like regarding a perfect brittle glass bowl and worrying that if you handled it too roughly, it would shatter in your hands. "I'm curious, Kamile," I said, glancing over at her, now chopping cooked bacon. "How did the competition go at the hotel in Rochester? I heard there were incidents there. *Many* incidents, some dangerous."

Frowning, she nodded without looking up, and crossed herself with her free hand. "It was as if the show was cursed. I felt it."

"What kind of things happened?"

"Oh, the electricity went out in the ballroom while we were taping. One of the crew fell ill with food poisoning, as did Lachlan. Brontay's costume was ripped. Alain tripped on loose carpet and fell down a flight of stairs."

"Did anything happen to you?"

She looked up at me, her eyes hooded, her expression brooding. "No. I was fortunate. Why do you ask?"

I felt a chill down my back. Moze Markunis was reportedly merciless as a businessman; people who opposed him disappeared or died. To what lengths would he go to have his niece win the competition, even if it meant ruthlessly taking out other competitors? "No reason," I said. I glanced at her sideways. "Your performance today was brilliant. The judges seemed pleased."

She didn't comment. Okay, so flattery could not win her confidence.

"What do *you* think happened to Gilda?" I asked bluntly, watching her.

She jolted, and bacon spilled. She scrupulously wiped the bits from the counter and carried them to the garbage, which I pointed out. She then washed her hands and turned to me. "I think she probably questioned the wrong person about the wrong thing. She was careless. She was meddlesome. She got in trouble." She paused, her eyes glittering in the pin spots over the counter. Then, with no change in expression, she said, "I should go and join the others."

With that, she turned and glided out of the room.

Twenty

Uneasy, I shivered as Virgil came in from the grill to get the steaks. He saw my shiver and encircled me from behind. I rested my head back on his shoulder. He asked what was wrong, of course. I turned in his arms and murmured my conversation with Kamile to him.

He looked troubled, breaking away from me and unwrapping the steaks, putting them on a platter, and prepping the Portobello mushrooms with olive oil and herbs. I watched him, noting the flexing jaw, the twitch of his shoulders, following some internal dialogue he was not sharing. "Speak up," I said, watching his face. "Tell me what you're thinking."

He sighed and frowned, and shook his head. "I don't know how to say this without it being offensive."

"You know you can say anything to me."

He turned and stared past me, his gaze unfocused. "There is something about Kamile, and I can't pinpoint it. My old cop instincts are clanging alarms like a bomb is about to go off. There's something . . . *something* wrong. Something . . . *false*. Like she isn't who she says she is." He shook his head and shrugged, perplexed.

Isn't who she says she is. Like, not Moze's niece? I didn't have a chance to follow up as Anne came in at that moment and said, "Merry, do you have any more of the white wine we had the other night? I *need* a glass."

"There are a couple of bottles in the wine fridge. Help yourself."

Virgil grabbed a bottle of beer and carried the steaks and mushrooms out of the kitchen to go out in the dark and grill. Anne retrieved a couple of bottles of the wine and examined the wine rack, which held the reds. "That is one handsome man you have there." She turned with the two bottles of white.

I smiled, then bent to take the baking sheet of baked potatoes out of the oven and set them on a rack. "He is, isn't he? He's one of the good ones."

"Virgil is a cop, right?"

"Was. When I met him he was sheriff of the Autumn Vale force. He's now a private detective."

She watched me for a moment. "Do you think he'd be willing to work for the production company?"

"What do you mean 'work for'?"

"I'm worried about the attack on Gilda. I'm not convinced that Sheriff Urquhart will solve the crime."

"Urquhart is a good police officer. He's smart and dedicated." I couldn't believe I said that, but I did believe it.

"Still . . . HHN would be willing to pay your husband to look into it," she said, staring at me intently. "They have deep pockets, you know."

I sighed. Virgil has been careful, since leaving the police department, about not interfering in anything Urquhart, his mentee, was investigating unless invited. "He's busy right now," I said, which was true. The missing and murdered girls' task force was taking a great deal of time and trouble.

"Not too busy to grill steaks for us. Surely he can hear us out?"

I knew he wouldn't take it on. He was *informally* investigating along with me, but I didn't want her knowing I was trying to figure out who had attacked Gilda in my woods and that I suspected one of them. However, it struck me that under the guise of "hearing her out" we might be able to winkle information from her about what she knew without betraying my own sleuthing. "I'll see if I can set something up. Would you have time this evening to talk to Virgil? If he's going to consider taking the case on, he'll need to hear what you have, first."

"I don't have *anything*. That's the problem."

"I wouldn't be so sure." I hesitated, watching her through squinted eyes, but then said, "Anne, you do realize that the most likely culprit to have attacked Gilda is among your crew or cast?"

Eyes wide with horror, she slowly nodded. "I knew that." She shivered and her eyes teared up. "I didn't want to admit it even to myself."

"So you may know more than you realize. We'll all be sitting down to dinner in a few minutes. Do you mind if my husband and I ask leading questions, or point the conversation in a certain direction? And will you play along with us? Then we can talk later."

She nodded. "Do it. I'm sick of looking over my shoulder and worrying. This shoot has been nothing but headaches and all I want is to be done with it and go home to my husband and my cats."

At the word *cats*, Becket rose from his spot near the hearth, ambled over to her and rubbed against her legs. She set the wine aside, picked him up and held him close to her face, inhaling deeply. "The hero of the hour, saving Gilda's life! You, handsome boy, have been out and about lately. I can smell the fresh air on your fur."

"You have a remarkable nose."

She set him down and picked up the wine. "That's why I love this so much," she said, waving one bottle around. "Good tea, good coffee, good wine. All smell divine." She sighed. "Maybe I'll take a bottle to bed to go with my sleeping pill."

• • •

I spoke to Virgil before we served, and he reluctantly agreed to help me pry information out of our guests as long as we shared anything we discovered with Urquhart. I agreed with alacrity. "I hate sharing our home with someone who would do such a thing, Virgil. I can't wait for this to be over and the HHN people to be gone."

Dinner was a success. For a while people ate steadily, with a minimum of chatter. Eventually, though, as hunger was sated and with the lubricating quality of copious amounts of wine, beer and even Pish's extensive liquor collection, which he threw open at my suggestion, our guests started to talk.

The twelve at the table in the breakfast room had various attitudes and expressions. Kamile was quiet, and ate sparingly. Alain ate with gusto and enjoyed copious amounts of red wine, while Lachlan ate a giant steak with no baked potato and drank only water. Brontay wanted a burger, while her mom ate the grilled Portobello mushroom and salad, as did Darcie; both women drank wine. Anne ate a burger and drank the wine, then started on a bottle of chardonnay, and moved to a zinfandel, quietly getting blotto. Sparrow watched her anxiously and ate like her namesake, her gaze flitting around the table; the woman was so nervous she made *me* nervous.

As the diners were finishing up, I raised my glass and tapped the edge with my spoon. I looked around at the faces turned to me. "I'd like to make a toast to you all, and to Gilda, who we all pray will recover from her injuries. Congratulations to all of you, the contestants, and to the producers, who have been working so hard to make a success of *Opera DivaNation*."

"Hear, hear," Anne said, raising her glass and sloshing white wine over the edge.

My eye caught on Brontay, whose gaze was anxiously roaming the group. She had claimed what happened to Gilda was all her fault. I wondered if Urquhart had questioned her about why she said it. I'd like to ask her myself, but this was not the time or place. Later.

Alain made a florid toast, almost as drunk as Anne by now. Kamile did not participate in any of the toasts, and drank little, just one glass of the red, which she was nursing.

I had whispered my plan to Pish, and he vowed to help. "I'm worried about that poor young woman," he said about Gilda. "I feel responsible. I never like to think I could have done anything to help and failed. What do you think, Sparrow; you seemed to be close to Gilda. Do you have any idea who she may have been going out to meet?"

She shivered and her eyes were wide, whites showing around the iris, but I couldn't tell if that was part of her habitual nervousness or fear. Was she worried about it happening to her?

"Do you know who she went out to meet?" I asked again.

"I *wasn't* close to her. I don't know where you got that idea."

"I understood you two were old friends." I watched her pale oval face. A panoply of emotions flitted across it, with a twitch and a grimace, as she shook her head in automatic disagreement. Lachlan eyed me with suspicion, and I worried I had laid it on too thick.

Darcie said, "I saw you arguing once—you and Gilda—in the hall at the hotel. What were you arguing about?"

"We *weren't* arguing," Sparrow said. "That's ridiculous. You're imagining things. She was after *you*, though, wasn't she?"

"After Darcie?" I asked. "How?"

Sparrow turned and glared at me. She was about to speak but Lachlan interrupted. "Darcie, surely you're imagining things, as our little bird says?"

"You *all* wanted to get rid of Gilda," Brontay burst out, glaring around the table. "Every *one* of you; she had stuff on everyone because that's the kind of reporter she was."

"Brontay, what are you talking about?" Pam gasped, setting her wineglass down too hard and slopping red all over the tablecloth.

I wouldn't have asked in front of everyone, but Darcie felt no such hesitation. "Brontay, what do you know about Gilda?" the singer asked. "Do you know why she was out that night?"

The teen looked guilty and miserable, but she nodded. "She got a note telling her to meet him—him, her, *whoever*—down by the woods."

"How do you know any of that?" her mother asked.

Because she's the mole, I thought but did not say. Her words confirmed what I had thought was a possibility. I flashed a look around the table. It was too dangerous for people to know that Brontay had been snooping and feeding information to Gilda. I sent the kid a warning look, then said, "Look, *if* Brontay knows anything for sure and isn't just guessing, then she should be telling the police, not all of us."

Virgil said, "I think we all say things we think are true when sometimes we are only guessing."

"What do you mean, Detective?" Anne slurred.

Some of the guests looked startled, in particular Sparrow, who narrowly gazed at her associate.

Virgil hesitated only a second, then said the most outrageous thing he could think of. "I *could* say that Lachlan and Darcie are feeling a strong physical attraction but are denying it."

I bit back a smile at my husband's brilliant misdirection; both of the singers denied it vehemently.

"Me an' Darcie? Hah!"

"Him? I'd sooner be linked with a baboon," Darcie said with a sniff and haughty tilt to her head.

"Isn't that the basis of almost every romantic comedy movie ever made, that people who argue constantly are trying to fight physical attraction? Like the whole bath situation," I said. "A sexy made-for-the-movies dilemma, right? Two people arguing about a bubble bath, one person banging on the door? It's like a scene out of a rom-com."

Darcie, her cheeks reddening, looked away, glaring at the buffet with frowning intensity. "I wanted a bath, for heaven's sake."

"I haird her, at the door, shoutin' and bangin'," Lachlan said with a devilish smile. "But I was otherwise occupied. And I was not thinking of our dear Darcie while I was so occupied, I can *promise* you that."

I don't usually blush, but my surmise that he was having phone sex with someone came to mind and my cheeks pinkened, I'm afraid. "What *were* you doing in the bath for such a *long* time, though? All joking aside."

He raised his eyebrows and then winked. "Why don't you ask where Darcie went when she *had* been so heated about the bath? She was nowhere to be found when I got out. Ask her roommate."

As Darcie spluttered a denial, I turned to Kamile. "Was Darcie in your room all night?"

"Now see here . . . that's a *definite* intrusion," Sparrow exclaimed, glaring at me. "What's going on?"

"It's nothing that you haven't probably already told Sheriff Urquhart, correct?"

Lachlan nodded. "Aye, it's true. I told the sheriff about our little bath problem, but I wasn't in the room when Darcie answered, so I dinna know what *she* told the copper."

I sighed. Lachlan was one of those guys who clearly like to make trouble, and enjoy the fallout. It was irritating.

"Anne, are we actually being questioned by our *hosts*?" Sparrow said. "What is going on here? It's *outrageous*."

Anne looked confused, blinking blearily at me.

"It was just a question," I said.

Kamile watched us both, not saying a word.

Alain spoke up. "I am okay with questions, having nothing to hide. Zeb and me . . . we both watched our videos . . . the ones the technical staff give us if we ask—I watched mine many times and took notes—then later Lachlan came in from the bath smelling like the rose, and we slept. What the ladies did, we cannot say, hein, mes amis?"

Brontay rolled her eyes. "There he goes again, with the Frenchie stuff."

"Brontay, enough," said Pam. "I'm done, and so is my daughter. We're going upstairs and locking ourselves in for the rest of the evening."

"What about dessert?" I said.

"We'll do without." She grabbed her daughter and hauled her away from the table.

"Tomorrow is the second-to-last day of taping, Pam!" Sparrow shouted.

"I know!" she yelled back. "Brontay will be ready."

"Drinks in the library?" I said brightly, glancing around.

Anne's head was already on the table, so I assumed that was a no for her, nor would she be up and able to talk about Virgil taking on the case. Sparrow sighed and said that if someone could help, she'd get her fellow producer to bed. Lachlan, a brawny lad (as he'd no doubt describe himself), offered to carry her, and Sparrow agreed, but ultimately Anne was able to stagger up the stairs supported on both sides by the two. Kamile murmured a goodnight, Darcie flounced off in a huff, Zeb offered to help clear—an offer I declined—and Alain flitted off speaking rapidly in joual on his phone.

Determined to find out about his aunt, I followed him out to the great hall and plucked at his sleeve. "Alain, when you are done with your call, may I speak with you?"

He nodded, distracted, then went on to rapid speech.

I don't know any joual, but I do know some French, and I know I heard a few familiar words and names, among them Tante Marie, and Sir Daffyd Rhys's name. It hardened my determination to get to the bottom of his history with the Welsh singer, and if he knew anything about Gilda's near-demise.

"I'm sorry that didn't go as planned," Pish said as he helped me tidy the table in the breakfast room. Virgil had been in the kitchen loading the dishwasher, but returned with the bus tray to load the rest of the china that wouldn't go in the dishwasher.

"Does it ever go as planned?" I asked with a sigh. "The night Gilda was attacked troubles me."

"Do we know what time she was last seen?" Virgil asked, dumping silver utensils in his tray.

"I don't think so . . . it's confusing. She was here, and then she wasn't. It was hard to keep track of *anyone* with everyone coming and going. She must have slipped out with no one to see her, unless . . ."

"Unless someone *did* see her and follow."

I nodded. "I was up and down all night because I had trouble sleeping, with you gone and Becket out. I saw and heard a few of our guests who appeared to have trouble sleeping." I related who I had seen and when, and that I had told Urquhart what I knew.

I remembered what Doc had said about the car in Autumn Vale. Could it have been Gilda's rental car? It had been returned to Batavia.

How long would that take? I worked it out in my head. Autumn Vale to Batavia is about ten miles, give or take. Five minutes into Autumn Vale and ten from AV to Batavia—less if someone drove like crazy—and ten minutes back to town, then five minutes back to Wynter Castle. Half an hour is all it would take if they had everything timed down to the minute but . . . they would need a ride back.

They'd need a ride back.

"There *have* to be two people working together," I said as Virgil carefully stacked crystal wineglasses on top of the silverware. "Because they would need someone to drive Gilda's car, and someone to drive a car to drive that person back here."

Pish clapped and said *of course,* while my husband's gaze remained hooded and oblique.

"You already knew that, didn't you?" I said to him with (I'll admit) an accusatory tone. He shrugged and I sighed. Of *course* he did, and Urquhart likely did too. I felt like a dummy for not thinking of it earlier, but I had been distracted. We weren't looking for one culprit, we were looking for two. What two could be working together?

I got a damp cloth and wiped the table down as my husband carried the bus tray back to the kitchen. Determined not to leave anyone out, I considered pairs. First, as silly as it seemed, Pam and Brontay? That was dumb, though Pam had been up and dressed and outside. I couldn't dismiss her entirely, but Brontay wouldn't have been involved, though the kid knew more than she had so far said. Pam could have been working with someone else, though.

Darcie was, according to Lachlan, missing for a period of time, and Sparrow was offended when the singer's roommates were prodded for information on her coming and going. Could Sparrow be in cahoots with Darcie? Gilda could have dirt on Darcie, who I suspected of doing whatever she felt she needed to do to get ahead.

It was a little much to imagine Lachlan, Zeb and Alain all working together, and they were present and accounted for during the essential time period, when Gilda presumably went missing and was attacked. One or two of them could have snuck out, I supposed, but it was unlikely.

There was another possibility: someone in the castle *could* be working with someone who was staying at the motel near Ridley

Ridge, a crew member, or even an outside friend. Again, unlikely but possible. One more possibility in a case that already had too many.

I was putting a clean tablecloth on the table in the breakfast room when Roma, who had been at Liliana's house with the other mentors and judges, sought me out. She looked troubled and watched me with a frown. "Sir Daffyd is angry. He's threatening a lawsuit," she said, but there was no venom in her voice. "He's threatening to sink this whole project, the Wynter Woods Performing Center."

"Why?" I yelped, my stomach squeezing in panic.

"He says you questioned him, accused him, then sicced the police on him."

"Me? I did no such thing!" Not exactly.

"He's angry. I guess Sheriff Urquhart spent an hour asking him about his movements."

"Shouldn't be a problem if he was at the party all evening, like he *says* he was," I said, giving the tablecloth a last snap and letting it fall in place. "But he wasn't. Pish says he was MIA for at least part of the evening."

She looked troubled.

Pish, who had followed her in, put an arm around her shoulders. "I'm not imagining things, you know. Daffyd was not there for at least an hour. I *had* to tell the police that."

She was silent and still.

"Roma, a woman is lying in the hospital in a coma," I said, my voice trembling. "If you know *anything* . . ."

She nodded, tears welling in her eyes, and glanced between us. "Rhys has . . . a reputation."

Pish watched her and knit his brows. "A reputation?"

"Among female opera singers."

I stiffened.

"A reputation for what?" Pish asked.

"For . . ." She moved her shoulders, as if she was trying to shrug off the truth, and the tears spilled over, running down her cheeks. "For not nice behavior."

"He's rude? Demanding? Hysterical sometimes?" Pish said with a smile. He squeezed her shoulder. "That is not new, my darling—"

"He's molested women, hasn't he?" I said, my voice hollow.

She nodded, looking down at her feet.

"In fact, he did something to you?"

She nodded. Pish gasped in horror and put both arms around her. Virgil made an inarticulate grunt of anger.

"What did he do? Why didn't you tell . . ." Pish trailed off and froze, staring into space.

"Roma, you don't need to tell us anything," I said, shaken to the core. "But if you *do* tell us, we'll only share it with Urquhart if you agree."

She looked over at me with gratitude. "Can we sit down somewhere?"

We left the breakfast room to finish tidying later and followed Pish to the library, where he sat on one side of her on the sofa and I sat on the other, while Virgil stayed in the shadows. Bit by bit Roma told the story, the usual tale of a starstruck singer in the presence of true greatness. Rhys was in a management position with an opera company—not the LOC—and Roma was in the chorus. She hung on his every word, and he invited her to come to his hotel room. There were drinks offered, and an advantage pushed. He was rough; he was demanding. But . . .

"He didn't *force* me," she said, looking into my eyes. Her chin went up, and her voice was high and tight as she said, "I sobered up and I made a decision; he could help me, he said, but it depended on me sleeping with him. And why not? I was no virgin. Better to get something more than a broken heart from sex."

The cynical quid pro quo of life in entertainment; even the elevated circles of opera and the symphony were not free, it seemed, of sexual excess. "Still, Roma, he took advantage of you. You may not feel it, you may excuse his behavior, you may blame yourself, but he took advantage of his position to compel you into something you were reluctant to do."

She nodded, acknowledging it. "The next morning he threw me out of his hotel room—physically *threw* me out into the hall—and said if I told anyone he'd make sure I was blackballed." She sighed. "I had sex with him willingly. What was I going to say? So, I shut my mouth and . . . he did help me. Payment received," she said bitterly.

"He's done this before," I said, watching her.

She nodded. "And since. That was seven years ago, and I've thought about it a lot over the years. I'm lucky; I have friends and close family. If I had been alone and friendless things may have gone differently."

"What do you mean?" Pish asked.

I watched her eyes. "She means that she could have walked away that night and he would have let her go. She means that she said yes and they had sex. But without that background support, which he no doubt knew about—"

"He did. We had talked about my family."

"—the story may have been different. There is a certain kind of man who knows how to assess a girl with no support system, knows how to manage her, how to bend her to his will," I said, still watching her.

Roma nodded. "There are other girls out there who had it rougher than I did, who Rhys treated much worse."

"Why didn't I know about this? Roma, you know me well enough to know . . ." Pish trailed off, his expression agonized.

Roma put one hand on his. "It's not your fault. We don't talk about it much . . . the other women, except little whispers to be careful around him. He's adept at hiding his behavior. I had heard he was not to be trusted, but I didn't listen to the woman who warned me. I wrote it off as jealousy. Cattiness. I figured he wouldn't give her the time of day so she was trying to destroy him." She sighed shakily. "That's how guys like him get away with it."

"Plus they have the power and money to threaten to sue if you say anything."

She nodded.

"What do you think he'd do if Gilda learned about his past and threatened to expose it?"

She shrugged. "He doesn't like being confronted or held accountable. He changes from Prince Charming to the prince of darkness pretty fast."

I met my friend's gaze across her. "Pish, you've already told Urquhart about Rhys being missing from the party. And we have proof that *something* happened in Rochester at the hotel."

"Rhys is who Moze Markunis fought with that got the whole production kicked out of the hotel," Pish said, nodding. "Rhys must have done something to Kamile, and that set Moze off."

"That likely lets Moze and Kamile off the hook though, because they would have no reason to attack *Gilda,* in that case."

"Don't jump to conclusions," Virgil said, moving from the shadows into the pool of light cast by the desk lamp. "Just because there seems to be no reason you can think of in that instance doesn't mean there isn't something else, something more. Look, if I read the situation with Rhys right, and excuse me, Roma, if I get this wrong," he said, glancing at her. "Reputation is important in the opera world. If there were whispers about Kamile and Rhys having an affair that had gone bad . . . if word was getting out that Kamile was the cause of the whole *DivaNation* production being evicted from the hotel in Rochester, whose reputation would it damage the most, his or hers?"

"Hers," all three of us said at once.

"*He's* the one with the star power," Roma said. "*He's* the one with legions of fans. *He's* the one with a cadre of lawyers at his beck and call and the money to employ them, and the friends in the industry to vouch for him. If it went further, if Kamile Markunis complained and was the cause of Sir Daffyd Rhys, legendary tenor star, losing his position, the girl could be blackballed even now, even with all that has happened lately. It's still going on, women being ruined when they come out with an accusation."

Virgil was right; there was potentially a motive for Moze and Kamile to want Gilda silenced if the journalist knew about the substance of the quarrel between Rhys and Moze. There was the danger to Kamile's future career, which was important to Moze, and there could be more to it, more than the problem between the two men. What if Gilda knew about something wrong with the relationship? That would give Moze a motive to shut the journalist up, and if he had enough power over Kamile, maybe she'd help him.

But Kamile was not necessarily involved. Much depended on whether Markunis had an alibi or not. I wondered about the car in Autumn Vale. Had it been Gilda's? And if so, was it possible that the man who Doc's friend saw toss the keys into the car was Moze? Who was he leaving the keys for? A man like Moze Markunis would likely have people on payroll ready to do any task.

"This is a mess, but we can't worry about Rhys's threat to us," I said glumly. "I don't want him associated with our project now anyway. He needs to be exposed for the slimeball he is. I wonder how much Anne and Sparrow know?"

"I'm so deeply shocked," Pish said, his eyes shadowed with worry. "I have to assume the two ladies know more than we do."

"We'll figure it out." I turned to Roma. "Are you okay? Do you need company tonight? We'll stay up with you if you do."

She smiled. "No. You know, it happened a long time ago, and I've made my peace with it." Her smiled died and she sighed. "Okay, I obviously haven't *totally* made peace with it, but I sleep better now than I did at first."

We all headed upstairs to our rooms, and it was only then that I remembered I had told Alain I wanted to speak with him. He had not sought me out, and had disappeared into his room, the door tightly closed. I was left wondering . . . what was Alain Primeau hiding?

Twenty-one

Saturday dawned. With everything that had happened I was hoping to get through the last two days of the *Opera DivaNation* competition and get them all—the cast, the crew, the producers—out of the castle. I had to have a serious talk with Anne about Sir Daffyd Rhys; what she knew about him and when, and what they planned to do about it. It *should* be done immediately, but I didn't know how to tackle the subject so I put it off. I had a fatalistic view that with a production as plagued by misfortune as *Opera DivaNation*, it would likely never be aired anyway.

I take full responsibility for the fact that I was procrastinating. Pish offered to do the deed, and I understood that he felt responsible for the fact that he had known the man for years but had never suspected his behavior went so far, however . . . I felt the information should come from me. I would do it, I just needed to think it over and decide how. I think I was stalling because once I told Anne what we knew and that we expected them to handle Rhys, the production might stall. If that happened we'd have a castle full of angry contestants whose chances at a quick entrée into the world of opera would be dashed.

I was most *deeply* concerned that we had someone among us who had attempted murder. Hopefully we'd catch whoever attacked Gilda. We hadn't ruled out *anyone* as Gilda's attackers. Urquhart was nowhere to be seen, but I know enough about police work now to understand that he was at work, investigating leads.

While Virgil still slept upstairs in our castle bedroom with Becket draped over his chest, I had morning coffee with Pish while I made muffins for the café and Golden Acres. After discussing what we would do if Rhys followed through on his threats, I let my mind ramble through all the things I had to get done. "Oh! I forgot to ask you," I said. "Pish, the window washer gave you a list of things that had disappeared from their truck. Have you tracked anything down yet?"

"I haven't had a moment to check."

"What's on the list?"

"Let me get it; it's on my desk." He came back with it in hand and donned his reading glasses. "Let's see: there are only three things."

"Three things too many, and I don't like the idea that we have a thief around, likely in this group of TV lunatics," I said, ladling batter into paper muffin cups. I know, a thief seemed like small potatoes when we had a homicidal maniac on the premises, but it was too much, *all* of it. I was fed up and ready to take action on each problem we were dealing with. "What are the items? I'll keep my eyes open."

"A drop cloth, one of their jackets, and a utility knife."

"Huh. Weird list." Or maybe not so weird. Was it connected to the assault? If someone was planning a murder the drop cloth *could* be used to move a body, but there was no indication that Gilda had been moved. A utility knife was suspicious, given that Gilda had apparently suffered stab wounds, but in my estimation a utility knife would not have a deep enough blade to do damage. Taken together, those two things could mean that the assailant's plans had gone awry, that he—or she—had intended to kill Gilda, wrap her body in the drop cloth, and take her somewhere to dispose of. But the Batavia Sparkle Clean jacket? Odd. I'd be sure to tell Urquhart when I saw him next about the missing items.

Janice and Patricia arrived with a laden van, and I helped them unload. Janice was having the time of her life and bustled around the kitchen singing bits from "O mio babbino caro." I finished my muffins and set them aside to cool; if you put them in plastic tubs too warm they get mushy. I was about to go upstairs to change my clothes to town-suitable wear when I got a text from Hannah; she had more information for me. I texted back that I'd be in town and drop in to see her at the library.

I was again about to leave the kitchen when Janice said brightly, "Do you need the muffin tins for anything for the rest of the day?" She held one up and waggled it.

"Nope."

"I thought for the craft services table I'd do up a selection of meals in a muffin tin."

"What did you have in mind?"

"Stuff my sons liked when they were young," she said. "The crew work up an appetite, so I have a whole slew of recipes for mini meatloaves, macaroni and cheese in a muffin tin, potato puffs, pizza bombs, things like that. My boys loved them because they could grab and go."

"You go for it," I said with a smile. Virgil was in the shower when I went upstairs so I shared a steamy kiss with him and told him I'd see him later. I changed into leggings, a tunic, boots and an oversized sweater coat with a scarf, donned chunky art-glass jewelry, and retrieved, from the kitchen, my plastic totes of muffins. I headed out, avoiding the production crew, who were setting up for the day's shoot, and Anne and Sparrow, arguing inside the dining room about missing music for one of the singers. I gritted my teeth; I would have a conversation with them later, but right now I needed to move.

I drove out of my lane and paused by the woods, where a police crew was still present. I watched for a moment, wondering what they had found. I wished Urquhart was more forthcoming with info. I do get why he can't be, but it's annoying. When Virgil was sheriff I could always wheedle information out of him. But Urquhart, despite all that, was a good guy. People are surprising. Sometimes, like with Urquhart, you start out not liking someone and then discover the warm, kind heart that beats beneath the chilly exterior. Or it goes the other way. I had built Sir Daffyd Rhys, legendary tenor, star of stage and screen, up in my mind to be extraordinary, but it turned out he was just a run-of-the-mill abuser.

I did my muffin drop-offs then headed to the library, where I found Hannah, who always opened on Saturdays for the villagers. There were a few patrons so I lingered, waiting for them to clear out. The last was a woman who was borrowing a cookbook of soup recipes and chatting with Hannah. She was middle-aged, a big woman, wearing a black coat that was covered in dog hair.

Isadore came in at that moment with her morning break apple and took a seat. She beckoned to me and pointed at the woman, who was finally done chatting with Hannah. "That's her," she whispered then took her seat.

"Her who?"

"The one who saw your cat."

As the patron turned away from Hannah, I approached her with a smile. "Hi. I'm Merry Wynter. I understand that you saw my cat in the woods along my property the other night?"

She looked startled but then nodded. "You're the lady who owns Wynter Castle," she said. She had a surprising voice, light and lively. "I've seen you in the coffee shop before. Big orange cat, right?"

"That's Becket. He finally came home the next morning."

"Oh, good to know." She was about to walk away, but then, lips firmed, she turned back to me. "I've heard that you found a dead body in that woods the next day. Is that true?"

The gossip mill was faulty, it appeared. Urquhart was not one to do press releases; he preferred to conduct his investigations with his cards close to his chest. "Not *exactly*. We did find someone with the help of my cat, but she is very much alive. I understand that you heard a scream as you stood at the edge of the woods looking for your dog. Could it have been Gi . . . uh, her? The woman?"

She started shaking her head right away. "No, no, it wasn't a *scream*, it was an owl. I said the eastern screech owl call *sounds* like a scream. It's quite startling, especially when you're standing by the dark woods."

So it *wasn't* Gilda who screamed. I'd hoped to pinpoint the time of the attack; she seemed quite sure. "Would that owl call if there was anyone—any human, that is—around?"

"Possibly. Why?"

That squashed another possibility, any hope of using her information to pinpoint the time evaporating. "I just wondered."

She stared at me for a moment then her gaze shifted, became less direct, more internal. "You know, I had a feeling, though . . . that someone was watching me."

I glanced over at Isadore and said, "I had heard that you saw a woman."

She frowned and shook her head, her cheeks pinkening. "No, I saw *something*, movement and a flash of white, but I couldn't say it was a woman."

"I heard that you saw a woman," I said stubbornly.

She sighed. "I may have . . . I mean, you know, when you get to telling a story, sometimes . . ."

I got it; she exaggerated.

"I did see a flash of white, though. I even called out. I thought it might be whoever owned the cat looking for him. So it wasn't you?" I shook my head. "Do you think it's possible there was someone there?" she asked.

"I don't know," I said. "Did you happen to note the exact time you were there, along the woods?"

"The sheriff asked me the same thing. I *did* notice the time. That was ten fifty. I drove home slow, still looking for my dog, and missed all but the last couple of minutes of my home reno show that starts at eleven. Laddy was on the porch when I got home, silly boy. He was probably out in the field chasing mice and ignoring Mom." She departed.

We were alone except for Isadore, which was like being alone. I trust Isadore. She's odd, but she's good people. I sat down in the guest chair by Hannah and we shared muffins as she finished what she was doing. "I've found out a bunch even since our video chat," she said, tapping away at the keyboard and bringing up notes on her monitor. "I'll send this to your email. There's breaking news; one of the chambermaids in that hotel in Rochester where *Opera DivaNation* was being taped gave an interview and said that one of the opera stars exposed himself to her when she went to clean his room."

My heart thumped, but after hearing Roma's story I wasn't so surprised. "Let me guess who it was; Sir Daffyd Rhys."

She nodded.

"Is he going to be arrested?"

"I don't think she's filed an official complaint yet."

I had been considering Rhys a front-runner as a suspect because of his disappearance during the party at Liliana's, but the more I thought of it the less I considered him likely to try to kill Gilda for threatening to expose his horrible behavior. People must have known of his conduct for decades and let it go. He felt untouchable, I'd bet, invulnerable to facing the music, to use a fitting cliché. But still . . . I shook my head. He remained on my list. There were too many variables and unknowns in this instance.

"And then there is what more I learned about Lachlan," Hannah said. "I came across a couple of news items in obscure foreign newspapers. They're a little hard to understand because I've used online translation software to interpret them, but here . . . you be the judge."

I read quickly through the news items. It appeared that Lachlan's departure from the Scottish Tenors happened immediately after trouble in Sweden. At a bar away from the concert venue he became embroiled in a drunken altercation after he made a pass at a girl. Her friend objected and he assaulted the fellow, which resulted in a broken jaw, a night in jail, charges and eviction from the country. There were no comments from the other singers in his group, but I could imagine the consternation at being ejected from a country, and wondering when it would happen next. The Lachlan I knew seemed abstemious, but maybe he had cleaned up his act in an effort to find solo success.

So Lachlan had a violent temper. Troubling, but I could not figure out how he fit into Gilda's attack. Though he had been listed in her notes as someone she was looking into, I had no indication that he and the journalist had clashed. And unless Zeb and Alain were lying, he was well alibied, his presence accounted for.

Though Darcie's was not. I blinked. Why had I not seriously considered *her* as a suspect? According to Lachlan, she was nowhere to be found when he got out of the bath. Who could she have been working with? One possibility occurred to me, and I didn't like it a bit. What exactly *would* she do for fame and fortune? She and Sir Daffyd Rhys were absent at about the same time. She was hugely ambitious and seemed to be teetering on a knife edge of uncertainty, a dangerous—and uncomfortable—place to be. Would she aid and abet a would-be killer to secure a career in show business?

"By the way, have you asked Alain Primeau about the information I gave you?" she asked.

"I have not," I said, shaking off my wool-gathering. "I will talk to him today. Is there anything else?" I asked.

"There is *one* thing. You know I don't like unanswered questions."

"I do know that about you. You will poke around until you find answers."

"Hold onto your hat, I've discovered something interesting."

What she told me next shook me to the core. She had dug deep in her research, made connections in the greater world, and with her nimble mind had deduced something potentially shocking.

"You are incredible," I said in awe, my mind numbed by what she had told me.

"I'm not positive about this," she warned.

"But you may be right, and if you are—"

"It may not have anything to do with the attack on Gilda."

"Still, Hannah . . . what if it's true? This is an extremely delicate situation. I need to think about this for a while."

I headed back to the castle, my mind reeling from Hannah's suppositions and reasoning. And yet I was becoming increasingly sure she was right. If so, this was going to take careful handling. What she told me made so many things fall into place and yet . . . she was one hundred percent right; it may or may *not* be connected to Gilda's attack.

I turned into the castle lane and through the new stone pillars and wrought iron gates that stand open all day (and usually all night; I'm not the best about security) and up the winding lane to the castle, pulling off to one side and getting out. I had a weird sense in the pit of my stomach that one way or another, this mystery—and possibly many more—would be solved soon. Maybe even tonight. I would do my best to discover who had lured Gilda out and attacked her, dragging her to the bowels of my forest and leaving her to die. Every time I remembered what she had suffered—a long lonely frigid night—I burned.

I pulled the empty muffin totes out of my car and set them down on the crushed gravel as my phone pinged. A text from Virgil, who had left after me to meet up with his PI partner: *We found one of the missing girls; Dewayne's brilliant . . . followed one of the girl's social media accounts to Buffalo. We've got to go and interview her for Urq and Baxter, make sure she left town voluntarily. Got a hockey game in RiRi after, so I'll be late tonite. You OK?*

I texted back that I'd be fine and put my phone back in my purse. With Virgil off on his task, it was up to Pish and me to figure this out. I girded my loins, so to speak, picked up the plastic tubs and headed into the castle. There was muted music echoing in the great hall. A scrawled sign on the dining room door announced that recording was in progress and to please leave them alone, so I headed back to my kitchen, where Patricia and Janice worked on prep for the craft services table and advanced prep for dinner.

"Wow, you've been busy!" I exclaimed, stacking the empty muffin tubs by the deep double sinks for washing. I examined the rows of muffin tins laid out to cool along the big trestle table that dominated the center of the kitchen. There were various iterations of muffin tin meals: mini meatloaves bathed in a crusted tomato herb sauce; tiny macaroni and cheeses with a garnish of cheesy bread crumbs baked on top; miniature quiches with finely chopped herbs; and a puff pastry pizza creation that looked and smelled wonderful "These are amazing, Janice. What a great idea! I'll have to steal this for hors d'oeuvres platters."

I washed and dried the muffin tubs, trying to decide how to proceed. I was still shaken by Hannah's deduction and couldn't decide if I thought it had any bearing on Gilda's attack. At that moment Dani, the window washer, entered the kitchen, looking for me.

"We're done," she said, thrusting her work-reddened hands in her windbreaker pockets. "Could you come out and have a look? We'd like to make sure everything is okay before we leave."

"Now?"

"Yes, please. We were supposed to start on our next job this morning, and we'd at least like to show up there today and make an appearance and let them know we'll be back Monday, so they know we're not abandoning them. It's getting nippy out there, and we won't be able to keep working if the weather turns."

I eyed her and nodded. The poor girl was clearly freezing, her cheeks red, her eyes watering. It must have been frigid in November on a ladder eighteen feet in the air. I owed them a debt of thanks along with their payment for what they had had to deal with. "Okay. I'll meet you out front."

"Before you do, could you take a walk around your building to check our work? If you have any questions we can answer them."

I did as asked, heading out the back door and circling the side of the building that faced the houses and parking lot. The windows were sparkling, and everything looked good. I circled back around to the dining room side and noted that the gothic windows that line the room were now pristine. I was happy. I headed to the front and admired the window over the double doors, then thanked them for a job well done. As Dani's husband packed the truck, I said, "I'm sorry about the missing items. I can't imagine who stole them, and we haven't found them yet. We *will* reimburse you. Please add the items on to your bill and I'll make sure you're paid."

"Thanks for that. It was a challenging job, with that crew of nutbars in there making everything more difficult," she said, indicating with her head the HHN cube van that was parked by the terrace. "The theft was bad enough, but moving our ladder . . . sheesh! They could have been hurt. It's heavy and awkward."

"Wait, what? They moved your ladder? I never heard anything about it."

"Yeah, the extension ladder; it was moved overnight. What day was that?" She frowned and looked down at the gravel. "Let's see, we started on Tuesday. Must have been Thursday morning when we arrived to find the ladder had been moved."

"From where to where?"

"Well, that's the weird thing; it was moved a few feet, from one window to the next."

"Show me," I said, getting an uneasy feeling.

She looked at me with a furrowed brow. "We're not upset now, though we didn't like our equipment being moved." Her cheeks colored, and she added, "Look, we shouldn't even have left it there overnight, but we didn't think anyone would touch it, you know?" She fidgeted, shrugged and huffed a sigh. "Look, I *swore* we took it down and laid it alongside the building Wednesday evening, but we *were* tired. I guess we left it in place, and someone moved it."

I could think of an alternate explanation. "Just show me. Please?"

She led me down the ballroom terrace and showed me the windows, about midway along.

"So, it was moved from . . . ?"

"The next window over." She pointed from the window next to it, toward the front, to where it had been left. "I mean, that's the one we were working on Wednesday, when we left. But it was moved, so . . ." She shrugged.

I counted the windows, knowing exactly which room was which. It didn't make sense. Not a bit, unless . . . "How much does the ladder weigh?"

"About eighty pounds," she said promptly.

"Can you move it by yourself?"

"Not if it's standing. I mean, I could *lift* it, probably, if it was already lying on the ground—I'm stronger than I look—but it would be too dangerous to take it down from a window by myself. My hubby can. It's not the weight, it's how awkward it is."

Troubled and puzzled, I thanked them for their efficient job—after apologizing for the crazy crew who made it more difficult—and asked her to bill me. I hoped the lovely sheen and sparkle would last until the film crew arrived in a week. Lizzie, my favorite moody teen, stomped toward the castle from the direction of the houses as the Batavia Sparkle Clean truck drove away. She looked up, saw me, and swerved to join me.

"What's up?" I asked, hoping for distraction from my gloomy and tormented thoughts.

"I'm worried," she said.

"About . . . ?"

"About the kid."

"Brontay?"

"What other kid is there?"

"Why are you worried?"

"She's been upset ever since Gilda was found. Like . . . *really* upset, and she won't say why. I don't get it. And she made that crack about it being her fault."

"We did talk to her last night at dinner and she said some stuff, but I got distracted. Let's see if we can find out what's up with her." I had other trails to follow . . . many *many* trails, and one nagging growing suspicion. One way or another, I was determined to follow those trails to their conclusions.

Twenty-two

I sat in on part of the day's taping. That day and the next were pivotal, as the production crew planned to be finished by the next evening. With all the new information, as well as what I now suspected and feared, I watched them all. There was a hum of tension in the room, but I wasn't sure if that was because of the attack on Gilda or something that would be there anyway because of the timeline and how close they were to completion. If all went well these singers, to whom this competition meant so much, would know soon who won.

Or the competition show would be canceled once I discussed with Anne Rhys's atrocious past behavior. I wasn't sure how to broach the subject and was still in procrastination mode. All I could think about was exposing who tried to kill Gilda. If it was one of the contestants, producers or judges the show might be over anyway, and my revelations about Rhys would be a nasty afterthought. I had my suspicions, but not enough evidence to back them up.

The judges were there. I watched Daffyd Rhys. With the recent revelations my crush on him had dissipated, like mist in sunlight. All I now saw was his posturing, his condescension and self-involvement, his utter snobbish certainty of his own superiority. Contrasted with Anokhi's resolute professionalism and Giu's kindness, it was cold and sterile; Rhys was an empty vessel with dead eyes.

Final performance videos were being shot. Zeb was filmed gazing out the window, take after take necessary to get the lighting right. He sang along with his own perfect track, finishing with one devastating, direct, down-to-the-soul gaze into the camera. He was a star, but I didn't think he'd win this opera contest.

After he was done, Alain was up. As he finished his take and left, I followed him out to the great hall.

"Alain, could I have a word with you?" I said.

A troubled expression on his narrow face, he stared at me for a long minute, his eyes shadowed in the dimness of the high-ceilinged expanse, then nodded. "Where?"

"Come to the library." I led the way to the deserted room and to a window seat the farthest away from the door. I motioned and he sat. I faced him, one leg drawn up under the other. Without evasion, I stared him in the eye and said, "Alain, I know about your aunt, how her career was ruined by Sir Daffyd Rhys's assault on her and his behavior after. Are you here to even the score? Did Gilda know about it and threaten to expose you to the production company?"

His eyes widened and he rapidly blinked. The bon vivant devil-may-care French Canadian disappeared to be replaced by a determined and angry young man. But he paused before speaking. Then he looked away out the gleaming window, staring off at a drift of leaves sent scuttering along the yellowing grass by a sudden gust of wind. "She trained me, you know," he said softly. "She trained me since a little boy. Teaching was her only solace. She is a beautiful soul, but broken, and now resides in a facility, for the time, to recover her sense, you know . . . to . . ." He shook his head. "To recover her . . ." He shook his head, impatient at his inability to find the right word.

"She's being treated for depression?"

"After she try to kill herself. My mother is gone; Tante Marie is the one who raise me from a boy, you see." His breath came faster; he leaned forward, his lean face drawn in anger. "She is a soft woman, sensitive, an *artiste,* and he took advantage." He balled a fist and shook it. "He used her, and then denied her."

"Let me be clear, Alain . . . was this a love affair gone wrong?"

"*Sacre,* no. He get her alone, he debase her, then toss her to the side like . . . like . . . *Crisse,* but I will see him done!" He trembled with anger.

"You were going to take revenge?"

He met my gaze, frowning. "Hein?"

"Were you going to attack him? *Kill* him?"

He drew back in horror. "What do you think me, like him? I was gathering . . . what do the movies call it . . . 'intel.' I want him to pay for what he has done," he said, jabbing his finger at me. "I want him to pay and pay and *pay*. I want the law to get him, but my aunt, she is not a . . ." He stopped and shook his head again, sadness overwhelming his expression, tears gathering in the corners of his eyes. He dashed them away with an impatient gesture, then shrugged.

"She's not considered a credible witness," I whispered. "The assault upset her deeply and made her emotional, so people write her off as a hysterical woman. Unstable. Unreliable."

"No justice for a woman because she cry." His incredibly expressive eyes were hard—flinty even—indigo stone.

He was angry, and despite his denial angry people do things they never thought they'd do. "What about Gilda? Did she know what you were up to?"

"*Ouais*. She was going to 'elp me. Until someone stop her. Who do you think *that* would be?"

It took a moment to get his implication, but then I gasped. "You're saying Daffyd attacked Gilda?"

"Of course."

"How do you know?"

He shrugged and grimaced. "Who else? He was not at the party at Madame Liliana's that night."

"How do you know *that*?" I asked, astonished. Neither Pish nor I had said anything.

His gaze slid away. "I went to find him. He was not dere."

"At Liliana's home? You snuck out and went looking for him."

He nodded.

"When? Why?"

"Lachlan was in his tub, you know, and Zeb . . . once he sleep, he sleep! I snuck out and went to the house on the edge of the woods and watched the party."

"And you didn't see Rhys."

He looked mulish for a minute, then shrugged. "I saw him. He was dere, yes, but so was someone else."

"Who?"

He smiled. "Miss Darcie, that is who. She was skinking . . . how you say that?"

"Skulking?"

"Yes! Skunking around that house and looking in windows."

I frowned. That explained why she wasn't in the castle when Lachlan got out of the tub, but why was she *there*? Was my conjecture correct? Did he and Darcie do the deed together? It was either that or she was there to confront Rhys about why he was ignoring her.

"Perhaps Sir Rhys snuck away after everyone went to bed and did the 'orrible attack on poor Gilda."

"Alain, to be clear, you saw Rhys outside?"

Evasively he said, "He come out and see Darcie, maybe?"

"But you didn't see him outside."

He shook his head. And yet . . . Rhys *had* been missing, though it wasn't clear for how long. "What time was that, Alain? Please, think."

He shook his head. "Is no good. I am not a watch person, you know? Always, I am late."

Rhys was inside, and Darcie was outside Liliana's home, but I wasn't sure what time. But maybe I had a clue. I checked my phone; Pish's call that night came in at ten-oh-seven. So Rhys was missing from the party at that point. But Alain was upstairs when I went up. "Okay, I came upstairs and checked in on you all, and you were there then. So you went out after your shower, right? Not before."

He nodded. "I wait until Zeb is asleep."

"And Lachlan was still in the bath when you snuck out?"

"Yes."

"So, that puts you at Liliana's house at . . . maybe eleven thirtyish. And you saw Rhys *inside* her house then, and saw Darcie outside skulking."

He shrugged. It was confusing and he wasn't much help, but I knew that Gilda had likely been attacked by ten to eleven or so when the woman was looking for her dog and saw Becket. I had a feeling that the flash of white she saw was Gilda either running from her attacker or being dragged. What I suspected was possible, if I was right about everything. It all hinged on who saw whom and when; Lachlan's testimony about Darcie being absent when he came out of the bath was pivotal if we could lock down the time frame. "So, did you hang around there long after you saw Darcie outside of the party?"

"What for? I wanted to learn more about him, but it look like he was going to be dere all night getting drunk and bragging, so I came home and went to bed." He frowned and twisted his lips. "I still wonder, though . . . what was Darcie doing?"

That was a good question, one I wanted to ask her in person, among other questions I had. What was her relationship with Rhys, and why was she stalking him?

• • •

I was almost certain Alain had nothing to do with Gilda's attack. It *seemed,* from my timeline, that Alain was in his room with Zeb at about the time Gilda was being attacked, but I couldn't be sure. That depended on whether or not I was right about the woman on the road and what she saw. The information about Darcie was much more interesting; I wanted to know why she was leaving the castle at all, much less at the time in question. Pish would have told me if he had seen her at the party, so . . . where did she go if she didn't go in? I would bet she didn't go in because Rhys came out to meet her. I emerged to the great hall in time to catch Brontay exiting the dining room after her taping session. "Hey, how are you doing?" I said softly, closing the library door behind me. "Where's your mother?"

She started at my voice, so deep in her own thoughts she hadn't noticed me. "Oh, uh . . . Mom stayed in to look at the video and be sure my section was lit right. She's picky about my angles. They'll be in for it if they catch my double chin," she said, sounding forlorn. She cuffed the sleeves of her sweater, pushed them up to her forearms, and sighed. "She'll screech and shout until they redo the whole bit."

"Can we talk?"

She stared at me for a moment, the shadow of gloom on her young, round face. Lizzie trotted down the stairs; she had been looking for me, and when she saw Brontay, said to both of us, "Let's go *out* for a walk. There's no place to talk in this joint without tripping over the wrong person."

That was a good idea. The moment Pam emerged from the dining room she'd demand to do a postmortem of Brontay's performance with her daughter. I grabbed jackets from the rack by the door, thrust two at my companions and we headed out, Becket racing to follow. I led the way, tramping the path toward the open construction area in the woods where the domed performance theater would be built. We walked in silence.

There was still a wooden stage there where Liliana Bartholomew had thrilled us all the month before with her and the church choir's rendition of "Go Tell It on the Mountain," so we mounted the steps and sat, Lizzie on one side of Brontay, me on the other, and Becket climbing the steps after us to sit at our feet and stare into the forest, his ears twitching this way and that as he listened to the screech of blue jays and chirr of chipmunks upset at our intrusion.

"Why did you say that what happened to Gilda was your fault?" I asked, turning to her.

"Because it *was*! She probably went out there thinking she was meeting me."

"Why?" Lizzie asked.

"Because we had met in secret locations before," she explained with that teenage eye roll that says *you're so slow*.

"You were feeding her inside information," I said. She nodded in confirmation. "Okay, you're the mole, her contact inside the contest. But why would she think she'd be meeting you? Are you *sure* about that?"

"No, but . . . I saw her and she gave me this look, and then whispered something like, *I'll see you later*. I didn't know what she meant, so I ignored it. When she was gone the next day I figured she was off investigating something."

"And that's it?" Lizzie said.

"Yeah."

"She may have gotten a note and thought it was from you," I mused, thinking of the note Urquhart had shown me. "But did you usually *write* her notes when you wanted to talk to her?"

"No, I'd text her."

"Did you usually meet at the same time?" I asked, thinking of the "usual time" mention on the note.

"Yeah."

"What time?"

She frowned and stared at me. "Lately I'd sneak out after Mom thought I was in bed at the hotel, at, like, ten. Mom would go back out and hang around at the hotel bar, hoping to talk to the producers or judges. Gilda and I met a couple of times at the hotel near the lobby washrooms."

It was starting to come together. "I do think she was lured out to the forest edge with a phony note she suspected was from you, but that's not your fault." I paused; there was still something nagging at me about the note—something I'd noticed—and I hoped it would come to me at some point if I left it alone. "So how long have you been feeding her gossip?"

"Since nearly the beginning. I think she had other sources at first. But once we got down to twelve singers I was it, her only source."

"What information did you give her?"

She slewed her glance sideways and reached down to scrub

Becket under the chin, his favorite scruffies of all. "Is she going to be okay?"

"We don't know yet. She's still in a coma. What did you tell her, Brontay?"

"Just . . . stuff. Whatever I overheard or saw." She stopped petting the cat, but he nosed up under her hands, demanding more.

"Like?" Lizzie was getting impatient.

"Gawd, I don't know! Just . . . like, I don't know."

"Come on, Brontay, you must remember *something*."

She sighed. "Okay, so like, Zeb met up a couple of times with this guy, sorta sneaking out of the hotel in Rochester, and I told Gilda, but she found out it was a writer who was doing a piece on Black opera singers. Then I told her how I saw Alain watching Mr. Rhys too much, you know, with this funny expression on his face, like he smelled something bad. And I told Gilda that a couple of nights Darcie snuck out of her room at the hotel and went to his room."

"*His* room . . . *whose* room?"

"Mr. Rhys's."

So, that confirmed the "relationship" I had suspected. It also bolstered the notion that she was outside of Liliana's house to meet Rhys the night Gilda was attacked. It did *not* explain what they did once they did meet up: sex, an argument, or attempted murder of a nosy journalist? "And what else did you tell Gilda?"

"Oh, just random sh . . . stuff, like that Lachlan can be a real jerk."

"What makes you say that?"

"He picks on people, you know? He picks on Darcie because she's always sucking up to the judges, and he picks on me for being a kid, and Kamile for being 'weird,' and yesterday he said right out that Alain is a peeping Tom who moved a ladder to stare into the girls' room one night—"

"He *what*?" I yelped. That was *not* what I had been expecting. Becket, offended by my screech, hunkered and hissed, then scooted down the steps into the forest.

"He said Alain moved that big ladder that the window washers use."

I was taken aback; I'd need to think about that. I had had my suspicions, but they didn't involve Alain. Maybe I was completely wrong. "What did Alain say to that?"

"Nothing. He stared at him like he was crazy." She frowned. "I'm not sure that he understood what Lachlan was saying. Between Lachlan's Scottish accent and Alain's rotten English . . ." She rolled her eyes.

"So you told that to Gilda?"

"That was *after* Gilda was missing."

"What else?"

She stared at me and narrowed her eyes. "You're trying to figure out who hurt Gilda, aren't you?"

"None of your beeswax, kid," Lizzie said. She had picked up the oddest expressions from Doc English, so her conversation was becoming sprinkled with old-timey phrases.

"It's okay, Lizzie," I cautioned as Brontay's expression became mulish. "If I *was*, what would you think?"

"That I'd want to help. Gilda doesn't treat me like a brain-dead toddler." She squinted. "But that's about it. I can't think of anything else right now, anyway." She sat up straight and her full lips thinned. "Except that Mr. Markunis is always bossing Kamile around, and she's afraid of him. He's a scary dude. I don't blame her for being afraid of him." She met my gaze. "She is, you know."

"Afraid of her uncle?" Lizzie said.

"Yeah."

"How can you tell?"

"Whenever he gets her alone he talks to her in that low scary tone that's worse than being yelled at. I think she'd do whatever he said to keep him from hurting her." Her eyes widened. "I didn't mean . . . I don't think—"

"It's okay, Brontay," I said, hand on her shoulder. "Anything else?"

She shook her head. "Have I helped? I feel so helpless and stupid, you know? No one will tell me anything. I'm not going to win this stupid competition anyway," she groused, kicking at the step with the toe of her running shoe.

"Why do you say that?"

She shrugged. "If a girl wins, it *should* be Kamile," she said, her eyes filling. "She's so good. I'm *pretty* good, but she's . . . I mean, Darcie is *awful*; I don't know how she made it this far," she said, with the naiveté that didn't allow her to connect Darcie sneaking into

Rhys's room with her advancement in the competition. "But Kamile . . . she's . . . *wow*. I could listen to her all day."

"Don't sell yourself short, kid," Lizzie said gruffly, buffeting her on the shoulder with a fist. "You're really *really* good."

"Thanks, Lizzie!"

"Thank *you*, Brontay, for being honest with us," I said. "If you think of anything else you told Gilda, will you let us know?"

She nodded. "Do I have to go back now?"

"You should," I said. "You've made a commitment to this competition and you should see it through."

"Hey, do you want to see the Fairy Tale Woods?" Lizzie said, jumping to her feet and startling Becket, who had returned to the base of the steps. "It's cool."

"What is that?"

"They are these crumbling little buildings the old guy who owned this place built way back when Merry was a kid."

Thanks for making me feel old, kiddo, I thought but did not say.

The other girl agreed and the two strode off together, deep in conversation.

"Lizzie, you get her back to the castle in half an hour!" I yelled after them.

My thoughts were gathering like a whirlwind, with new suspects—hearing that Alain moved the ladder had made me rethink my dismissal of him as a suspect, and yet I had to consider the source of that statement—and mulling over what Brontay had said about Moze. I try not to be swayed by unthinking prejudice; because Moze Markunis was a scary dude did not mean he tried to kill Gilda. It didn't mean he hadn't either, and that was something to consider. I tested that theory—that Moze Markunis, in an effort to keep a deep dark secret about Kamile, had attacked Gilda—and didn't find it compelling. He seemed ruthlessly competent. If he wanted Gilda dead, she'd be dead.

But I couldn't rule him out.

"So this is where it'll be, your grand performing arts theater?"

I looked up. Lachlan was staring into the open space behind the wood stage. Becket stood to greet him, but the singer ignored the cat and my furry dude got in a huff and tore off to chase chipmunks, who scolded and shrieked at him from tree trunks.

"It is. We had hoped to break ground before the snow flies, but there have been quite a few delays so it will probably be spring. We're still going to have a ground-breaking ceremony though. We have all the utilities placed. The dome will go up quickly once they get started." At his invitation we strolled the open space and I explained the dome, the rehearsal facilities, how many it would seat.

"It sounds grand! What I wouldn't give to sing here."

"Maybe you will," I said to him, wondering how he'd respond.

"Aye, maybe."

I sighed and gazed toward the castle, though I couldn't see it from where we stood. "I suppose I'd better get back and oversee dinner." We began the long stroll back, and I said, "Someone told me that the real reason you left the Scottish Tenors is because of problems while you were on tour. Is that true?" I was watching him, but he neither flinched nor looked upset.

"There *were* problems, but I wasnae happy, and it's true that the boys were not happy with me. We parted ways. But it is *also* true I wished to pursue my own solo career. Two things can be true at the same time, you know. All I care about is the singin'."

"It seemed that you were having a few vocal problems when I sat in on a rehearsal the other day. I know from Roma that overuse of the voice can be a big problem. Has this competition been hard on your voice?"

He shrugged but his voice was tight when he said, "No more than the others."

He was stonewalling me. I reflected on what Roma had said, that one of the competitors was using steroids to improve his or her voice. Was that Lachlan? Was he losing his voice and getting desperate? Brontay's accusation against the Scot came back to me, so I said, "You enjoy teasing and tormenting the other competitors, Darcie in particular."

"You notice many things," he said, and stopped, turning toward me. "You don't like me much, do you, Ms. Wynter?"

I met his gaze, taken aback by the accusation. "I couldn't say, Lachlan. I don't know you well enough to decide. Does being confronted with your behavior irritate you?"

"I can tell when a woman has come to an unreasoning conclusion. It's the curse of your sex, you know, to let emotion guide you."

I had nothing to say in reply. We circled the arborvitae and came out to the full view of the castle, windows gleaming in the afternoon sun.

"It's a lovely place you have here, madam. You're fortunate. Surprising, considering how many people have lost their lives here, in this lovely spot. I canna imagine how *that's* come about . . . all those deaths."

I stiffened. "What do you mean by that?"

He turned to me and smiled. "Now you see how implications based on a poor understanding of the circumstances can sting. It does, doesn't it? I can see it on your face. You've done nothing wrong, but looking at it from the outside it appears you either have a liking for violence or you invite it to your home."

He smirked, and I'll admit the impulse to the violence he spoke of was there; I wanted to smack his face.

"Nouw, I must get back. We're taping my last mentoring session this afternoon, and I have to charm the estimable Signor Giuseppe Plano, which should not be difficult, given his liking for a handsome face and willing manner." He strode away, leaving me flummoxed and sputtering.

Of all the *nerve*! Of all the insufferable, inconsequential, overbearing . . . I took a deep calming breath and admitted the justice of what he had said. From the outside, our series of misfortunes at Wynter Castle would seem to be far too full of coincidences to be coincidental. I knew none of it was our doing, nor even our fault, but an outsider might not see it that way. So, too, the string of events that had led to him leaving the Scottish Tenors could easily be explained. He had lost his way, gotten in trouble, left the group, cleaned up his act and moved on. He was abrasive, yes, but *that* was no crime.

And yet sometimes things were simpler than they seemed. I stared steadily toward my castle, so lovely in the clear, clean golden November sunlight. Dry leaves skittered past me with an arid rattle. One more time I would heal the pain and violence that had assailed us here at Wynter Castle. I had a few more avenues to explore in the search for a villain. I had my suspicions, but I wasn't quite sure yet. Time—and the right questions asked of the right people—would tell.

Twenty-three

The first thing I did when I returned to the castle was seek out Pish. He was in his sitting room office working on his next book. He is a writer of note, with several books to his credit relating the history of confidence men, scams, financial boondoggles, Ponzi and pyramid schemes that cheat people rich and poor out of their life savings.

He turned from his newest venture, a book on the world of online fraud, and gazed at me. "You know something," he said, brows raised, as he examined my expression.

"I do," I said, and told him what I had learned from Hannah, saving the most interesting tidbit for the last.

His response was all I could have hoped for. He rocked back in his chair and his raised brows did not relax, nor did his mouth close for a good thirty seconds or more. When he finally took in a long breath, he said, "Are you sure?"

"No," I responded. "I'm not. But Hannah's research is convincing, and it would explain a lot. I'm not so sure, though, that it has anything to do with this attack on Gilda, and that's my primary concern right now," I said. "I have more, though." I told him of my chats with Alain, and the timeline of him being outside Liliana's house, seeing Darcie there, and seeing Rhys inside.

Pish swore that if Rhys was inside at eleven thirty—or whenever Alain saw him—that he must have been there only briefly and gone back out. Pish had not seen Rhys before leaving at about one in the morning. That left the tenor open as a suspect in Gilda's attack. He *could* have done the deed, returned to Liliana's briefly, then met up with Darcie outside.

I then told him what I had learned from Brontay and Lachlan, and my thoughts on all three. We discussed what I had learned, and it helped me order my thoughts. I had a new perspective on Lachlan's revelation, that Alain had moved the ladder outside, an interesting and pivotal piece of information. "Thanks for talking me through this, Pish."

I returned downstairs to find that the production had broken for a late lunch, contestants, crew, producers, judges and mentors all scattered to eat in various locations, to get a breath of fresh air, or in some cases a breath of smoky air. As I came out the front door I saw Alain pacing in the drive, yelling into his cellphone. It seemed to be an emotional conversation, but as it was in joual I didn't understand much beyond a few words.

I rounded the front corner to the ballroom terrace side and spied Darcie and Sparrow at the far end, where the tables and chairs were clustered. They appeared to be in an intense conversation, and my curiosity was piqued; what did those two have to talk about? I wanted to ensure that the ashtrays were empty and all was neat.

I approached in time to hear Darcie say, "I won't be thrown over, Sparrow, I mean it. And you tell Anne I said that. This is all I have." She stabbed out her cigarette in the ashtray in front of the associate producer, then hastened past me, leaving Sparrow alone. A paper plate holding remnants of Janice's muffin tin concoctions sat in front of her, along with a paper cup of cold scummy coffee and a full ashtray.

I should have brought a garbage bag. "You and Darcie were chatting?" I said brightly.

She shrugged and huddled deeper into her black puffy coat.

"How are you doing?" I said. "Mind if I sit?"

She blew out a long stream of smoke. "It's your castle!"

"How is it all going in there? Does your timeline look good?"

"Do you mean will we be done tomorrow?" she said, eyeing me. "Anne has been bitching nonstop about how you've been harping on our exit date."

Nettled, I retorted, "Since we've done you all a massive favor—"

"—for which you are being paid handsomely—"

"—I don't think it's unreasonable for me to be concerned, when I have to be sure the castle is in tip-top shape for the *next* lot who will be coming to film. I didn't plan on this, but you're here now so—" I stopped and took in a deep breath. I had not intended to get into a squabble with the associate producer. "But that is neither here nor there. I was actually asking if you were satisfied with how it was all progressing. The show . . . is it going well? Will it be a hit?"

"That's the question," she said, stabbing out the cigarette she had been smoking and lighting another. She checked her phone, then sat back, blew a stream of smoke straight up and sighed. "It's impossible to tell at this stage."

"Sparrow, I can see that this is hard on your nerves. Is this better than being a writer?"

She eyed me coolly. "Why are you harping about that old writing thing? It's the best thing that ever happened to me, losing that story. I'm a fricking TV producer! Do you know how hard it is to write anything that sells anymore? People expect to get articles and books for free."

Touchy! "What a nice bunch of competitors you have, though. Who do you think will win?"

"You know I can't speculate on that."

"I'd bet on Kamile. She's the best singer."

She eyed me stonily.

"Or Alain; he's the best male."

"*Gawd*, no!" she blurted out. "Lachlan is better by a long shot than that asinine, parading French-Canadian idiot."

I smiled. "I know your secret!" I said, chuckling. Brontay had said that Sparrow was in love with one of the competitors; I'd bet it was Lachlan.

"What do you mean?" Her cellphone chimed. She looked at it and stabbed her cigarette out. "Gotta get back to work." She stood, gazing at me steadily. "I don't think you know a thing, lady," she said, then stalked away.

So much hostility! I emptied her ashtray in the receptacle and gathered up her discarded dishes to take in to the trash rather than leaving them to blow around in the increasing wind. It was going to be one of those nights, I thought, looking up at the sky as I approached the front door. Clouds were gathering. There'd be a storm.

• • •

Anne staggered into the kitchen, hand to her head, as I washed pans that had been soaking in the sink. "Good heavens, are you okay?" Janice and Patricia were restocking the craft services table during the lunch break, so there was just me.

"The beginning of a migraine," she said, slumping down in one of the wing chairs by the fireplace.

"Can I help?" I asked, drying my sudsy hands.

"What?"

I regarded her for a long minute, then went and got a towel, wrapped a few ice cubes in it, and returned to her. "Here, put this around the back of your neck and close your eyes. Relax." I turned her in her chair and approached her from behind, applying my fingers to her temples and pressing lightly for fifteen seconds and then massaging, alternating these treatments for a few minutes.

"Mmm." She sighed. "My husband does this, but he's not as good at it as you are."

I stayed silent and kept it up until I could feel her relax. I stopped and sat on the table in front of her as she opened her eyes. "Now, take a couple of whatever pain relievers you're used to, with a cup of decent coffee, and it will help."

"Thank you. It's starting to ease up a little."

I got her the coffee—some of Pish's secret stash—as she took a couple of pills out of a small fanny pack she had around her middle.

"Lifesavers," she said, shaking the prescription bottle. "Between these and the sleeping pills, I manage when we're on location. At home I don't need them; my cats and my husband are all I need." She put two on her tongue, then gulped the coffee. "This is *wonderful,*" she said, raising her cup.

"Thank Pish for that." I let her drink, thinking of what Sparrow had said. I tussled in my mind; should I raise the topic of Rhys's past behavior now, or later? "Anne, please know that if you need another day or two to finish up, I won't ride your butt, I promise. You have time." I watched her eyes.

She sighed deeply. "Thanks for that. I think we're going to be okay, though. If I can keep everyone on the schedule we've been following, we should be done by late tomorrow. You may have done me a favor, making such a point of your schedule. Trust me; I don't want to take any longer with this than I have to."

"I have a question, and I don't want you to think I'm suspicious or accusatory."

"Okay," she said warily, drinking down the rest of her coffee. "Shoot."

"How are decisions made in this competition? Will the best singer actually win?"

"That's a difficult question. Talent is subjective, isn't it? No two people hear the same. Personally, to me the best opera singers sound like strangled cats. And yet consider this: I'm a big fan of Bob Dylan and love his voice. I think his singing is gritty and real and it soothes me, you know? But many find his singing nasal and unpleasant."

She had something there; even the most popular singers have detractors. "But this is an opera competition with knowledgeable judges from the opera world. How do they choose? Is it a consensus thing, two out of three judges?"

"Pretty much, in consultation with the mentors."

That didn't explain how Darcie had made it so far. There must have been better opera singers competing. "So, no deal making? No, *I'll vote for your favorite singer if you vote for mine*?"

She stood and shook her clothing into place, giving me an annoyed look. "You know, my migraine is starting to come back. I'd better go and get this damn show put to bed. We'll be done by tomorrow night, come hell or high water."

I sighed in exasperation. I had been tiptoeing toward Rhys's possible behavior with Darcie, but she was touchy. As she stormed off my phone chimed; it was Urquhart, and he had more questions for me about something I hadn't considered. It made me think. They had found prints on Gilda's comatose body . . . glove prints. The assailant had come prepared. These were not just any gloves, he said, they were rubber gloves of a particular size and brand, which he named.

"Urquhart, I'm missing my favorite pair, and they are that brand and that size!" I said urgently.

"When did they go missing? Do you know?"

"I *do* know," I said, and told him when I knew they were gone by. I also thought of something else. "Urquhart, I'm also missing a filleting knife."

"A *filleting* knife?"

"From my kitchen. It's my favorite, with a long, thin, flexible blade."

"How long is the knife? And how thin, especially the handle?"

I told him.

He was silent for a moment, but then said, "Okay, that's important. I can't tell you *how* important, but . . . it's important."

"There's more." I told him about the missing items from Dani's truck. "I wonder . . . do you think the murder was planned on the fly?

Like, the killer was gathering things, then maybe found better items, like my filleting knife instead of the utility knife from the window cleaners' van?"

"It's possible. If so, it's someone who is used to improvising."

One more thing suddenly occurred to me. I asked if he could text me a picture and he obliged. After I'd looked at it for a long moment, expanding the view considerably, I called him back and told him my idea. I wasn't sure it meant anything, but it could. I told him all I had learned and pondered and surmised in the last day, holding back nothing.

He and one of his officers would be by in the evening to conduct another search, now that he had an idea of what he was looking for. I was becoming increasingly convinced that though there were other possibilities, whoever tried to kill Gilda would most likely be sitting at my dining table for dinner. And with new information I had received I was sure I was right.

"Don't do *anything* more, Merry," he said. "I know Virgil is not there right now. If anything happened to you, Virge would kill me."

"Yes, he would," I said softly. "I promise; I'll wait for you."

• • •

Finally, the day was at an end. It was eight by the time everyone came to dinner, and there were many bags under the eyes and weary sighs huffed all around. Janice helped serve the chicken marsala—thin, tender chicken breast medallions in a light wine sauce—and the accouterments she had provided—a crisp broccoli salad—then wearily headed home, too tired to even stay and enjoy the company of the talented contestants. Pish and I did our best to keep conversation going, but these were people who were already spending almost every hour of every day with each other and had nothing left to say.

So as people silently ate, or murmured to their immediate companions around the table, I observed. Given the information from Urquhart and my own reasoned conclusions, I was viewing each one in the light of a potential killer, or two potential killers. I was pretty sure of my conclusions, but not positive. I was determined to keep my eyes and ears open so I could tell Urquhart anything else I learned, but I would hold to my word and not do anything until he arrived.

Darcie was sulky, picking at her food, stabbing at the chicken pointedly and glaring at Lachlan, who raised his glass to her as she glowered. The Scot knew how to push people's buttons and seemed to enjoy antagonizing others. I was virtually certain that Darcie had used her influence with Sir Daffyd Rhys to get him to sway the judges to let her stay in the competition when she did not deserve her spot. It's hard to say no to a friend, and the judges *were* friends and had been for many years. The only way I could explain Darcie's place in the final three women was if Rhys went to bat for her, but I had a sense her influence with him was waning, and she was becoming increasingly anxious as that happened. Her career was vitally important to her, but was it important enough that she'd try to kill Gilda if the journalist threatened to reveal her "jury management," so to speak?

This led me to Lachlan, who—even tired—was baiting Darcie with snide remarks about her performance. He had a checkered past, but he had freely admitted it to me. Even if he was alibied to the hilt, no alibi is that perfect. So, the case against Lachlan, if I was seeking motive for getting rid of the journalist? He badly wanted to win. Gilda was most certainly investigating him. To believe he had attacked her, though, I had to think there must be something more he was hiding than an assault conviction in Sweden and possible performance-enhancing drugs—he was the one taking steroids, I was fairly certain—that were not illegal when prescribed by a physician.

One thought made me pause and eye both Darcie and Lachlan through squinty eyes; surely their enmity was over the top? Could it be that these two had together committed the perfect plot, concealing that they were working together? I shook my head. That was unlikely at best.

Alain was murmuring to Kamile, and she smiled. It was good to see her smile. But my own smile died. If Hannah was right, Kamile had a secret. It didn't seem like such a big deal to me, but in my experience what seems minor to one can be life-altering to another. Though I couldn't picture her stalking and trying to kill Gilda, I had no problem imagining Moze Markunis doing it, and Kamile was under his thumb. Could she have played the part of the nonlethal partner? It was not out of the question.

When Urquhart arrived I was going to ask if they had tracked down Markunis and discovered if he actually left the area when he said he was going to. I could picture the man lurking, in his black car with the tinted windows, on a back lane until he could lure Gilda out and attack her. I had speculated that he was too ruthlessly competent to leave her alive, but he could have been interrupted, or the woman looking for her dog could have spooked him.

And even Alain was not out of the running. He had ample motive, if he was there to bring down Daffyd Rhys and Gilda threatened to get in his way. Perhaps Gilda discovered why Alain was there and was about to warn Rhys. A smile and a joke, the singer's usual demeanor, could cover up the most evil of intent, but I had seen the serious side of him, the passionate defender of his family. He was a definite maybe.

And then there was Sparrow; based on my observation of her as a woman walking a tightrope, it was possible that she was involved. She had *ample* reason to be angry at Gilda for stealing the story and ruining her career as a journalist, despite what she claimed, that Gilda had done her a favor and she was happy working as a TV producer. She did not *seem* like a happy woman. I didn't know a thing about her personal life, so she could certainly have a partner on the outside, someone who was her ride or die, as the saying goes.

Dinner was over. I glanced at my watch and said, "Will you join me in the library for dessert, coffee and wine?"

Pish said, "Splendid idea!"

People paused and looked at each other with consternation. There were murmurs of dissent, but I knew Urquhart would want their rooms free—where *was* he?—so I said, with determined bon vivant hostess jollity, "Oh, come on, pretty please? It may be your last night! Tomorrow night if you're all done, you'll no doubt be busy packing. I'd like to get photos with each one of you, if you don't mind."

Pish and I managed to herd them all into the library and got them sat down, then went around and closed the drapes, making it a cozy spot. We got quite a few nice photos of all of us together, *for the Wynter Castle scrapbook*, I said, and the contestants gathered around the piano.

Becket strolled in to the group and greeted some with a friendly head butt, while avoiding others. He allowed Brontay to pet him, Zeb to chuck him under the chin, Alain to admire him, and Anne to get down on the floor, eschewing all dignity as only a middle-aged cat lover can and will, to tickle his tummy and pepper his head with kisses. But it was Kamile to whom he belonged body and soul. He eventually leaped up and kneaded his way into slumber on her lap. Dogs, I've observed, are indiscriminate lovers of all, but cats choose their people, completely disregarding that person's feelings about them. Kamile was his people whether she wanted to be or not.

When the door knocker clattered, echoing through the great hall and into our library, I jumped, even though I was ready for it. I ran to the door and let Urquhart and his female deputy in.

He wasted no time. "I have a warrant, Merry," he said, handing me a copy to read. "That's why I'm a little late. I took your information and went to the judge, and we thought this was best. I didn't want any resistance or evasion from your guests."

I nodded and turned on the chandelier, glancing over the document, noting the high points, among the legal gobbledygook Urquhart was surprisingly good at, mentioning the knife, the gloves, and the source of the information supplied . . . me. This was getting real, and the idea that I was hosting a killer in my library started me quivering. If Virgil had been with me I would have been calmer, but I was not about to rely on my husband for everything. I am a strong independent woman . . . except that I wanted my husband so badly I could feel it in my bones.

I nodded in acknowledgment and handed the warrant back to him.

Anne emerged into the great hall. "Merry, I'm so tired," she said, plucking orange cat hairs off her chest, looking down with a squint, her chin doubled as she tried to get every one. "I know you're trying to be a good host but we have an early call tomorrow morning and I think they all should—" She looked up and stopped, staring at Urquhart and his deputy, who were striding toward the stairs in the glare of the brilliant overhead light. "What's going on here?"

"I'm afraid no one will be able to go to bed for a while," I said, my voice shaky.

"What's going *on* here?" she repeated, her voice rising in volume, echoing off the marble floors in the great hall.

A couple of contestants, stretching and yawning, bumbled out of the library and stopped dead, staring as Urquhart ordered his deputy to wait at the top of the stairs. He glanced back, saw the group, and murmured something to his deputy. She immediately used the radio clipped to her epaulette, muttering into it hurriedly.

Urquhart, meanwhile, stepped up onto the bottom step, allowing him to look down over those gathered, his expression bland, his manner unyielding. "My apologies to you all," he said, using his official voice. "But we have new information and a warrant that allows me to again search all of your personal belongings. I thank you in advance for your cooperation."

"You can't *do* this!" Sparrow blurted, her voice a high whine of anxiety.

I watched her. She was agitated; something was wrong, and I thought I knew what it was.

"Ms. Wynter, please let them know that you've seen the warrant and what it says," Urquhart said, raising his voice over the mutter of the contestants. "I'm willing to answer questions—later—but in the meantime, we will be searching *every* room. We can work best and get you all back into your rooms fastest if we get down to it."

The deputy's radio sputtered to life and she moved back, spoke, and then murmured to Urquhart. He nodded. I could hear the heavy throb of a motor outside, and more deputies entered. One moved to the base of the stairs while the others climbed them, their heavy-booted footsteps echoing in the hall. The one who stayed at the bottom folded his hands in front of him, spread his feet slightly, and stood staring ahead with an impassive expression.

Most of the contestants grumbled and sighed, but trooped back into the library to slump in desolation on the sofas and chairs, listlessly giving in to the inevitable. But two of my guests in particular appeared more anxious. I watched them, uneasy. I had a feeling . . . I can't say what kind of feeling, but not a good one. I went to Pish, telling him my fear while I eyed all the contestants.

"Should we have the sheriff keep an eye on those two?" I whispered. He nodded. There was a sudden commotion out in the great hall, yelling, a furious voice hectoring and bullying the officer on duty. I bolted to the door and saw Moze Markunis, his face red, holding his suitcase in front of him and facing down the deputy, two more behind him at the open door, with the cold air gusting in.

At first unintelligible in a stream of Lithuanian, he calmed enough to speak in English. "Why was I prevented from coming in this place? What is going on? Where is my niece?"

The deputy, one hand on her baton, said, "Sir, please calm down. This is an ongoing investigation."

"Investigation of what?" he roared.

I approached, trembling, and said, "Mr. Markunis, Kamile is fine. This has nothing to do with your . . . your niece. Please come to the library to wait until the sheriff and his deputies are done with their search."

He whirled to face me, then his gaze went over my shoulder. I turned to see Kamile in the doorway, face pale, clutching the doorframe with both hands. She melted back into the room. Without another word he pushed past me and strode into the library. I gave the deputy an apologetic look and followed.

The library seemed emptier. Someone—some *two*—were missing. Pish had pulled Kamile aside near a window and talked urgently, but that stopped as Moze shouted, "Kamile! We are leaving." He stomped over to them and pulled Kamile away, holding her by the arm and furiously muttering into her face, a steady stream of Lithuanian.

This I would not allow, not until we had straightened a few things out. Call me a meddler, I just couldn't let it go. I exchanged a glance with Pish, who nodded to me; he had confirmed what Hannah suspected. We approached the two.

"Pardon me, Mr. Markunis," I said as politely as I could manage. I glanced at Kamile, then back to the Moze, his wild brows lowered over angry eyes. "I won't have you treat Kamile that way in my house. We know the truth. We know *everything*."

His face turned a deeper shade of red, an angry crimson suffusing his skin in blotches. "What do you know?"

"We know that Kamile is your daughter, not your niece."

Twenty-four

"Shut up!" the man roared.

We had gathered the attention of the others. Alain, looking grim, started toward us. I put up my hand to stall him, and he nodded, backing away. He turned and guided the others back to the sofas, then stood watch, alert to any sign we needed him.

I turned to the contestant while Moze fumed, shuddering with fury. "Kamile," I murmured. "We know who you are, that you are Moze's daughter by a woman who was not his wife, and that he has been promoting you for years as his niece because . . . because he took you away from your mother." I stopped, frowned and turned away from the young woman's shocked face to confront her father. "Why *did* you take her away from her mother?"

Pish muttered, "Merry, delicate, *please*. We don't know the whole truth yet."

I nodded and turned back to Kamile. I put one hand on her shoulder and gazed into his eyes. "Kamile, unless you wish to go along with your father willingly, we can help. You don't need to stay under his thumb."

"He threatened my mother," she said in a tight voice, her gaze darting between Moze and me. "He said he'd have her thrown out of her home if she did not let him take me. I was only thirteen, but I told her to let me go."

"But he's wealthy. You're his daughter. Shouldn't he have given her support for you?"

She shrugged, tears welling in her eyes. "She didn't know better, and I was just a child. He said he'd destroy her, take away everything. We would live in poverty. He said he'd take care of me and give her money to live. He said he'd make me famous, and then I could take care of her for the rest of her life." She shrugged. "But his wife, she was alive then, you see, and it would have been scandal, so he says I am his niece."

I understood more than she likely did. I didn't think scandal was his worry. Businessmen have affairs every day, and it's no big deal, it was just a way of manipulating her mother. He was using Kamile, from what I had gleaned through Hannah's research, as a way to move from country to country with impunity, and to launder money, even, taking money as loans or "investments" that he would supposedly use to promote his "niece." I avoided looking at the angry man and said, "What do you want right now, this minute, Kamile? You're an adult; we'll abide by your decision and not say another word if you go with him, I promise."

"I want to stay here and finish the competition," she said, her voice a ghostly whisper.

Anne approached. "And so you will," she said. She put her arm over Kamile's shoulders.

Moze was in as foul a mood as I have ever seen anyone. Perhaps he knew that his daughter had in those few moments—with loving support from others—slipped beyond his control. He blundered over to the bar cart and poured himself a tumbler full of scotch.

I looked around, meeting the puzzled gazes of the others. It was not my place to explain, so I passed them by in my search for the two who *weren't* there. And *another* presence missing. "Where's my cat?" I asked, looking around. "Where's Becket?" I wasn't alarmed, just curious.

Brontay said, "Sparrow picked him up and they went off to the dining room."

"What? Sparrow doesn't like cats."

Brontay shrugged. "She and Lachlan snuck out of here and headed down to the dining room, that's all I know. I followed them to the door and watched. Beats me why."

"Sparrow and *Lachlan*?" I felt a stab of alarm deep in the pit of my stomach. I bolted from the library and dashed down to the dining room, yelling to the deputy to follow me. He didn't—it would be worth his job to leave his post because Urquhart is a stickler for following orders—but I heard him yelling up the stairs for backup. I wasn't about to wait. I raced into the dark room, tripping and stumbling over wires, crashing into the directors' chairs. I picked myself up, rubbing my knee. Gleaming though the far gothic windows I could see that the motion sensor lights outside had been activated; a cold breeze swept though the room.

"No!" I yelled. *"Becket!"* I limped and staggered across the dining room and found the open window, climbed through it, and erupted onto the terrace. *"Be-ecket!"*

A distant yowl answered, and I heard a voice yelling *shut up* and *stop that*. Shadowy figures moved swiftly across the lawn toward the far woods: Lachlan, Becket and Sparrow. Becket yowled again, and Lachlan screamed. My cat would be doing damage with the claws I let him keep long and sharp so he could defend himself.

But this was a lethal pair, and I was not going to lose my boy to them! I followed, looking back over my shoulder. My cat screeched wildly, Lachlan screamed again, and I knew I could waste no time. I ran, gasping, panting, out of breath, following as they headed for the woods.

A car radio squealed behind me and I heard Urquhart's voice, amplified, "Merry, stop! Let us handle it!"

"No!" I yelled over my shoulder, in my loudest voice, which I have been told is plenty loud. "They have Becket!" My voice was a hoarse out-of-breath panicked screech, but I could not stop, not while they had my poor cat in their evil clutches.

The murderous pair had entered the woods. The only reason they had taken Becket was to have a bargaining chip, I thought, which meant they must be pretty sure the police search was going to unearth something, probably bloody rubber gloves, and/or my fillet knife, and possibly, I thought, remembering a zippered piece of clothing peeking out of Lachlan's suitcase, the Batavia Sparkle Clean windbreaker.

I stumbled and staggered to the edge of the woods and stopped; the duo had entered the woods at the only path in, but what was their plan? Did they even *have* one? Huffing and puffing, I entered the forest, holding up my cell phone with the flashlight app glowing, and paused, listening. It was quiet, except for my pounding heart and the blood rushing in my ears, but with that sense that there were people nearby holding their breath. "Becket?" I called.

Yowl!

"Lachlan? Sparrow? I know you're near." My blood was still rushing and panic spiraled through my stomach. "Let the cat go; all he's going to do is slow you down. I won't follow you if you let him go. *Please!*"

There was silence for a moment, but then Lachlan said, his voice flinty, "I'll no' let him go 'til you leave us alone. I'll kill the cratur first. It's his bloody fault all of this has happened. If he hadn't brought back the damned bow, you'd not have found Gilda 'til she was dead."

"Until you had time to go back and finish her off, you mean!"

"Shut up, ya blathering witch."

"*You* shut up! You did what you could to blame everyone else, even to saying it was Alain who moved the ladder, when it was really you, but we still figured it out!"

Silence. A sob caught in my throat; I should not infuriate him more. I softened my tone to wheedling. "What is this getting you? Come on, Lachlan, *think*! This is ridiculous. Let Becket go. I only care about him, I swear it. I'll let the police deal with *you*."

I heard someone approaching behind me, the faint thud of footsteps, unguarded and swift, and a swish of branches, which could only mean that Urquhart or one of his officers had followed me to the forest opening. I didn't want Lachlan to know that though, so I rapidly went back to talking . . . "Lachlan, come on! Let the poor cat go." Becket yowled again and I heard a stream of Gaelic-accented swearing.

"Sparrow?" I called out. "Make him let the cat go. Don't ruin your life for that man! He almost killed Gilda. He'll hurt you the first time you don't do what he says." I had no idea if that was true, but my plan was to muddy the waters, to set them at odds with each other if possible. This was a ridiculous scenario. Lachlan had been panicked into bolting, and was now thinking no further than the next few minutes.

My scalp prickled . . . someone was close by, but I dared say nothing until I knew if it was friend or foe. I extinguished my cellphone light by clicking out of the app and slipping it into my pocket and stood, listening. I heard the footsteps a split second before being seized from behind and jerked off my feet. I yelped in distress, hearing my voice as if I was out of body, a shriek of fear. Lachlan had me; he was strong, and dragged me backward into a thicket, one meaty hand over my mouth, his hand smelling of disinfectant and damp, with a smear of sticky metallic-tasting ooze. He grunted and breathed hard hauling me backward, while I struggled to gain footing, flailing and twisting as he grunted expletives.

My mind swirled into panic as Lachlan's strong arm twisted my neck until it felt like it would break. My breathing was becoming jagged, painful, like I was suffocating. As I cried and struggled I heard sounds, impressions; things were happening around me, but the light was going out as I was being dragged, suffocating and losing consciousness: Becket yowling; Sparrow shrieking . . . or was that the owl? A shout, a cry, a howl, then . . .

My vision dulled; everything was starting to go black. Then, in an instant, the pressure on my neck was suddenly released and Lachlan was jerked away from me. A blessedly familiar voice cried out, "Stop hurting my friend!"

"Gordy!" I croaked, my voice choked and odd-sounding.

There was a whacking sound, then silence. "Merry, it's gonna be okay." It *was* Gordy, my friend and champion.

I felt his hand take mine and he jerked me to my feet with a surprisingly strong tug. Together we ran/stumbled away through a thick slurry of leaves and sticks and mud as two cops with flashlights came toward us. "Back there . . . Lachlan and Sparrow!" I hoarsely cried, coughing and gasping and wheezing.

"Let me help you, Merry," Gordy grunted, shoving his bony shoulder under my arm and hoisting me upright.

Another yowl, closer now, and Becket was suddenly there, jumping into my arms, clawing his way up to nuzzle under my chin. "I . . . I can't," I said to Gordy as I slipped from his grip, falling with a thump to the forest floor, sticks jutting into my butt.

I heard an outcry and a wail, and it was over. The female deputy, flashlight clipped to her epaulette, frog-marched a weeping, smeared, dirty, bedraggled Sparrow past me on the path, followed by another officer with Lachlan securely in his grip, hands zip-tied behind him. I looked up and in the momentary bobbing beam of a flashlight saw the singer's face; it was covered in claw marks, long angry red trails down his forehead and cheeks, with blood smeared down his chin. He roared agitatedly when he saw me and Becket and tried to lunge at me, but the officer gave him a sharp kick in the back of his knees and he buckled.

Good job, Becket. Now I knew what the metallic tang on Lachlan's hands were; his own blood.

With the help of Gordy I got to my feet and staggered the short way out of the woods. On the path across the leafy damp lawn, I stopped; I heard a heavy motor rev and a car screech to a halt with a spray of gavel.

"Merry!" Virgil pelted over the slight rise and straight for me.

Sobbing, weeping and shivering, I collapsed into my husband's arms and let him half carry me up to and inside the castle, where Pish greeted us in almost hysterical relief. I motioned toward Gordy, lingering uncertainly at the door with Becket cradled in his arms, and my friend ran to tug the young man in, to be with us and be tended to as well, as he had sustained bruises and scrapes from his brief scrap with Lachlan.

The police took the two miscreants to the hospital first to attend to their feline scratch wounds—bless my ferocious cat—and a paramedic tended to me as a couple of the singers and Anne clustered around the fireplace out of the way, casting worried glances my way. I refused to go to the hospital, had a few scratches cleaned up, and agreed to see my doctor to be sure my throat/windpipe/esophagus had not sustained permanent damage.

Gordy, meanwhile, was being introduced to Brontay, Pam and the others, and was now retelling his part in the ordeal, which I overheard as Virgil held me close. The police were finishing their search upstairs, but Urquhart had muttered to Virgil that they had, indeed, discovered my fillet knife with the extremely slim handle stuck down in a tall bottle of bubble bath in Lachlan's toiletries, along with bloody gloves stuck in the back of the toilet tank in the bathroom. I whispered hoarsely to Virgil about the Sparkle Clean windbreaker I thought I spotted in Lachlan's luggage. The first search had not uncovered it because the scope of the search did not encompass our guests' luggage, while the second did, thanks to my information. Urquhart was a by-the-book sheriff, trained by my husband, the best by-the-book sheriff.

Soon, I would have to summon the energy to tell Urquhart what I thought had happened; Lachlan's long bubble bath was a ruse to give him an alibi. Earlier, with a Batavia Sparkle Clean windbreaker on—in case anyone witnessed his shenanigans—he had moved the long ladder to the bathroom window, then he had made the whole ruckus about having a long bath. I suspected he had used a recording/ playback app on his phone—similar to what Brontay had been using to record her practice—so *that* is what I heard murmuring seductive nothings to no one, literally. I was not going to bust in on someone having phone sex in the bathtub, he had no doubt reasoned, and he was right. Besides, the door has a privacy lock from the inside which he would have engaged before climbing out the window. We would have had to bust the door in.

He had lured Gilda out with a note. The picture Urquhart had sent me of the note that had been found near her confirmed it, but it had taken me a while to recognize it. When Urquhart showed me the note in person I noticed one thing that nagged at me—besides the edge of the castle graphic—but it took me a while to realize that what I was seeing was part of Sparrow's iconic signature, with the row of V-shaped birds winging away. The note was no doubt from Sparrow to Lachlan to meet her at the usual place, so Lachlan tore off her signature and slipped it under Gilda's door. She found it and thought she was meeting Brontay, her mole, who would have information.

He used Sparrow. I wondered . . . did she know his plans beforehand or was she recruited after, to move the car to Batavia? I remembered how weary she looked the next day. Anne would have been out cold on a combination of sleeping pills and wine through the whole thing so Sparrow could have been out most of the night and the producer would not have known.

She almost certainly had a hand in promoting Lachlan as winner. I suspected that Daffyd Rhys was behind both Darcie making it as far as she did in the competition and, at Sparrow's behest, getting Lachlan to the finals. Perhaps Sparrow used her knowledge of his finagling Darcie into the final three to blackmail Rhys into helping Lachlan. And all those incidents in Rochester? Some, at least, were likely planned by Lachlan, who had been in college for electrical engineering. I was almost certain that he was the one who had electrified Gilda's shower curtain rod. It could have killed her, his plan, no doubt. I had tipped Urquhart off to my suspicions, and he had the Rochester police investigating.

I didn't know what happened that night, but I suspect Gilda slipped away to meet Brontay, was attacked by Lachlan but got away from him, then got lost in the woods. He beat her, stabbed her, barely missing her heart, and left her for dead, intending to come back and handle the body. He must have driven Gilda's car to Autumn Vale, leaving it for Sparrow, who followed in an HHN company car. He probably drove the HHN car back to the castle, leaving his accomplice to return the rental to the lot in Batavia. How did she get back to the castle? I still didn't know so much. It would all be up to the police to sort out.

Becket finding and retrieving her glittery black hair bow, with her recognizable hair in it, was a stroke of luck for Gilda; as Urquhart had said the night we found her, she would not have lived another night in the woods. Why Lachlan had attacked her we *still* didn't know for sure. All of my suspicions were suppositions. That he would kill her to keep his spot in a singing contest seemed absurd.

With Virgil's support, I gave Urquhart my statement. One tiny additional clue came pinging onto my cellphone, which had been recharging. The Glasgow police wanted to know why I had been messaging on social media—and leaving my cell phone number for—the Gaelic woman singer who had been Lachlan's girlfriend. She was missing and feared dead. *That* was information Lachlan may have tried to kill Gilda to keep silent.

Two hours later, in the wee hours of the morning, Urquhart and the rest of his crew cleared out of the castle, though there was still a police presence, as the press always puts it, at the edge of the forest.

I had no words to thank Gordy; tucked into my husband's comforting embrace I gazed steadily at our vigilant friend in the doorway as he was about to leave. He shifted awkwardly on his feet, staring down at them, his balding pate gleaming in the chandelier light. I found my voice, scratchy and hoarse as it was, and gave him effusive thanks, which he received with silent embarrassment. His cheeks and neck were flushed a dull read.

"Why were you there, Gordy? Why were you in the woods?" I croaked.

Virgil cleared his throat and I looked up at him. I looked from my husband to our friend.

"That would be me," Virgil said. "I was stuck in Batavia and the car lost power. I got this awful feeling that you needed me. I'd call it dumb if it weren't for what happened. I couldn't get Dewayne on the phone and I didn't want to alarm *you* needlessly, so . . . I called Gordy and asked him to check in on you."

"I was comin' up the lane when I heard and saw that jerk hightailing it across the lawn with the poor cat, and you after him," Gordy said. "I was by the woods and know a better way in from the lane, so I cut in thinking I'd head him off. But I got kinda turned around, until I found him hauling you by the neck."

"And you saved my life," I said, tears welling and dripping down my cheeks.

"Yeah, well, it's nothing. Don't think twice, I was just lucky," he said rapid fire. "And . . . and I'd better get out of here. I borrowed my uncle's truck."

And he was gone, his face and neck brick red. That was probably the most he had talked to anyone in a month. I'd have to think of something I could do for him to show him my appreciation.

With a tender hug from Pish, carrying my hero cat and supported by Virgil, we went upstairs and I collapsed into a deep, deep sleep. Of course I had nightmares, one horrible one with me in an endless chase through a forest, an owl hooting, Becket crying, and me screaming and thrashing. But with Virgil's tender ministrations, I made it through to morning.

Twenty-five

Virgil brought me coffee in bed and sat while I drank, telling me that Patricia and Janice had it all well in hand for the final day of taping, which was going ahead. Moze Markunis and Kamile had an argument, and, supported by Anne, the young woman told her father to take a hike, or words to that effect. Markunis had stormed off, one step ahead of the FBI, who wanted to detain him for a federal tax fraud and money-laundering case they were building. I was relieved; I didn't know how that was going to go, but it sounded like Markunis's legal trouble might keep him from interfering in his daughter's life from now on.

Virgil had heard from Urquhart; Sparrow was singing, now that she was facing a conspiracy to commit murder charge, among others. The sheriff told my husband—in confidence, Virgil told me, with a warning to keep it to myself—that there was far more to Lachlan's past than anyone knew.

The Scottish singer had an outstanding international warrant from Sweden; the fellow he beat up had since died as a direct result of the injuries he suffered at the Scot's hands and it was considered murder. It had not yet been reported, but Gilda had done some deep digging and contacted a source in Sweden and was *about* to include that fact in her story, along with other unsavory revelations, including the mysterious disappearance and possible murder of Lachlan's former fiancé in Glasgow. It was chilling.

These revelations would have ended his competition hopes even if he didn't wind up in jail. He had roped in the infatuated Sparrow, she claimed, but not in the actual commission of the crime. As I suspected, after he left Gilda for dead in the forest—she had stumbled away from him and he was alarmed by the sound of a motor and a woman calling out, the woman looking for her dog—he knew he was running out of time and figured Gilda would die, if she wasn't already dead. He slipped back to the castle, texted Sparrow, and she retrieved the keys to the HHN car and followed him in the middle of the night into Autumn Vale. He left the keys in Gilda's car for her, then drove back to Wynter Castle in the HHN car. He couldn't leave the bathroom door locked forever, after all. Sparrow returned the rental to Batavia, then had to take a Greyhound back and walk from the nearest bus drop-off point, a curbside stop one road over from Wynter Castle. Urquhart had verified her story with the Greyhound driver.

As I sipped my coffee Virgil relayed the news he had learned from the *Opera DivaNation* people: there had been a meeting the night before at Liliana's that included her, the mentor Carlyle O'Connor, Roma, Anokhi Auretius, and Giu Plano. They were aghast at the revelation of Rhys's assault in Rochester, they claimed in a press release issued early in the morning from HHN publicists. I read it on my phone as I finished my coffee, skeptical that no one knew about the Welsh singer's past bad behavior, but . . . spin would be spun.

After learning about the allegations against Rhys—and there had been many over the years that had been swept under the carpet—Anne had an early morning conversation with the powers that be at HHN. The network agreed that too much money and resources had been put into the show to abandon it now but there *would* be changes. In a second press release HHN stated that they had reconfigured the judge's bench for *Opera DivaNation*. Sir Daffyd Rhys had been dismissed. Liliana would step in. Carlyle and Roma remained the mentors. With all the footage they had, they thought they'd be able to cobble together a decent show, even if they removed every scrap of footage with Lachlan. They didn't use those exact words, but I could sense how they were scrambling to save network dollars.

"Anne must be reeling," I said. "I mean, it's a lot: Lachlan arrested for attempted murder, Rhys arrested for what he did, and Sparrow arrested for, what?"

"At the very least accessory after the fact, but it will depend on whether they believe her story that she didn't know what Lachlan had in mind beforehand. It'll be up to the DA."

"Yeah. It's a lot," I said, setting my empty mug aside and touching my throat.

"Are you okay?"

"I will be," I croaked. "So . . . we were talking about Anne?"

Virgil knit his brow. "She seems oddly energized. Sparrow's arrest shocked her to the core, but she's a professional," he said with grudging admiration. "She's taking it in stride and working it out."

I sighed. I hoped Rhys's fall from grace signaled change in the opera community. There had been, in some opera companies, a conspiracy of silence that allowed abusers free reign. I was happy to learn, from Virgil, that Anne had decreed *more* changes in the competition: they were scrapping the nasty interviews Sparrow had overseen in favor of more uplifting "packages" where each contestant would get to speak to struggles they had overcome and their hopes for the future. There would still be a winner of *Opera DivaNation,* but the contest would be about more than that; it would be, the HHN press release had stated, a beacon of hope for change toward a bright, inclusive, diverse, artistic future in the opera community.

I was hopeful.

After a shower and dressed, with a pretty scarf to cover up a choker of bruises around my neck that made me look like an escapee from a hangman's noose, I descended to be overwhelmed by the effusive love of Patricia and Janice. They would not let me do a thing; I must sit by the fire with a cup of tea and hero-cat Becket.

That lasted a half hour until I got bored and wandered into the dining room to watch the last tapings. Kamile sang a fresh take on "Voi che sapete." With her new openness, it was lovely. Alain was back to his giddy flirtatiousness, Darcie was still sullen but appeared to have accepted that she was not going to win, Zeb was as focused as before, and Brontay even more ebullient and youthful. Lynn had, for the first time, come to see the singing, now that Rhys was gone. She said she had a "feeling" about him from knowing him in the past.

I sat with her, my arm around her thin shoulders, and as Zeb again sang "Somewhere" tears streamed down her face. She whispered to me that he was the nicest fellow she had ever met, and an absolute dream to style. It was like he had intuition that she was staying upstairs and away from the taping; he brought her treats: coffee, snacks, and sweets. If he wasn't too young for her, she said, she could fall in love with him. "I'm going to miss him so much when he's gone," she said wistfully, watching him as he finished.

"Who says he's too young for you?" I asked.

She gave me a look. "I do. My life is complicated. I wouldn't wish me on anyone."

I didn't know how to respond to that, so I gave her a hug. *Don't count yourself out,* I thought, as I caught Zeb's warm glance toward her.

It was another long day and everyone was exhausted. The change in direction for the show was going to take a lot of editing, retakes, and much thought. But Anne—after apologizing for her many missteps—told me that there would be a lot they could do in the studio, so they would be leaving the next day as scheduled.

"Can you make it later in the day?" I asked and told her why.

She nodded with a smile. "As anxious as I am to get home, we can make time for that."

• • •

The next day we had a party. I invited many Autumn Vale friends for an informal brunch buffet, to celebrate with us and meet the contestants. Patricia and Dewayne, Janice and Simon, Binny, Hannah, Gordy, Zeke, and even Isadore, among others, all accepted our invitation. The judges and mentors attended as guests, as did Anne, though she had sent the technical crew back to HHN studios in New Jersey to begin work on the next phase of the *Opera DivaNation* competition. Of course, with so many singers it inevitably became a performance, and it was revelatory. My lovely dining room, cleared of equipment, cameras, director chairs and with a crackling log fire blazing in the hearth, late autumn sun gleaming through the pristine gothic windows . . . it was breathtaking.

I say there were no cameras, but Lizzie was there with a digital camera given to her by the lead video technician from HHN, filming it all for social media. Her viral video of Liliana Bartholomew had now reached over a million views and was picking up speed. She was determined to have another to upload to capitalize on the popularity of Wynter Castle Videos, as she had named her channel.

After food and chat, the singers took turns on the "stage" near the fireplace or piano, whatever they chose. Brontay, who had become Lizzie's little buddy, sang, then retreated to sit with Hannah, Zeke and the hero of the hour, Gordy, at a table near Lizzie's video camera. Darcie actually surprised me—and herself, I think—by choosing a modest rendition of a sweet older Britney Spears song, "Sometimes." It was suited to her soft uncertain voice; very pretty. Zeb Wolfe played the piano—a skill I did not know he had—and sang (to Lynn, it seemed to me) a John Legend song, "All of Me."

Alain crooned a song by the French-Canadian legend Ginette Reno, who I had only known from her English-language hit "Second

Hand Man," a tune my mom used to sing around the house. "Je Ne Suis Qu'une Chanson"—"But I'm Only a Song," he told us it meant in English—was an absolute revelation. Alain, with his charm and magnetic personality harnessed, would be a star. Hannah was enthralled, and when Alain went to sit with them, charming her with sweet flirtation, she was breathless with admiration. Zeke took her infatuation manfully, shaking Primeau's hand.

But Kamile was the real star. Dressed for the first time in more relaxed garb, a soft drapey sweater and jeans I recognized as Lynn's, she approached the microphone and with no music sang a lovely, haunting Lithuanian folk song that she introduced as being about an orphan girl mourning the loss of her parents. I looked over at Anne, and there were tears in her eyes; she had "adopted" Kamile, she told me, and would be her American mother, not to replace the one she had but so she had someone to turn to even in America while she sorted out her new life, away from the clutches of her controlling father.

• • •

A couple of hours later our castle was empty again, except for Lynn, of course, and Lizzie, who wanted to consult with Pish on the book of photos she was creating, and Roma, who was staying on for a few days. So, not empty at all, really. I was tired . . . *so* tired. And a little sad, but at the same time, happy.

Gilda was awake and recovering, I was relieved to learn. She had been speaking to the police, filling them in on what she remembered. I asked Virgil to take me to visit her in the hospital. He would have preferred that I take it easy, but I was determined. However . . . I was devastated when I saw her; she seemed so frail, in her hospital bed, head bandaged, springy hair sticking out at all angles, hooked up to an IV, weak and gray. I held back tears; she didn't need to see me weeping. There is nothing scarier when you're in the hospital than seeing someone crying over you. Her mother was hovering over her and she was recovering. When her mom left the room to go down to the coffee shop for a break, I sat down beside her hospital bed.

"Gilda, I'm so sorry," I croaked.

"Sorry?"

"For what you went through at my castle, my home . . . I'm so *sorry.*"

She rolled her eyes. "My own fault for being so set on a story that I didn't even guess that the note wasn't from Brontay. What an idiot I was." She paused to catch her breath, then spoke a little more. A lot from that night was foggy, but she did remember slipping out of the castle to the terrace. Once there, she heard a summoning whistle, and followed it across the damp grass to the edge of the woods, where she found Lachlan. She was mildly alarmed, given what she had already dug up about him, and was about to turn away. He said he had something to show her. She refused to go with him. He attacked her and dragged her into the woods.

Everything was blurry after that and she didn't remember the attack at all. She did remember something else, though; "It's so odd," she said softly. "I got away from Lachlan, I think? I staggered through the woods and fell. I heard . . . I think I heard a woman calling out?"

"Yes . . . there *was* a woman. She was looking for her dog, and she spent a good few minutes there calling and shining her light into the woods. I'd bet she scared Lachlan off, plus he was running out of time," I said, explaining the ruse he had used of being in a bubble bath.

"I drifted off again, but through that night I felt something. I'm probably imagining it, but I felt a warm spot, a little furry critter that would not leave me alone. My ghost animal." She smiled. "It nestled right up close to me. Sometimes I woke up, and I could hear it. I'd almost *swear* it was purring!"

I smiled through tears; that was my Becket . . . independent and brave and sweet.

Gilda was tiring, so we left her with her mom fussing over her and returned to the castle.

Urquhart was there tying up loose ends and took my husband aside. Sparrow, at her lawyer's urging and in an effort to cut a better deal, had guided the police to the journalist's purse and laptop. Lachlan had taken them from Gilda's room, used her keys to lock the room, then wrapped the two items in a garbage bag and hid the package in the bottom of the trash can on the terrace. Lachlan had intended to recover the items at a later date but fortunately for us, Gilda, and the investigation, misfortune plagued him at Wynter

Castle. His bad luck continued after his arrest. The singer had been denied bail; he was a definite flight risk. Sweden, Scotland and the United States were fighting over who would prosecute him first, and for what.

As the sun slanted down through the trees, Virgil and I drove back to our home and parked, then walked inside arm in arm. Becket followed us in and headed for his food bowl, of course. I sighed as we entered and turned on lights. Our home; our retreat. We locked up, climbed the stairs and, after feeding Becket, went straight to bed, but not to sleep.

No, not to sleep, but to love away all the pain and sorrow and fear. *Then* to sleep, and to wake, only to love again. It was paradise, a lovely well of blissful happiness I was grateful to fall into.

Recipes

For recipes from this book and others, sign up for Victoria Hamilton's newsletter at victoriahamiltonmysteries.com.

About the Author

Victoria Hamilton is the pseudonym of nationally bestselling romance author Donna Lea Simpson. She is the bestselling author of three mystery series, the Lady Anne Addison Mysteries, the Vintage Kitchen Mysteries, and the Merry Muffin Mysteries. She is also the bestselling author of Regency and historical romances as Donna Lea Simpson. Her latest adventure in writing is a Regency-set historical mystery series, starting with *A Gentlewoman's Guide to Murder*.

Victoria loves to read, especially mystery novels, and enjoys good tea and cheap wine, the company of friends, and has a newfound appreciation for opera. She enjoys crocheting and beading, but a good book can tempt her away from almost anything . . . except writing!

Visit Victoria at: www.victoriahamiltonmysteries.com.

CPSIA information can be obtained
at www.ICGtesting.com
Printed in the USA
LVHW030458090721
692210LV00002B/291

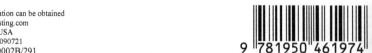

9 781950 461974